A SOLDIER'S CHRISTMAS

WORLD WAR II ROMANCE

A COMPELLING CHRISTMAS WARTIME SAGA

GRACIE SHAW

PUREREAD.COM

CONTENTS

DEAR READER, GET READY FOR ANOTHER GREAT STORY...

A WARTIME ROMANCE

The war is over, but one woman's battle for her husband's heart has only just begun...

Turn the page and let's begin

any Years Later...

Ok, I'll admit. Most stories don't begin, *"many years later"*.

But this one does. With me, a keen and somewhat spunky grandson, trying to prise some juicy details about the war from my granddad.

Little did I know the rollercoaster story I was about to hear...

Oxford, 2005

We were in Year Six when Miss Fullerton assigned us a project in History.

It wasn't a group project, which was a relief because it meant I wouldn't have to be paired up with any of the idiot boys in my class. I always ended up doing all the work in those kinds of things, anyway. No, I was pretty excited about the project at first, though of course I wouldn't have admitted that to any of the others because *I* wasn't an idiot. I wasn't about to tell them, either, that I'd got a bunch of history books last Christmas and that I'd asked for more this year.

Anyway, I was excited because the project was going to be on World War Two, and I was already a bit ahead of the others on that subject. That's because, to put it simply, I was *obsessed* with World War Two. I knew everything there was to know about it – really, I did. I even got Mum and Dad to let me sit up late and watch *Schindler's List* when it was on TV one night. Susie (that's my older sister) cried her eyes out. David (my older brother) said it was "depressing". Molly (my other older sister) fell asleep halfway through the film. But I was fascinated from beginning to end. Of course, I thought it was really sad, too, but it was so *interesting*. I got *The Diary of Anne Frank* out of the school library after that and read it in a few days.

And I kept talking about World War Two and asking Mum questions about it until she got annoyed. She said it wasn't her "area." (Mum lectures History in the university.) But I think she felt bad about saying that, though I did stop asking her questions. She said it was good that I was so curious and interested in things. And I think that's why she bought me the history books for Christmas. She pretended they were from Santa, and I pretended to believe her.

But that was in Year Five. In Year Six, when Mrs. Fullerton assigned us that project on World War Two, she said we couldn't just go home and look up things on the Internet about it – that we'd have to talk to elderly relatives and ask them what it was like.

I had my hand up, because I was going to ask if it would be OK to get facts from books, if we had them at home, instead of the Internet. But I didn't put it down quick enough when she said that thing about "elderly relatives," and she looked right at me and called out my name in front of everyone and said, "I know *you* have a grandfather who fought in the war."

Everyone looked at me then, and they kept asking me questions for the rest of the day, about if he was a hero, did he have medals and that kind of thing. It was so annoying. I don't even know how Miss Fullerton knew that about my grandad. Maybe she saw something on TV about it – there was that ceremony last May that he went to.

Anyway, I knew then and there that the project was going to be a failure, because, plain and simple, my grandad didn't talk about the war. And since he was the only grandparent I had who was still alive, it wasn't like I could ask anyone else about it.

My dad said before that Grandad fought in Burma, which is now called Myanmar. I thought that was confusing – not just the name change, I mean, but why didn't Grandad fight closer to home? Didn't he care about what was happening with Hitler and the Jews? I knew the Japanese came into it somewhere, but I wasn't sure where exactly.

I wished there was a way I could get Grandad to talk about these things. He would be coming to Oxford on the 21st, and staying until Boxing Day, just like he did every year. Mum and Dad always tried to get him to stay for longer, but I don't think he liked being away from home. But since my other aunts and uncles lived farther away, it was Mum and Dad's job to make sure Grandad was all right at Christmastime.

I decided to do everything I could to make Grandad talk. I went with Dad to the station to meet him off the train. He had this old brown suitcase, and moved with a slow, shuffling walk. He shook Dad's hand and ruffled my hair. I think he couldn't remember my name. I suppose he has a lot of other grandchildren.

But it wasn't as if any of them were making as much of an effort with him as I was. None of my siblings were, anyway. They couldn't have cared less that he was around. David and Susie were out with their friends most of the time, and Molly spent hours and hours shut up in her room, talking to people on MSN messenger. So that left me, and I really did try. At least, at first.

I told Grandad about my project the first evening after he came to stay. There was a fire crackling in the hearth and our great big Christmas tree was spreading its lovely smell around the room, and I felt relaxed. Grandad looked relaxed, too. He was looking through a book of postcards Mum had shown him earlier, and he seemed to like the pictures. I don't know why – I glanced over his shoulder as I was passing by and they looked pretty ugly: they were all industrial towns, not nice and old like Oxford. I asked if he liked Oxford.

"What?" He frowned at me. I had to repeat myself three times before he understood what I was saying. I don't think it was his hearing, though; I think he's just not used to the way we talk. He has a much thicker accent than we do. But finally he shook his head and said no, he'd never liked Oxford.

"Didn't you go to uni here?" I asked, curiously. He kind of smiled and shook his head. Then he asked what *I* thought of Oxford, and I talked for a bit about a class trip we'd had a while ago. Miss Fullerton had brought us around the city showing us interesting things, like the lamp-post from *The Lion, the Witch and the Wardrobe* and a cross on the street where these three bishops had been burned at the stake. I finished up by telling him about the World War Two project.

"How old are you?" he asked.

"I'm ten years old," I told him, patiently. "I'll be eleven in March. And I'll be going into secondary school next year."

He nodded, and then told me all this stuff about the war that I already knew, like about rationing and the Blitz and Winston Churchill saying *we will fight them on the beaches*. I was annoyed because it's always annoying when adults think you're stupid. So as soon as I could, I butted in, "What about you, Grandad? What did you do?"

He leaned back on the couch so that the frame creaked. He said he'd fought in Burma, in a battery in the 28th Field Regiment. I asked what kind of guns he'd fired, and he said all kinds, he didn't really remember. And then he started warbling a tune under his breath and I didn't want to interrupt so I stopped asking questions.

The next day, Dad brought him into town, and I didn't see him till evening. We didn't get a chance to talk because Mum and Dad put on a *Yes, Minister* on the TV, which they seemed to think was really funny and which sent me right to sleep. But when I woke up the next morning, there was a book on my nightstand. I asked Mum, and she said that Grandad had brought it back from Blackwell's for me.

I tried to read it at breakfast, but I was pretty soon disappointed. It was boring. It was called *Singing the Lord's Song in a Foreign Land*, and some minister had written it about being in Burma. But he used a lot of big words and there was barely anything about war, just a lot about "the grace of God" and stuff like that.

When we were in the living room again that evening, while the others were playing Cluedo, Grandad asked me what I'd thought of the book, and I told him there was too much about God in it and he laughed. It was funny when he laughed because his mouth made a strange shape, and you could see his dentures come a bit loose.

"Anything you want to know about Burma," he said then, "it's in that book."

"Maybe you can tell me instead," I said hopefully, but he shook his head and said it was a long story, and anyway he didn't remember most of it.

I gave up after that. I left the book at my bedside and spent most of the next day playing *video games* at my friend Eric's house. It was pretty fun. In the evening I stayed in my room wrapping presents.

The next day was Christmas Eve, and everyone was cross and stressed. Susie burst out crying three times. David said he wished his family was normal. Mum kept asking me to do jobs like peeling potatoes or whatever and then she would just do it herself because she said I wasn't doing it right. And in the evening time, she told me I had to stay behind with Grandad while everyone else went to church.

I thought that was so unfair. I knew Grandad preferred to go to church on Christmas Day, but Dad normally went with him. Why was it my job this time? I was used to us all going to church together, and it was always kind of exciting at night, passing by all the houses with candles in the windows. You could almost believe Santa was real when you looked up at the dark rooftops. Plus, it meant you could sleep on in the morning. So, I felt kind of weird when I heard everyone piling into the car, their happy voices fading away with the rumble of the engine.

Then it was just me and Grandad. He was looking at his book of postcards again. I brought down a book and started reading it. I was a few chapters in when Grandad coughed and said, "Do you know what this is?"

I put down my book and went to look over his shoulder. He was pointing at a black-and-white photo of a big building that looked like a department store or something, with a small park in front of it. The date at the bottom read *Broadgate, Coventry 1953.*

"It's nice," I said, though I was just being polite.

"A friend of mine helped build it," said Granddad. "A lot of Coventry was bombed during the war, you see. They had to build a new cathedral, too." And then he rested his shaky hand on the page and said, "I can tell you a story about Coventry, if you want."

"Is it about the war?" I said, hopefully.

Grandad frowned and said no, not really. I rocked back on my heels, disappointed. He said the story started at the end of the war. He said if I listened, I might learn something. But it wouldn't be the kind of learning you got from books.

I supposed I didn't really have a choice about it. I went and sat down on the carpet, on the other end of the coffee table between me and him. I had my back to the fire, and I was comfortable enough. I watched his eyes get far away as he started talking...

PERFECT HAPPINESS

oventry, 1945

They were married in the Methodist church in Coventry. It was a quiet ceremony, as Luke's sister was still serving overseas. On Teresa's side, there was only her sister and brother-in-law, who had closed up the shop for the day. Teresa's parents had died in a motoring accident ten years before.

Luke's father had also died some years ago after a long illness, so it was just his mother in the front pew, with neighbours and friends in the rows behind her. Teresa knew most of them, too, from the shop, though when they were shaking hands with her outside after the ceremony, none of them would acknowledge the relation. Maybe they thought she would be embarrassed if they brought up the fact that until recently (until the day before yesterday, in fact), she had been working behind a counter. Or maybe Mrs. Carmichael didn't want to be reminded of how she'd kicked up such a fuss last Tuesday because her sugar ration wasn't yet available.

They gave her blissful smiles instead and pretended that they were meeting for the first time, and Teresa didn't mind because she was feeling blissful inside. Luke, standing beside her with his auburn hair slicked back and a white carnation on his lapel, looked so handsome today. Coming down the aisle a few moments ago, her hand had been entirely enclosed in his, and though they weren't touching now, she caught his eye every now and again. She couldn't seem to stop smiling. He didn't smile at all, but no one really expected him to. At any rate, he got his shoulder squeezed and his face kissed plenty of times, and it was plain that he was just as well-loved in the neighbourhood as his mother.

"My head aches," said Luke in the car on the way to the hotel – the first words he had spoken since "I will" – and Teresa took off her left glove and put a cool hand to his forehead. He closed his eyes and let his head drift back against the seat. They were happy that way for most of the drive, apart from being disturbed by a car horn.

Luke didn't like loud noises, on account of the war, but fortunately he still had a good appetite, so he seemed willing enough to put up with the bustle around him during the wedding breakfast. Teresa didn't eat as much as him, but not for lack of trying. It seemed that every time she lifted a forkful to her lips, someone else would come up to talk to her. They generally said something about how wonderful the Parrishes were or how handsome Luke was looking – "Just like his old self again" – remarks which Teresa was perfectly willing to agree with.

When her sister and brother-in-law came up to talk to her, however, their congratulations were more subdued. Kathleen made a promising start by telling Teresa that marriage wasn't what she thought it was.

"And what, exactly, do *you* think that I think it is?" Teresa wanted to know, and she had to bite her lips to prevent herself from actually saying so. She reminded herself that she was a blissful bride, and said instead, calmly, "I suppose I'll learn soon enough."

"Maybe you won't," said Kathleen, darkly. "Some people never do. They just go on hoping it'll get better, and never actually do anything about it."

"It's true," said Brian, who didn't look in the least put out by his wife's disillusioned remarks. Leaning an arm over the back of Kathleen's seat, he closed a fist to demonstrate to Teresa, "You've got to work and *work*."

"Well, I've never minded a bit of work."

"It's not you I'm worried about," said Kathleen. There was a pause, and then their gazes all turned to Luke, who was sitting a few seats away, just out of earshot. He had finished eating and was staring off into the corner of the reception room, his sinewy hands folding his napkin into smaller and smaller squares.

"Do you know," Kathleen went on, lowering her voice as she leaned towards Teresa, "that when we went to talk to him just now, he didn't say a single word to us?"

"He smiled," said Brian.

"He *nodded*. He didn't smile. Tess, was he really like that before?"

Teresa thought back to the time when she had first started walking out with Luke. 1939 seemed like an age ago now, and they had only gone on a few dates before he enlisted. She was seventeen then and thrilled that the older boy had noticed her. She remembered chattering away the whole time when they went to the cinema together; she couldn't even stop when the picture was on. "He was always…quiet."

"But he was able to string a few sentences together, wasn't he?" Kathleen prompted. "And I'm sure he smiled a little."

Her voice had gotten a little louder on the last few words, and Teresa gave her a warning look. Anxiously, she looked down the table at Luke, who gave no sign that he had heard anything. His napkin had been ripped into shreds by now.

"Please keep your voice down," she said, turning back to Kathleen. In a whisper, "Remember what I told you last night. I want to take care of him. I want – "

But she got no further, because Mrs. Parrish had just come up, taking a seat in the chair beside which Brian had been hovering and sparing not a glance either for him or his wife. Her gaze, instead, zeroed in on Teresa, and she said, "Ah! Here you are," as though she was surprised to find her at the high table. "My dear, I don't want to worry you, but Mrs. Lyndon just ate the cardboard icing off her slice of cake. The caterers should have taken it off before they cut it, of course; if I told them once, I told them a hundred times..."

"Goodness, is she all right?"

"Well, I think you'd better check on her, my dear. She's in the cloakroom." Patting the back of Teresa's chair, Mrs. Parrish watched as her daughter-in-law got to her feet, and remarked, as though continuing some earlier conversation, "Yes, it *is* a good thing you wore something that will be useful later on. White is pretty but hardly practical."

"I think blue suits Tess much better than white," Kathleen countered, so that Mrs. Parrish was forced to turn around and acknowledge her presence for the first time. "With her dark hair, you know."

"Yes, she *is* dark," said Mrs. Parrish, looking Teresa over. "But you should really perm your hair, dear. I'm sure it was very patriotic of you to give up that luxury, but you're a married woman now, and you know most of us do it. I'll send you to my hairdresser when you're back from your honeymoon."

Keeping her composure with some effort, Teresa thanked her mother-in-law. "And now I should really go and check on Mrs. Lyndon." With gratitude, she ducked out of the crossfire, and she did her best to avoid Mrs. Parrish, Kathleen, and Brian for the rest of the reception. It was not too difficult, as within another hour she and Luke were on the road anyway, setting out for Blackpool while there was still light in the day.

They drove in a borrowed car to the train station and found a compartment to themselves. Teresa supervised the loading of their luggage while Luke sank into his seat. He was positively grey with exhaustion, and his tie was wrinkled and off to one side. He groaned, half-asleep, when the whistle blew, and shifted on his seat trying to find a comfortable place until Teresa said, "Lean on me, darling."

He opened his eyes and turned them on her. Up close, she could see that they were brown with flecks of green. She held her breath for a moment, but then he closed them again and nestled against her shoulder. His head was heavy, and it only grew heavier as the journey went on. But Teresa wouldn't have moved for all the money in the world. When she was sure he was fast asleep, she raised his hand to her lips and kissed his calloused palm. Then she intertwined it with her own and watched out the window as the scenery shifted from city to country to sea.

Luke didn't mind the rain so much, though Teresa said it spoiled things. She got up every morning earlier than him, with plans made out for walks they were going to take along the cliffs, or beaches they were going to visit, only to twitch back the lace curtains of their hotel room to see that the sun wasn't shining, after all. So they would go walking along the south pier or the promenade instead, bumping into people and dodging trams. Teresa kept a firm grasp on Luke's arm after the first time he nearly walked out in front of one.

He couldn't help it if he didn't notice things the way other people did. In a place like this, he barely even noticed the days passing, because everything happened in the same sequence, over and over. Morning – bad weather, Teresa disappointed. Afternoon – prom, pier, shops. Evening – dinner, walk along the pier again. Night bed, hurtling into sleep as soon as his head hit the pillow.

The mist came down on the third or fourth day of their holiday. Luke, of course, wasn't keeping count, and this led to even more dismay on Teresa's part. They still attempted a walk every afternoon, clad in oilskins, and bowed their heads under the slanting rain. But now, walking up the south pier, the shapes of people loomed out of the mist at them, invisible one minute and practically in their faces the next. Luke didn't like these unexpected meetings, and when Teresa inevitably suggested they turn back, he was always relieved. The sight of coiling mist and the sound of lapping water had taken on a sinister character for him, and while it wasn't much better in the hot, crowded recreation room of the hotel, at least when they were sitting there, he knew where everyone was.

The one good thing he could say about being in Blackpool was that his usual nightmares seemed to have taken a holiday, too. His dreams at night were confused and often a little sickening, placing him back in Yenangyaung with the 28th Regiment or back in the hospital, but he didn't wake up in a cold sweat like he did at home. In fact, the first real disturbance to his sleep came from outside, announcing itself with a hammering at their door one night.

Luke woke first, of course, his hand reaching for a weapon that wasn't there. It collided with the nightstand instead and knocked over a glass of water. The sound woke Teresa, and she sat up with a gasp. She was on the other side of the bed, a long strip of bedclothes between her and Luke. He wasn't sure how that arrangement had started, but he had made no attempt to cross the uncharted territory and neither had she.

The hammering at their door continued, accompanied by a voice which Luke didn't recognise, which told them to get up right away and leave their things, to keep calm and vacate the hotel by the nearest exit. Luke kept calm, all right; he kept deadly calm. As the person outside their door, whoever it was, moved on the next room, he found Teresa's hand in the darkness and squeezed it. "Come on," he said.

He smelled the smoke as soon as they were in the corridor. Keeping Teresa behind him – he was now gripping her arm, and she kept saying that he was hurting her, but her words barely made a dent on his consciousness – he proceeded towards the staircase. He could hear frantic cries from downstairs, feet rushing down the stairs. More doors opened behind them as other guests vacated their rooms and asked what was happening. But Luke didn't look around or join in their queries. He knew what was happening. It was what he had been waiting for, what he had always known was lurking on the horizon, through all the victory celebrations. They had told him that it was all over, but he had never really believed it.

Teresa had fallen silent now, but he could hear a faint snuffling that told him she was probably crying. "It's all right," he told her in a whisper as they descended the stairs, step by cautious step. "It's going to be all right."

But when they reached the bottom of the staircase, he found himself proved wrong. A flurry of footsteps behind them, a cry of alarm from Teresa, an exhaled breath on the back of his neck, and Luke moved on instinct, throwing a punch in darkness. Pain shot through his knuckles as it landed, and he heard a crunch and then a thump as whoever it was hit the floor.

And then, someone shone a torch, and Luke saw the young man in his nightshirt, collapsed on the floor with his hands over his nose. He had seen the guest a few times in the recreation room. Looking now at the blood running over the man's fingers, Luke had the first, queasy sense that he might have made a mistake.

Apart from that terrible air-raid in '40, it was quite possibly the longest hour in Teresa's life. They were herded out of the hotel and into the street, where they huddled together in their night clothes and listened to the hiss of the sea on the dark shore behind them. Rumours flew among the guests about how the fire had started, how big it was, and how the place was going to be devoured in a matter of minutes if they didn't get help. By the time the brigade arrived, the owner informed them ruefully that it had, in fact, already been doused. Then they had to wait another half hour before they could go in, and all the while that this was going on, recriminations and accusations were pouring from the wife of the man Luke had hit.

Young Mr. Fletcher, who was also in Blackpool on his honeymoon, had panicked when he heard about the fire and rushed ahead of the other guests, including his own wife, to get to the entrance first. In bumping past the Parrishes on the staircase, he had not imagined himself rushing into further danger, but Luke, already shaken, had mistaken the man for some kind of enemy, and his fist had met Mr. Fletcher's face, and now Mr. Fletcher had a broken nose and a whole world of trouble was waiting for them.

This trouble centred itself around Teresa rather than Luke, because he hadn't said a word since the incident. The way that his face had drained of all colour, and his eyes had gone so very wide and glassy, was telling enough, and seemed to alarm Mrs. Fletcher and most of the people assembled in front of the hotel. It even alarmed Teresa a little bit. She had touched his hand once, and she found that it was cold as ice.

The arrival of the police meant that, thankfully, Mr. Fletcher had to be brought to the hospital. He was helped into the patrol car, his wife trailing behind. Then the hotel owner told them that it was safe to return to their rooms. The fire had, after all, spread from a discarded cigarette and only burnt a few curtains in the rec room. Under the wary gazes of the other guests, Teresa told Luke to go back inside. She had to repeat herself a few times until he finally acknowledged her, with a shake of his body and a quick nod. Slowly he moved to the door.

On the distant horizon, a grey patch on the sky, like a seeping dampness, foretold the dawn. The police inspector was waiting by the door of the patrol car with his notebook, and raised his eyebrows when Teresa came up. "What's your name, ma'am?"

"Teresa Evans – I mean Parrish. It's Parrish now."

"Mrs. Parrish, I'll want to speak to your husband too."

"Can't you just talk to me? Please," she added, quickly, as the inspector opened his mouth to object. "I can explain it all. Luke's shell-shocked from the war. With everything that happened tonight, I think he was spooked. He didn't mean to hurt Mr. Fletcher. He didn't mean to hurt anyone. He just thought he was protecting me."

"Well, all the same," said the policeman, noting something down, "I'll want to speak to your husband to get his side of things. What time today would be convenient for me to return?"

"He won't tell you anything," Teresa said, and then, seeing the look on the policeman's face, "I mean he won't tell you anything *sensible*, Inspector. He's in a kind of a fog at the moment."

"That sounds a little alarming, Mrs. Parrish."

"I don't mean...of course he'd never hurt anyone! Not willingly." Teresa sighed shakily, folding her hands in front of her chest. "Please, inspector, he just had a shock. He's seeing a doctor back home and we hope things will get better soon –"

"Where's home?"

"Coventry. We're on our honeymoon."

Something in the man's demeanour softened, and he glanced up at Teresa. "I suppose you came for the weather?"

"Yes," she said, coughing out a desperate laugh. "We've been sunbathing."

"I can imagine. Mrs. Parrish." He became all business again. "Mrs. Parrish, while I do have sympathy for your husband's condition, unfortunately boxes still need to be ticked. If the Fletchers decide to press charges, then I will have to visit you again and speak to your husband. Whether or not I can get anything *sensible* out of him, as you say."

"Yes, Inspector. I understand."

But the policeman did not return that day, because the Fletchers did not end up pressing charges. A visit from Teresa to the hospital, complete with tears, was enough to soften even Mrs. Fletcher's heart. It was late afternoon by the time Teresa returned to the hotel, and Luke was still asleep. At dinnertime she woke Luke so that they could go down and eat. She spent the rest of the evening packing their things.

They were not due to leave Blackpool until Friday, and it was Tuesday now. But between the curious whispers of the other guests, the mist, and the rain, Teresa felt she would not be altogether sorry to have to cut their holiday short, and so she booked them a train back for early the next morning. Mrs. Parrish would want to know why they had come back so soon, of course, and Teresa wasn't sure whether she should make something up or tell her mother-in-law the truth. She would just have to think it over.

It was difficult to think back on the pre-war days, because Luke felt like he was looking at a different person altogether whenever he revisited that version of himself. What had he eaten? What had he done for fun? What had he wanted to do with his life?

He remembered Teresa, though, simply because she had always been around. Her family lived down the street from them in Hearsall Common, and her father had been employed by Luke's father in his motorcar factory. Teresa often called on the Parrishes when Luke was growing up, inviting him out to various neighbourhood games with children whom his parents would have preferred him not to associate with. His sister Lily, though she was a few years older, joined them in these games a few times, and it was she who first warned Luke that Teresa fancied him.

"She talks about nothing else," Lily had said, with an indulgent smile that had infuriated Luke at the time, because it seemed to take for granted that he *must* like Teresa back. Well, he didn't, because she was a silly, gawkish kid who never knew when she wasn't wanted. The girl could never take a hint. And anyway, she was much younger than him. Luke was anxious to dispel any misconception that might have arisen on this point, and so he stopped playing British Bulldog around the Common, much to his parents' relief, and started going out with girls his own age, much to Teresa's chagrin. She cried over him. He knew this both from having been told by other people and from seeing her hanging around blotchy-faced outside Burneys' grocery shop where her older sister worked. A few months after Luke had decided to take this course of action, Teresa's parents were killed on the road, and he felt awful every time he saw her around after that, like his stomach had dropped out of his body.

He started at university in Birmingham in 1936, at the same time that his sister was finishing her medical studies there. He'd had some intention of going into the law, which he thought at the time was his own impulse but which he could now see, looking back, had been a decision undertaken entirely to please his father, with little consideration of his own actual suitability for the profession. For two and a half years Luke struggled, sank deeper and deeper into indifference, and watched his friends doing apprenticeships and getting into professions while he read dull texts all day. The rumours of war actually came as a relief, because Luke had no scruples about dropping his books and enlisting. It was all done under the guise of patriotism, and no one questioned his decision.

Around this time, he came across Teresa again, and he discovered with some surprise that she had grown up. Where she had been all sharp angles before, she was now soft. Her brown hair, swept off her smooth forehead and bobbed to her shoulders in the latest style, was soft and shot through with gold strands when the light caught it. Her blue eyes, previously round and innocent as a baby's, now had a strength of understanding to them. She was walking out with one or two young men in the neighbourhood when Luke came back to Coventry, but she quickly dropped them once Luke had made it clear that his feelings to her had changed.

Or maybe his feelings hadn't changed at all, because she still infuriated him, just in an entirely new way. She had picked up a few coquettish tricks, and she had clearly been warned by someone, probably her sister, not to take things too far with him. They went to the pictures together a few times, but there were no snatched kisses in the dark of the cinema. They went dancing, too, one time, and Luke couldn't remember where else. He just remembered going to train in Halifax shortly after that, and his whole life re-orienting itself around the war.

He and Teresa had never made any promises to each other, but her face had lingered in his mind, and the idea of her came back to him at various times in the war: during the Coventry air raids in 1940, during the retreat from Burma to India in 1942, and during the assault by the Japanese on their base at Kohima in 1943. Things got foggy from that point on, and Luke didn't even try to delve into those more recent memories. He just knew that somehow Teresa Evans had come back into his life yet again. She couldn't seem to stay away.

And now here she was, sitting across from him on a hot, crowded train. There were dark shadows under her eyes, but every time she dozed off, she would sit back up again straight away, guiltily. He had heard her tossing and turning most of last night. She had even almost crossed the uncharted territory between them once or twice. From what he understood of it, she was worried about what excuse they should give his mother for coming home early. Mum had been wired in plenty of time and everything was arranged for their return, so Luke didn't know what she was so worried about.

"We'll tell her it was because of the bad weather," Teresa had said this morning at breakfast, and Luke had just nodded. Then, while they were waiting for their train at Central Station, she took it into her head that it would be better to tell her the truth altogether, but once they were en route to Coventry, that resolution changed again.

"We'll say there was a mix-up at the hotel," Teresa said finally, after their compartment had emptied at the Birmingham stop and they were alone again. "We'll say they thought our booking was only for a few days, and that it was too much bother to change it." She was looking at him eagerly, so Luke raised his eyes to meet hers and nodded again. And then, a sudden jolt of the train made

Teresa throw out her hand to the edge of her seat for support, and he saw a couple of bruises going up her right forearm. He flinched.

"It's all right," said Teresa, evidently thinking that he had been startled by the movement of the train, before following his gaze. The eagerness evaporated from her expression as she looked down at her own arm, and he saw her swallow. She turned her gaze out the window and covered her arm with her cardigan sleeve.

"I'm sorry," said Luke, and it was her turn to flinch. He suddenly, desperately, just wanted her to look him in the eye again. "I didn't realise I was hurting you the other night."

"You were just trying to protect me," said Teresa, but she was still looking out the window.

"No," said Luke, shaking his head. "No, that's not... I shouldn't have..." Why wouldn't the words come? He could feel the words that he wanted to say, but every time he got close it was like he was cut adrift again, set loose in the bobbing sea of his thoughts.

He got up from his seat instead and came around to sit at Teresa's side, moving her bag out of the way. He gently took her arm in his calloused hands and pushed up her cardigan sleeve. She breathed in audibly, and he wondered if she was frightened of him. But when he looked up into her eyes, the expression in them was not what he would have called fear.

Luke ran a finger over the bruises, very lightly, and said again in a low voice, "I'm sorry." And then, on a sudden impulse, because of the way she was looking at him, he added, quickly, "Are you… happy?"

At those words Teresa's face broke into the radiant, trusting smile that she had worn all day at the wedding, the smile which Luke could hardly believe was real, especially since it seemed to be reserved for him. She reached up and cupped his cheek with her hand, and the churning sea of his thoughts stilled as she said, "Of course I am, darling. I'm with you."

WAR STORIES

*M*rs. Parrish, as it turned out, accepted their early return from the honeymoon without question. She had never approved of Blackpool as a holidaying spot in the first place. She had, as she informed Teresa, spent a miserable week there with Lily and Luke back in '41, not long after Mr. Parrish's death.

"Rained on for the full seven days, we were, and Luke got such a chill. Oh! It broke my heart to send him back overseas in that state."

"You were in Blackpool during the war?" Teresa said, glancing at her husband across the breakfast table. He didn't look up from his toast. "I didn't know."

"Well, he didn't often get leave, you see, dear. That was one of the only times we were all together, before his accident, I mean, and what a waste! When I think of sending him away on the Victoria train, and the rain still

31

pouring down outside. My dear, he looked so pale and small in his uniform, you can't think."

Luke's knife fell off his plate and he quickly picked it up again, leaving a smear of margarine on the tablecloth. Teresa looked at him anxiously, trying to read some sign in his face that he wanted them to change the subject. "They say it's been one of the worst summers in years," she said, hesitantly. "Normally you'd get at least one fine day in Blackpool. When I was there with my sister last year, we got two, but it was so bad this time we couldn't even go for a bathe."

"Well, Luke doesn't like sea bathing, anyway."

"He – he doesn't?" Teresa asked, finally resigned to using the third person since Luke showed no intention of joining the conversation.

"Not anymore. He loved it before his accident, of course. His father taught him, you know, and he was like a fish, and now Luke won't go near it. Though, I suppose..." Mrs. Parrish stopped for a moment, looking at her son for the first time and then, when he did not acknowledge her glance, flicking her eyes away once more, "... I suppose he must have had to swim a great deal when he was overseas. They had to cross rivers, you know, dear, with heavy equipment. And in Burma, of course, monsoon season starts in April or May, and the mist comes down and the rivers flood, and any man who can't swim then... well."

She shook her head and began humming cheerfully as she poured herself another cup of coffee.

"I know so little about that part of the world," said Teresa. "It's hard for me to even picture him there."

"Yes, I suppose you've never left England, have you, dear?" Satisfied by her daughter-in-law's shake of the head, Mrs. Parrish went on, "That was one thing about the war; it got young people out in the world. I often think that's the only reason Luke signed up to begin with. He couldn't wait to get out of the country. He often said it to me, he'd say, 'Mum, there's nothing for me here.' And then when he first got to Burma he used to write me such long letters. 'Mum, you can't believe how beautiful it is here at sunset. I wish you could see it.' He was in Mandalay then, before it fell to the Japanese, you know. And the colours in the sky, he used to say, the colours were different to the colours you see here."

Luke had finished his toast and drunk only half of his coffee. He got up from the table without looking at either of them and he left the kitchen.

"Maybe I should –" Teresa began, thinking of their packed bags in the hall.

But Mrs. Parrish resumed,

"He was different then. You can't think how different he was, dear, because you didn't know him before. But he was so clever, so warm. He looked around him and saw things, not like now. And he thought the world of me."

"I *did* know him before, Mrs. Parrish," Teresa now found it necessary to interject. "I've known Luke almost my whole life."

Her mother-in-law just stared at her, the corners of her mouth turning down and an almost frightened look in her eyes. Luke had her eyes, brown flecked with green, and perhaps that was why Teresa relented after a squirming minute and said, "But of course I didn't know him that *well*. I'd love to look at one of those letters some time, Mrs. Parrish, and see what life was like for him then."

"I threw them all away," Mrs. Parrish said, abruptly rising from the table and starting to pile the dishes into her hands. She slapped a plate on top of a bowl and dropped a mess of dirty cutlery on top of it. As Teresa moved to help her, she waved her off. "I couldn't read them again, you know, not after what happened to him. He was so bright, so brave. Why, he might have gotten the Victoria Cross."

"I'm sure he would have," Teresa murmured, trailing her mother-in-law to the sink with nothing in her hands. "Can I help with –"

"But it's no use talking of the past like this." Mrs. Parrish dropped the dishes into the sink with a clatter. "You'd better unpack. I've left your wedding presents in Luke's room, though I'm afraid the new bed hasn't arrived yet, so you'll have to sleep in Lily's old room for now." Turning, for Teresa had made a surprised noise at this, "You don't mind, do you, dear? Luke's bed isn't big enough to fit both of you. Though of course, if you have your heart set on staying together –"

"It's all right, Mrs. Parrish." By now, Teresa was blushing deeply. "If you just show me where to go, I can bring my things there instead."

The Parrishes' house was a semi-detached that had been built in the 1930s, located in a row of houses just off Kenilworth Road. Theirs, along with that of their next-door neighbour, of course, the widow Mrs. Lyndon, was the only house on Wragby Row that had not been bombed out during the war. Now it was surrounded on all sides, all day, seven days a week, by the sounds of drilling and hammering. Like much of Coventry, the whole neighbourhood had become a building site, with cranes towering into the sky and scaffolding encroaching on the pavements below. It was, perhaps, not the best abode for a soldier recovering from battle fatigue.

But for Luke and Teresa, living anywhere else had not been an option. Even apart from the money that they didn't have, there was Mrs. Parrish to consider. Teresa had known her more than ten years by now, even if Mrs. Parrish pretended not to remember her, and she still had no idea what was going on inside the older woman's head most of the time. Though she was not a woman who wore her heart on her sleeve, it was clear that she had suffered, and that she had lost, and that to leave her alone now would have been cruel. Her husband had died during the worst year of the war, and she couldn't even blame the war for it. The son that she had known, if her talk about throwing away his old letters was any indication, had been lost somewhere in the monsoons of Burma, and her daughter was now halfway across the world, tending wounds and treating ailments in a malaria-infested country.

Teresa did her best to keep all of this in mind during the first week or so after she and Luke had returned to Coventry as a married couple. She was sleeping in Lily's old room, which was the smallest room in the house, on a camp-bed so creaky that she felt like she was keeping the whole house awake with her tossing and turning at night, amid environs so dusty that she seemed always to be either sneezing or waiting to sneeze, so these reminders about what Mrs. Parrish had suffered were necessary.

On the third day, she tried to clean up the place a bit, but had to stop when Mrs. Parrish discovered her and seemed suspicious that Teresa was using the task as an excuse to rifle through her family's personal effects. She did not express this suspicion openly, but Teresa was made aware of it, nonetheless.

"You're probably imagining things," said her brother-in-law Brian, in that tone of voice he always used when he imagined he was giving helpful advice. "From the sounds of it, you've been getting on with one another. You cook together every day, don't you?"

"More like she cooks, and I fetch and carry," said Teresa with a sigh. She had dropped into Burneys' grocery on her way home from town, and she was leaning against the counter with her shopping bags clustered at her feet. "Though I *have* been trusted with baking a lemon cake for this evening. Mrs. Parrish's invited the minister for tea. Well, I say 'invited', but the poor man really had no choice in the matter. Mrs. Parrish came up to him after service last Sunday and wouldn't take no for an answer."

Kathleen, who was fixing one of the displays in the front window, gave a snort of laughter at this, but Brian's attention had been caught more by the mention of the minister than by the jab at Teresa's mother-in-law. "Is this the fellow who was a prisoner-of-war?"

Teresa nodded. "He was an army chaplain, in Burma, actually, like Luke. He was repatriated just last month."

Brian gave a low whistle, and Kathleen, returning to her spot behind the counter, said thoughtfully, "I don't suppose they would have met out there?"

"I thought the same thing, at first," said Teresa, wistfully. "It would be so nice for Luke to have someone to talk to about it all. Most of the men in his troop are dead now, but I suppose it was a big place, Burma. And even if they did meet, I doubt Luke would know the difference. He says he doesn't remember much from back then."

"I'm sure he doesn't *want* to remember it," was Kathleen's sensible response, and her husband, shaking his head, mused,

"The things those men must have seen. I'd say they've got stories that would make your blood run cold."

"Luke gets nightmares, sometimes," said Teresa, thinking of last night when both she and Mrs. Parrish had been woken by an inhuman scream. But she didn't mention that, because the look in her brother-in-law's eyes was now far too eager for her liking. Instead, she just said, lamely, "So maybe he *does* remember more than he lets on."

Kathleen, no doubt noticing her sister's discomfort, nudged her husband and said, "But that doesn't mean you'd get any stories out of him. He wouldn't even say two words to us at the wedding. What makes you think he'd want to talk about the war?"

"A man can dream," said Brian, and on seeing the glares they both directed at him, lifted his hands. "What? I was counting milk coupons while these men were fighting for our country. You can't blame me for wanting to know more about it."

"They wouldn't have had a country to fight for if not for us," Teresa pointed out, and her sister hummed in agreement. "What would people around here have done for food if our shop had closed down during the worst of it?"

"But you can't compare what we did to what *they* did." Brian picked up an empty ration book from the counter and brandished it at Teresa as though to prove his point. "And if you understand *that*, Tess, you'll understand your husband better too. We might have lived in Hell for a while, but they've never left it."

The Reverend Timothy Albright was a small, dark-haired man, who smoothed down the doilies on armchairs before he sat into them, hovered his hand a few inches below his mouth when he was eating a biscuit so as not to get crumbs on the floor, and in general seemed so fussy and immaculate that it was difficult to imagine him anywhere other than at a pulpit or in a parlour. Yet Teresa had it on good authority that he had, in fact, lived elsewhere, and in the inhospitable environment of a prison camp, for quite some time.

After Mrs. Parrish's 'invitation' to him last Sunday, Teresa had asked around and gathered from various neighbours an idea of the man's service during the war. He had served as a chaplain first on the Northwest Frontier, then been transferred with his Gurkha battalion to Burma, where he had assisted in the evacuation of Mandalay and been present for the long and torturous march that had constituted the British retreat to India in 1942. He had been captured by the Japanese close to the Indian border, and he continued to serve as chaplain to the other prisoners-of-war in Rangoon.

Whatever gaps still existed in this story were filled in obligingly by the man himself. Mr. Albright told them, as Mrs. Parrish poured his tea, of the malaria and starvation rampant in the prison camp, of the firing squads that had dealt with those who attempted to escape, and the tropical conditions that had made the trains transporting weapons and troops so unbearably hot. He was, all in all, not shy of talking about his experiences. And while at first Teresa had failed to see the marks of his experience on his physical person, the longer he sat and talked, the more she began to notice them. There was the beginning of an angry welt showing just above his collar, and his complexion had the leathery look of a delicate skin that had spent long hours out in the sun. Then there were his eyes, which were strangely arresting. When he had first arrived, they had appeared to be a muddy green, but after a time they darkened, and it was difficult to tell if the effect had been produced by the waning daylight or by the nature of the tale he was telling.

Luke, Teresa noticed, listened attentively to Mr. Albright, his elbows propped on his thighs as he leaned forward in his chair. Whenever the minister would direct one of his remarks to Luke, however, in a gentle nudge to join the conversation, he would only get a nod or a shake of the head. Both men, it seemed, had once woken up to the same sun and seen the same stars at night, but only one of them was willing to talk about what it had been like.

Through all of this, in fact, the only person who did not seem very interested in what the minister had to say was the one who had been so anxious to invite him in the first place, Mrs. Parrish. She sat and fidgeted as he spoke, sometimes contributing an observation on 'the East' only to be politely corrected, and then her left fist would clench and unclench on the article from *The Daily Express* praising the generals of the Burma campaign which she had brought exclusively for Mr. Albright's perusal, and which he had taken one glance at before launching back into his own account. Her ire finally found a target when Teresa brought out the lemon cake that was supposed to be their dessert.

In this instance, Teresa could hardly blame her. The cake *was* a bit of a disaster. She had used too much baking powder and the batter had risen too quickly before collapsing in the middle. It looked rather sad and floppy on the plate, and though everyone (everyone being Mrs. Parrish and Mr. Albright) declared that they were sure what it lacked in presentation it would make up for in taste, they were soon proved wrong. The cake tasted bitter at the first forkful, and there was an edge to it that seemed like it might seep into your tongue and burn it. Teresa quickly put down her plate and urged the others not to attempt to have any more. They obeyed, all but Luke, who had already eaten his, and Mrs. Parrish began apologising to the minister and making excuses about the difficulties of making do with rationing. *That* Teresa could understand, but she thought it was going a bit overboard when her mother-in-law rose to her feet and practically dragged her out of the room.

"What is it?" she asked as soon as they reached the kitchen, and Mrs. Parrish rounded on her. She was flushed and breathing hard.

"What is it, you ask? Didn't you see the minister's face?"

"He seemed like he didn't mind too much," Teresa said, in her most placating tones. "He said he'd eaten worse in Rangoon –"

"He was being polite, you little *fool*." Mrs. Parrish made a lunge forward. "What do you think he'll say about my house after this? This is a man of God, a man who fought for our country and you serve him a cake that's not even fit for the dogs in the street. It's an absolute disgrace!"

Teresa had dealt with plenty of angry customers before, and she knew that the best thing to do was to put some distance between her and them. This she accordingly did, retreating to the other side of the kitchen so that there was a whole table and chairs between her and Mrs. Parrish. Her action seemed to calm her mother-in-law somewhat, too, who took a few breaths and mopped her brow with her shirt sleeve.

"I'm sorry about the cake, Mrs. Parrish," Teresa said, quietly. "Really I am. I wanted this evening to go well as much as you did. I think it's important for Luke to be around people who..."

"Is there anything you can do?" Mrs. Parrish asked, lifting her head so that she was looking her daughter-in-law square in the face. Her eyes, Luke's eyes, were cold and assessing.

"Anything I can do?" Teresa repeated, thrown by the odd emphasis in the question. "Do you want me to bake another cake, or..."

"I mean, is there anything you can actually *do*? Any way you can make yourself useful? Because if there is, I've yet to see it. You haven't helped around the house since you got here –"

"You won't let me," Teresa spluttered, but Mrs. Parrish ignored her and went on,

"You haven't done anything to bring Luke out of his shell –"

"But I think he's getting better! Didn't you see him this evening when Mr. Albright was telling his story –"

"You can't even stop him from disgracing himself in public." Mrs. Parrish lifted her chin, grimly satisfied at Teresa's silence. "Oh, yes. I heard about Blackpool. I know you didn't break up your honeymoon because of bad weather. The landlady of the hotel rang me up the very next day. She remembers me from when I stayed there before, you see, and she was worried about Luke."

"But I fixed it," Teresa protested. "The Fletchers didn't take things any further. I made sure –"

"You're embarrassed about him. Aren't you? That's why you lied about what happened when you came back." Mrs. Parrish's voice grew quieter. "You're ashamed of my son, of your own husband."

"I'm not!" Teresa was furious at herself for crying. She knew it made her look helpless, and she would have preferred to be anything but that right then. But the hot tears kept coming, and the room blurred before her eyes, so that Teresa heard rather than saw Mrs. Parrish moving to leave.

"I've left our guest alone for long enough. Clean yourself up before you come back in."

Teresa, though she was apparently useless in every other regard, did manage to do that. She stepped out into the evening air, ignoring the midges that dove for her face, and took some deep, quick breaths. Then she went back in and splashed some cold water on her face in the bathroom and looked in the mirror as she forced a smile once, twice. By the third time her eyes were looking a little less watery. She gave it another five minutes before she returned to the parlour, and neither of the men seemed to notice anything amiss.

Mr. Albright stayed for another hour, was very admiring of the late Mr.Parrish's Dickens collection, and even agreed to take a loan of *Little Dorrit* and *Dombey and Son*, all of which served to raise Mrs. Parrish's spirits considerably. He did ask Teresa to help him carry them out when he was leaving, which was a little strange, but then again, as he said himself, his hands were full with his briefcase and umbrella.

Dusk had come down by now, and the midges were thankfully gone, the neighbourhood around them finally free from the noise of construction. Mr. Albright seemed in no hurry to get to his car, which was parked a little way down the pavement, next to a builder's van. Instead, he gazed up at the evening star that had winked into being in the dreary sky and hummed to himself. Teresa slowed her pace to match his. She was a little taller than him, but there was something about his presence that made her feel dwarfed. She was surprised when he turned and cast his still dark eyes on her, and, seeming to read her thoughts, said,

"Well, I've had a splendid evening. Talked about nothing but myself for the full two hours and didn't let anyone else get a word in edgewise. Please tell me honestly, Mrs. Parrish, if you think me a bore now that you've had to sit and listen to my stories all evening."

"I found your stories very interesting, Mr. Albright, and I do hope you'll come for tea again." Teresa hesitated, and then added, a little shyly, that he could call her by her

Christian name, mainly because being called 'Mrs. Parrish' still didn't sit right with her. There was only really one Mrs. Parrish, after all.

"Then you must call me Tim. Oh, yes," Mr. Albright added, catching her protest before it had even escaped her lips, "Because I can tell already that we're going to be good friends. I knew from the moment I saw you in church last Sunday. And the next time that we meet, I will listen to all of *your* stories, and I promise not to utter a single word about myself."

"I don't have very many stories," Teresa said, with a half-smile. They had reached the car, and she hovered uncertainly while Mr. Albright leaned down to place his umbrella and briefcase onto the passenger seat but made no move to take the books from her. He straightened instead and turned to face her, with his back to the car door.

"Then you shall have to tell them very slowly, so that we can fill the time."

Teresa's smile became a full one. Mr. Albright regarded her for a moment longer, and then said, more seriously, "How is your husband?"

Teresa rubbed a thumb on the worn spine of one of the books she was holding, and chose her words carefully before replying, "He's not always himself, these days. But I think he enjoyed your visit this evening. I know he must have seemed quiet to you, but he doesn't usually concentrate like that on what people are saying."

"He *did* seem quiet," said Mr. Albright, tilting his head as he considered. "But he didn't seem uncomfortable, either, with my stories. I tried to tell the less grisly ones, of course." He laughed at Teresa's look of disbelief. "Oh yes, there are worse ones, I'm afraid. But what I mean to say, Teresa, is that I think this is an encouraging sign. It shows that he might be open to talking about such things in the future, provided he's in the right setting, with the right people, and so on."

"It's hard for me to know what to say to him," Teresa admitted, dimly aware that she was unburdening herself to a practical stranger but not wanting to stop. Remembering Brian's admonishing words, she added gloomily, "I can't possibly understand what it was like out there."

"But it seems to me that that in itself is a kind of understanding." As Teresa looked at him, confused, Mr. Albright elaborated. "Much worse to insist that you *do* understand, as so many people do. I've only been back in England a few short weeks, and I've been approached more times than I can count by people who try to explain to *me* about inhumane conditions in Japanese P.O.W. camps, about how the Burma campaign was won and so on." He hesitated, and then, "Your mother-in-law is, unfortunately, one of those people. But I don't mean to say that those people have bad intentions. I simply think they frustrate communication by insisting that they know everything already."

"But if I don't understand," said Teresa slowly, for his argument had spun her mind into knots, "then how can I help him?"

Mr. Albright drew a deep breath, and she thought for a moment that he was going to launch into another lengthy, slightly contradictory sermon, but instead, he abruptly said, "There's a book."

"A book?"

"Yes, a book that's luckily fallen into my possession, that may help you understand, if not your husband's experiences, then at least some of his behaviour. *The Traumatic Neuroses of War*, by a Dr. Abram Kardiner. He's an American, but we won't hold that against him, will we?" With a chuckle, Mr. Albright took the Dickens books out of Teresa's hands and piled them onto the front seat. "You may visit me tomorrow and borrow it, if you like?"

"Y-yes, all right," said Teresa, because he was looking at her expectantly, and then she shook his hand rather limply and watched him walk around to the driver's side of the car. She stayed standing on the pavement for a minute or two after his car had disappeared, bemused by the man's strange manners. As she walked back inside, she put a hand to her face and discovered, with some surprise, that she was smiling.

RADIO SILENCE

*T*here was little that drew Luke's attention these days. He had no curiosity about his neighbours, and the frenzied construction going on mere doors down barely registered with him, beyond the fact that the sounds sometimes made his head hurt. He nodded to his wife and mother in the mornings, but usually tuned out their remarks unless they required anything beyond a 'Yes' or 'No'. This was made easier by the fact that Teresa did not sleep in his bedroom, an arrangement which the elder Mrs. Parrish put down to the incompetence of deliverymen, who had, as of yet, failed to produce the bed apparently ordered weeks ago. As those weeks turned to months, her explanations died away, and Luke and Teresa went on sleeping apart. Teresa broached the subject with him once, but dropped it after that, evidently seeing that Luke preferred to leave things as they were.

Luke lived his life in a haze, apart from one daily occurrence that always had him on high alert. He was on his feet as soon as he heard the tell-tale squeak of a rusty bicycle wheel on the street outside, and he had always reached the downstairs landing by the time the postman rang the doorbell. Luke would take the pile of envelopes from the man without a word, sifting through them and plucking out any that were addressed to him. When he was upstairs again, Luke stuffed the letters in the same place where he kept his service medals, in a trunk with a heavy lid. He could have just thrown them away, of course, or burned them, but to go to such extremes seemed to him too terrible, too definitive. He settled instead for never reading them.

This routine continued through autumn and into the winter months. Sometimes he would have to sort through a large number of envelopes very quickly, and that led to the occasional slip. On one of these occasions, Teresa managed to get her hands on an envelope addressed to Luke, but it turned out to be only a letter from the Royal British Legion. He had a lucky escape that time, but he knew he had to be more vigilant from then on. He started lying in wait for the postman, sometimes haunting the hall a full half-hour before he was normally due, just in case the man should happen to come early. These tactics paid off, as there were no more slips, and the postman, for his part, got used to not having to ring the doorbell if he had any parcels. Luke would have the door wrenched open as soon as he heard footsteps crunching the gravel outside.

But then, one day, there was silence. It was not a Sunday, or a bank holiday. Of course those were the first things Luke checked as soon as he realised something was amiss. Figuring that the postman must have been delayed, he headed upstairs to his room and had his hand on the doorknob when he heard voices outside on the street.

He hurtled down the stairs so quickly that his foot caught on a step, and he had to grab the banister. Then, once he had righted himself, he sped through the hall and out through the open door. Teresa was standing on the path with a couple of envelopes in her hands, talking to the postman.

"A birthday present from the missus," the man was saying. "Said she was getting tired of all the noise the old one made."

Turning at Luke's approach, Teresa said cheerfully, "Darling, look at Mr. Bowman's new bicycle! Isn't it fine?" Luke snatched the envelopes from her hands and stormed back inside, reading the addresses as he went. One was for Mum; he threw that down on the hall table and took the other upstairs, handling it as delicately as though it were a grenade. Even after he had locked it in his trunk, and locked his bedroom door for good measure, his heart continued its hard pounding against his ribcage.

"Luke," came the distant voice of his wife, from the other side of the door. She sounded as though she was close to tears as she knocked over and over. "Luke, tell me what's wrong!" But Luke had his hands on his head and his chest was rising and falling rapidly, and his frightened eyes watched the doorhandle as it turned and turned again, to no effect. Eventually she gave up, and he praised his own foresight in locking his door. And if, later on, he stopped outside Lily's old room on his way to dinner to listen to the soft sound of crying, if he pondered for a little too long why Teresa had chosen to skip the meal, well, it was only natural to feel a little sorry for her. He would have felt sorry for anyone as in the dark as she was, who knew so little of the real importance of things.

"I know I shouldn't have done it," said Teresa the next day as she was sitting opposite Mr. Albright in his parlour. Her visits to the minister's house had now become so regular that his housekeeper, Mrs. Henshall, had started adding two extra custard creams to the plate which she usually brought in with the minister's tea. She held out the plate to Teresa now, who eagerly took one and thanked her.

"What shouldn't you have done?" Mr. Albright said languidly. He was only half-listening to her as he leafed through some notes. She still could not think of him as Tim, despite his telling her more than once to call him that, and so she tried to avoid using his name where possible.

Teresa waited until the housekeeper had left the room and then repeated herself, patiently. "I've written to one of the men in Luke's old troop."

A light frown appeared on Mr. Albright's forehead, bringing into sharp relief a crescent-shaped scar on his temple. He scribbled something down in the margins of his notebook and then asked, his tone nonchalant, "Which one?"

"His old sergeant. A man named Bill Farley."

Even the least perceptive of observers could not have missed the sudden alertness in Mr. Albright's posture, or the new tension in his hand as it hovered over the page, pen still held between his middle finger and thumb. Teresa, who was more attuned to his moods than most, instantly realised what it meant. "You know him, don't you?"

There was a pause, and then Mr. Albright put down his notebook and looked up at last. "Yes, as a matter of fact, I do." He rose from his chair, replacing the notebook in a drawer. Once this task was done, he returned his eyes to Teresa and said, "Sergeant Farley was in the same camp as me, for a time."

"He was a P.O.W.?" Teresa watched the minister carefully, noting the sad cast of his mouth. "When was this?"

Mr. Albright thought for a minute and sat back down in his armchair. "It would have been the summer of 1942, not long after I was taken prisoner myself. Farley was moved from Rangoon in July of that year to another camp, along with some of the other prisoners. I didn't see them again." He glanced up at Teresa again. "But since you're writing to him, I take it he's still alive. I'm glad to hear it."

"1942 was the year before Luke was sent back home shell-shocked," Teresa said slowly, trying to keep it all straight in her head. "During the retreat to India, is that right?" Mr. Albright nodded. "I didn't know anyone in Luke's troop had been captured."

"It was common enough in those days. The enemy was right on our heels all through that retreat, at least until the monsoons hit and drove them back." Mr. Albright reached for his tea. He always took it black, and he left the cup to cool for a few minutes before taking it up. He took a sip and continued cautiously, "Might I ask how you got hold of Farley's address?"

"That's the difficult part," said Teresa, with a sigh. At the minister's quizzical look, "I went through the trunk where Luke keeps his old medals and found a whole pile of letters there. Some of them are from Farley. I didn't open them or anything,– just took down the return address on the back."

"Teresa…"

"I know, I know, it was snooping. There's no excuse for it. Except –"

"Except?" Mr. Albright prompted, and his tone was gentler now, for he had noticed the tell-tale shine in Teresa's eyes. She looked away, so that he could only see her profile.

"Except that I can't go on like this for much longer."

Mr. Albright waited. After a minute or two, Teresa gave a sniff and looked back at him. She seemed to have stemmed the flow of tears, at least for now, and kept her voice steady as she said, "Yesterday he threw a fit because the postman got a new bicycle. He always watches out for him in the mornings, and hears him coming by the squeak of the brakes. Well, there was no squeak yesterday on account of the new bike, and Luke couldn't stand it. It's that – that hyper- whatever your American psychiatrist would call it…"

"Hyper-vigilance."

"Yes, that. Well, even knowing what it is, knowing something about what's going on in Luke's head, it doesn't really help anymore. Because I don't know how to make it go away. And we've tried, haven't we?" Teresa stared at Mr. Albright, a wild hope in her eyes, as though he were about to suggest some miracle cure that he had neglected to mention until now. He didn't. She continued, "These past few months, we've tried talking to him, or just sitting with him in silence, and even *praying* with him, because that seems to be something he likes doing, but it obviously doesn't give him any comfort because he still screams out in his sleep and watches for the postman and..." She stopped. Her voice had risen with her distress, and she suddenly remembered that they were not alone in the house.

Mr. Albright, on the other hand, looked unshaken. He took another sip of his tea. "It's as I've said to you before, Teresa. You can lead a horse to the water, but you cannot make him drink. Luke will only talk about his experiences if the desire to talk comes from within himself. And all *we* can do is make sure we have furnished a safe environment for him to talk to us, to me, or you, as the case may be, when he is ready."

"He's not going to talk to me," said Teresa, with such conviction in her voice that the minister, halfway through raising his cup to his lips, put it down again. "Not ever. With you, there's a chance, and with someone like Farley, who he looked up to, well, that's why I had to write to him. You see that, don't you?"

She was looking at him so anxiously that Mr. Albright had to nod. And when he spoke again, a moment later, he did his best to keep the trepidation out of his voice. "Will you ask him to visit?"

"If he's willing." Teresa glanced at her watch, and then shifted in her seat. "I must be going. Luke has his check-up today. Thank you for the tea."

"I can drive you home," said Mr. Albright, who had already risen from his seat. Teresa gave him that startled, grateful look which she always seemed to get when someone offered to do something for her. It was strange to see it on a face as pretty as hers. After all, shouldn't she have grown accustomed by now to people doing things for her? But the minister quickly cast away that thought, recognising the feelings from which it stemmed and resolving that he would not tolerate their presence any longer.

Mrs. Lyndon, the Parrishes' next-door neighbour, did not drop over very often, as she was now well into her seventies and preferred to sit listening to her wireless for hours on end. Whenever she *did* make a visit, it was to relay an important piece of information, and Mrs. Joanna Parrish was therefore rather disappointed, on this occasion, to find that it was only the usual nonsense about her daughter-in-law and Mr. Albright. She had a pretty good idea where the report had originated, with the minister's housekeeper, Maggie Henshall, who was an incorrigible gossip, and was able, as with all other such reports that had come her way since autumn, to refute it fairly easily.

"It's impossible, Agnes," she said, adding copious amounts of sugar to her neighbour's tea, just as she knew she liked to take it. "Tim Albright must be forty, at least, and he's seen so much of the world. As if he'd look twice at someone like Teresa."

"*I* hear he looks at her quite a lot," said Mrs. Lyndon, who always took things too literally. "Maggie says whenever she comes over to see him, he never gets any work done. He's supposed to be working on a book, you know. And after she's gone, he spends such a long time just standing at the window staring out at nothing."

"Well, he's a man with a lot on his mind. He was taken prisoner by the Japanese, probably tortured. You should hear some of his stories."

"Goodness me, I'd rather not." Mrs. Lyndon shuddered, swirling a spoon in her tea. "But anyway, Joanna, you'd better watch out for this girl. I don't like to repeat this, but some people have been saying, well… because of the way your son is these days you know, that she might…"

"I'd believe anything of *her*," Mrs. Parrish interrupted. "But not of Mr. Albright. We've known the man for years. Why, he was a great comfort to us when my Richie first got sick. Anything he's doing for Teresa now, it's just out of the kindness of his heart. He's a man of God, you know. He can't ignore anyone in his flock."

Mrs. Lyndon made a disappointed sound and raised her cup of tea to her lips. "Have you anything besides Digestives?" she asked after she had swallowed, with a meaningful glance at the plate that had been put before her, and Mrs. Parrish sighed and went to fetch the good biscuits.

When she came back to the parlour, she heard, with the sudden subsiding of the hammering that had been going on all morning, the purr of a car engine in the street outside. Quick as a flash, which was certainly quicker than Mrs. Parrish had thought the older woman capable of moving, Mrs. Lyndon got out of her chair and hurried to the lace curtains, twitching them back to see who it was.

"It's the minister," she said after a moment, the triumphant tone in her voice unmistakable, and of course Mrs. Parrish had to go and look then too. Sure enough, it was Mr. Albright's car that had pulled up in front of her house, and as they watched, he got out in a sprightly movement and went around to the passenger's seat to open the door. Teresa climbed out, adjusting the duffel coat, which was draped around her shoulders. The two stood close together talking for a minute or two.

"He has dropped her home," Mrs. Parrish said, finally breaking the painful silence. "Very kind. And of course, he must have come to see me."

But after another minute or so of talking, Mr. Albright touched Teresa's elbow as though in parting and went right back into his car without another glance at the house. Mrs. Parrish dropped the lace curtain in disgust.

"Well," she said, and cleared her throat.

"Well?" Mrs. Lyndon was looking at her expectantly, but Mrs. Parrish resolved not to give her neighbour the satisfaction of seeing her annoyed. Accordingly, she went out to the hall to greet her daughter-in-law as she came in, spoke loudly about how Luke had been missing her, took her coat, and suggested that she get some rest before they headed to the hospital. Teresa, looking baffled, but of course that was no surprise as the girl never appreciated anything Mrs. Parrish did for her, obeyed and went upstairs. Mrs. Parrish returned to Mrs. Lyndon, and for the rest of the short visit, pretended not to see the mischievous glint in her neighbour's eyes.

They were talking about his medication again, discussing whether Luke ought to be put on stronger sleeping pills. Or at least Dr. Jackson was, and Mrs. Parrish was pretending to listen but kept shooting murderous glances at Teresa over the examination couch. Yes, Luke noticed those glances. He wasn't exactly the most perceptive person, but then they weren't exactly subtle. The strangest thing was that Teresa didn't seem to be surprised by the open hostility on his mother's face. The few times she met Mrs. Parrish's gaze, her lips just pressed in a thin line, and she went a little pale before returning her attention to Dr. Jackson.

There was something Dr. Jackson said which eventually penetrated Mrs. Parrish's consciousness, so that she turned her attention from Teresa and said abruptly, "Sodium – what? What did you say?"

"Sodium pentothal," repeated Dr. Jackson, patiently. He was well used to Mrs. Parrish's manner, having known her since Luke's father had died in that same hospital. Back then he had been on the house staff, but now he was the attending physician, and there were a few more white streaks in his shock of black hair. "It's a sedative that has been used before, and with some success, on patients such as your son who experienced psychiatric collapse during their time in combat."

Mrs. Parrish opened her mouth as though to protest, but Teresa got there first. "Psychiatric collapse? Is that what you'd call it, doctor?" Her mouth was now pressed in such a thin line that her lips had all but disappeared.

"Well, yes," said Dr. Jackson, brooking the opposition calmly. "The term 'shell-shock' is considered somewhat outdated these days, after all."

"You told me before that sodium pentothal is dangerous," Luke's mother interrupted, her attention fully centred on the doctor now. He tilted his head at her question and considered, flicking through Luke's chart.

"It is not so much that it is dangerous, more that the process of administering this particular sedative is complicated. It would need to be administered, in conjunction with a delicate psychoanalytic process. And this treatment was considered risky when it was first pioneered a few years ago." Dr. Jackson paused, glancing down at Luke, his gaze sweeping up and down his face and form but never quite meeting his eyes. "I would need to refer your son to a psychiatrist, who would be present during the treatment."

"He's already seen psychiatrists," Mrs. Parrish said. "He saw plenty of them in the hospital, when he was sent home from Burma. Didn't you, dear?"

Luke couldn't remember. There were copious gaps in his memory from back then, and even now, time still didn't progress in the most straightforward way. Sometimes he felt as if he'd always been married to Teresa. Sometimes, as in Blackpool, he thought that the war must still be going on. But Luke had never been so irritated as he was right now at these gaps in his memory, because he didn't like the sound of this treatment Dr. Jackson was suggesting, not one bit. Every word that came out of the doctor's mouth sent another prickle of discomfort down his spine. He cleared his throat and struggled to sit straighter on his examination couch. His mother put a restraining hand on his shoulder, easing him back, and when Luke cast a look of appeal at Teresa, she didn't notice. She was still staring at the doctor, blue eyes round as saucers.

"What is it?" she asked, and there was no mistaking the tone of her voice. It was hopeful. "What's the 'delicate psychoanalytic process'?"

Dr. Jackson glanced down at Luke again. "Well, the patient should not know too much about the treatment before it is administered, or it may hinder its success. But what I *can* tell you is that it has to do with delving into the patient's trauma and releasing it in a controlled environment."

There was a pause as everyone took this in. Then Teresa began, hesitantly, "That sounds…"

"It's out of the question," said Mrs. Parrish, and Luke sank back against the examination couch in relief. "How is remembering those things again supposed to make him better? My son doesn't need more psychiatrists, he needs to be able to sleep the night through and get on like ordinary people do."

"But maybe he needs to remember what happened so that he can –"

"Wait outside, please, dear." Mrs. Parrish turned to Teresa, cutting her off again. "I'd like to have a word with the doctor myself." She waited while her daughter-in-law stared at her in disbelief, waited until she had padded to the doorway and stepped out. Then, turning back to Dr. Jackson, she said, "You should put him back on the embutal. He was on that a year ago and slept much better than he does now."

Dr. Jackson had been watching the drama unfold with a stiff half-smile on his face, but now his demeanour changed, and he became more familiar. He ran a hand through his hair and sighed. "But the side-effects, Joanna…"

"So maybe he'll be a bit drowsy during the day. I can certainly think of worse things." Mrs. Parrish paused, and then, fiercely, "I won't hear any more about this new-fangled treatment. And you're not to let her try to persuade you, do you understand, Raymond? Any decisions about Luke must come through me first. That girl doesn't know the first thing about him."

"Mum," said Luke, and they both turned towards him in surprise. It was the first time that he had spoken for the entire appointment, and his voice was hoarse from lack of use. He wanted to say that he agreed with her about the treatment, but that he didn't like her talking that way about Teresa. He wanted to thank her for knowing so intuitively what he needed, but also to warn her to tread more carefully when it came to his wife.

But Mrs. Parrish just planted a hand between his shoulder blades and rubbed comforting circles between them, as though he were a sick child. "Yes, yes," she said, extending her arm until it was around his shoulders. "Yes, Luke dear, Mummy's here. It'll all be over soon, and we can go back home, I promise."

Since talking to Luke, as a possibility, was not looking any more likely now than it had when they first got married, and since Mrs. Parrish had shot down the doctor's suggestions, to Teresa's mind, there was only one card left to play, and that was Luke's former sergeant, Bill Farley.

She had sent a letter of gentle inquiry to the Birmingham address that she had found on the back of one of Luke's unopened envelopes, and she allowed a few days for the man's response. Luke still watched for the post every day, of course, but since Teresa had made it very clear that Farley should direct his letter to her rather than to Luke, there was no danger of its being intercepted by her husband. Day after day passed, however, and the morning post brought only disappointment. Hearing her sigh on one of these occasions, Mrs. Parrish said, as she was going up the stairs, "Expecting a letter?" With her tone of voice, she might as well have said, "Who would be writing to *you?*"

But her mother-in-law had a point. Teresa's whole world was contained in Coventry. It was where her parents had lived and died, where her sister and brother-in-law lived and toiled day in and day out, and where Luke and Mr. Albright had both returned after wandering halfway across the world.

A week passed, and still Bill Farley did not write. Teresa began to wonder if she had copied down the address wrong. She was tempted to go back to Luke's trunk and check, and had Mr. Albright's voice not been in the back of her mind admonishing this instinct as soon as it surfaced, she might very well have done it. *He* thought, of course, that it was all a good thing, that it had been a mistake for her to write to Farley in the first place and that now nature had remedied that mistake. Teresa disagreed, but their difference of opinion on this point did nothing to taint their friendship. If anything, it added life to it, and on her visits to his house, they would often sit and argue back and forth about the best way to help Luke without noticing the hour passing.

It was a Monday afternoon and Teresa was just about to embark on one of these visits – Mr. Albright had asked her at church yesterday if she would come over and help with indexing his book, though she knew they were likely to spend more time arguing than actually doing any work, when Bill Farley arrived. She had no warning, not even the ring of a doorbell. She simply wrenched open the front door, which always stuck when it had been raining, and found him standing on the doorstep.

"Good after – oh, I'm sorry, were you going out?" he said, looking her up and down. She knew straight away who he was. He was in civvies, but he had that faint tan and thinness that both Luke and Mr. Albright shared. Only this man was thin as a rake, thinner than either of them. It was difficult to tell his age. He might have been a few years older than Luke, or even Mr. Albright's age. His moustache and receding hairline served to narrow his face further, and Teresa could see that his skin was stretched tight over his cheekbones when he made an attempt to smile. "I should have rung ahead."

"No, not at all," said Teresa, and gestured for him to come in. She divested herself of her coat and hat again and moved to take his.

"I would have settled a time and date with you, too, but I didn't want to give him a chance to change his mind."

Teresa had been about to hang up his coat, but lingered at this last remark, raising her eyes to the man's face. It was difficult to see his expression in the dimness, but the emotion in his voice was hard to mistake as he said, "Do you know how long I've been writing to him? And never a word back. When I got your letter I – well, I..." His voice cracked and he ran a hand over the balding part of his head.

"I'm glad you've come," Teresa said as she went to the coatrack, grateful for the chance to turn her back for a moment. Her heart was thumping, and her throat was dry, and suddenly she was hit with the reality of what she had actually done. Luke wasn't ready for this. Goodness, she wasn't even sure *she* was ready for this. What had she done?

"I'm sorry, I should have introduced myself, shouldn't I?" said the man when she had turned back. "My manners are not what they used to be. So I've been told, anyway. My name's Bill Farley. I expect you knew that already."

Teresa shook Farley's hand. "I'm Teresa Parrish." She managed a smile. "I expect you knew that too."

"Yes. Well, I'm glad I didn't get the old lady," Farley said, and then he seemed to realise what he had said, and he glanced at her anxiously. "Meaning no disrespect, of course."

"Luke's mother is out shopping," Teresa told him, not bothering to hide the relief in her tone. Somehow, she had a feeling Mrs. Parrish would have been even less in favour than Mr. Albright of Teresa writing to a member of Luke's troop. "And Luke's upstairs. He's probably asleep."

Farley nodded, casting his eyes towards the ceiling. His eyes, Teresa saw, were a very pale blue, so pale that they looked as though their colour had faded from too many washes. They were not murky like Mr. Albright's, but clear and –

Mr. Albright. Teresa slapped a hand to her forehead.

"What's the matter?" Farley asked.

"Nothing – nothing," Teresa said quickly. "I just forgot to do something. If you want to wait for me in the parlour…"

Farley went into the room she had indicated, and Teresa went to the telephone to dial Mr. Albright's number. His housekeeper answered after a few rings, and she sounded surprised that Teresa was cancelling her appointment with the minister. "And who is this unexpected visitor, if I may ask, Mrs. Parrish?" Teresa could picture the woman with her notebook and pen at the ready, gearing up to jot down the name so that she could relay it to her friends later.

"He's just an old friend, Mrs. Henshall," Teresa told her shortly. "Please give Mr. Albright my apologies." She wasted no time in hanging up the phone, and she turned to see that Bill Farley was standing beside the open parlour door, staring at her.

Her first instinct was to apologise again, which she very quickly did, stumbling over her words as she explained about how she had been about to meet Mr. Albright when Farley called to the house. But when no acknowledgement or answering apology came from Farley's lips, Teresa started to feel more than a little put out. He'd said that his manners were not what they used to be, but she was sure that he still knew it was considered rude to eavesdrop on a telephone conversation. And now that he knew she'd had another appointment, he could at least apologise for keeping her from it. She folded her arms over her chest and said abruptly, "You met the Reverend Albright in Burma, isn't that right?"

Farley blinked his very pale blue eyes, as though the question had startled him, as though, indeed, he had been far away until Teresa had asked it. Then he looked down at the floor. "Yes, that's right, Mrs. Parrish. I'm surprised to hear that you know each other. I didn't realise he'd come back to Coventry."

"He was surprised to hear that you were back in England too." Teresa was watching the man carefully. The similarity in his and Mr. Albright's reactions to hearing one another's names couldn't but strike her as odd. For the first time, she wondered whether Mr. Albright's disapproval of her writing to Farley had been entirely motivated by concern for Luke.

Farley's eyes flashed up again to meet hers, in a silent question. "I told him I'd written to you," Teresa added, by way of explanation. "He said he's glad you're still alive."

"Oh, I'm sure he is," said Farley, with such venom in his voice that Teresa took a physical step backwards. A moment later, he went on. "We went our own ways a long time ago, of course. There are many like him, men I thought I'd never hear from again. Speaking of which, Mrs. Parrish, might you wake your husband and tell him I'm here?"

Teresa took her time before replying. Her eyes on Farley, who was now avoiding her gaze, she said, "I'll go up now. Of course, he mightn't be up to meeting anyone."

"Of course," Farley echoed, and turned on his heel to go back into the parlour. Teresa, without being sure why, waited until she had seen the door close behind him before she climbed the stairs to Luke's room.

Luke had been dreaming that he was back in his tent outside Yenangyaung, so it didn't seem all that out of place when he opened his eyes into soft darkness to find Teresa shaking his arm and telling him that Sergeant Farley was looking for him. There was a sound from outside his tent, a drilling that kept starting and stopping in a most irritating way, which, Luke guessed, was coming from the men setting up Nissen huts at the other end of the camp.

He was going to go as he was, since whatever the Sarge wanted, it sounded pretty urgent. But Teresa said he'd better get dressed first, so Luke got out of bed and let her help him. As she was pulling his nightshirt over his head, it struck him that her being here, so far from home, was a bit odd. It was odd but also quite nice; he wasn't complaining at all. But he thought he'd better check that she was real, and so when the nightshirt had fallen to the floor, he put a hand to her cheek.

She went absolutely still and looked at him, lips slightly parted. Something else struck Luke then, a fact even stranger than the last. He realised that he had never actually kissed Teresa. He thought it was an awful shame, after all this time apart from each other, that he finally had her here with him and didn't seem to be making the most of the opportunity.

His hands closed around her forearms, gently but firmly, and tugged her towards him. She didn't seem to be breathing. He wondered if she was afraid. He wondered if she'd ever kissed anyone before. He knew she'd been out with other fellows, of course, but whether she'd kissed them or not was another matter.

"Luke," Teresa said softly, and started to shake her head. He continued to close the distance between them until she put a hand on his bare chest, restraining him. The thing was that she had put her hand right over his heart, and so could feel how fast it was beating. Her eyes widened in surprise. Luke brought up his own hand and put it over hers. He was not ashamed. He had never tried to hide how he felt about her, not since he was a boy who didn't know any better.

"Luke..." Teresa's voice was more uncertain than before. But then she said, "You're not yourself."

To be told something like that was quite a shock. It was not the first time, of course, that he had been told that his self was not his self. But that did not make the transition any less violent. So, when Teresa said the words, Luke fell through the intervening years, thumping through ceilings and over rafters, air whistling past him, and crashed back into his own bedroom, in 1945, in Coventry. It was dim because the curtains were closed. The sound of drilling was coming from the neighbourhood outside, not the camp. He had been dreaming.

The only thing that still didn't fit was Bill Farley, who, as Luke discovered when he came downstairs a few minutes later, was really sitting in the parlour under the portrait of the king. He was not supposed to be here. Luke had counted on keeping him away by not answering his letters. But when he looked towards Teresa for some explanation, he saw the parlour door closing soundlessly, the handle slowly turning up until it was back in the neutral position.

"I asked your wife to leave us alone for a few minutes," Bill said. Luke looked back at him, at his thinness, his stretched smile and shaking hands. Then he flinched away again, unable to stomach looking at the man any longer. "Hope you don't mind, Lucky. Thought it might be better this way. You haven't told her about the commemoration ceremony next May?"

"I'm not going," said Luke flatly.

"You deserve a medal as much as the next man. If someone has said or done something to make you think that you don't –"

"No one's said anything to me. It's got nothing to do with that." Luke was almost spitting his words out now.

Bill's smile remained in place, but he screwed up his eyes a bit, as though he too, was finding it hard to look at Luke. "Look, I've been trying to get a hold of the boys from our old troop. Not too many of them around anymore, of course, as you know, but I thought if we get enough together, we might have a reunion before the ceremony, catch up. Lucky, sit down, won't you?"

"I don't have to follow your orders anymore."

"For God's sake, Lucky…"

"Stop calling me that."

"You realise you're the only one who hasn't written back?" Bill rose to his feet and Luke shifted his footing, facing him head on. "Some of these men lost everything. You've got a nice wife and your mum wasn't bombed out of her house and you've still got your arms and legs, haven't you? Fair enough, you mightn't want to get together with myself and the other lads. I can understand that. But you won't so much as show your face at the ceremony? You'll throw away your medal like it means nothing?"

"Take it, if you want," Luke said coolly. "Or give it to someone who bothered to show up."

"That's not how it works, Parrish."

Luke inhaled sharply through his nose and then strode to the door, wrenching it open. Teresa was standing on the other side, and she jumped back a few steps. "I'm sorry! I wasn't listening, I was just…"

"How did you get here?" Luke said, ignoring her and addressing Farley over his shoulder.

"The train," came the slightly confused response.

"Did Mum bring the car when she went to town?" Luke asked Teresa. His wife was still staring at him, guilt written all over her face, and took a moment to process his question.

"She – no. She went with Mrs. Carmichael."

"Can you drive Mr. Farley to the station, then?" When she nodded, Luke glanced back at Bill Farley again, briefly. "I'm sorry you had a wasted journey."

Upstairs, Luke watched from his window as the small black car backed slowly out onto the street. He himself had not yet been cleared to drive. Mum wouldn't be happy knowing that Teresa had been at the wheel of her car either, of course, but there was no helping that. Luke had needed some time to get everything straight in his head, and he had acted accordingly.

Now he had time, and as he lay on his bed and reflected on what had just happened, he came to the conclusion that he would have been better off if he had stayed asleep, ensconced in the past. This new, grey, bustling world was not his own, and with each day that dragged him deeper into it, he liked it less and less.

"I think we got off on the wrong foot earlier, Mrs. Parrish," said Bill Farley, when they were a few minutes away from Station Square. Teresa glanced at him sidelong before stopping to let past a van that was coming the other way. She murmured something non-committal and put her foot on the ignition again.

But Farley was evidently not going to let it go. "I'm afraid your mention of the Reverend Albright caught me off guard. As I told you, I had no idea he was back in England." He hesitated the barest of moments before continuing, "And it's not really my place, I know, but I would advise you, Mrs. Parrish, to keep your distance from him."

Teresa almost felt like laughing, it was all so ridiculous. "Mr. Albright is our minister. And besides that, he's been a good friend to me these past few months. I understand that you might have a grudge against him, Mr. Farley, but as far as advising me to avoid him, I'd have to say that you're right. It's *not* your place."

Farley stared out the window at the crowded street. Flecks of rain appeared on the glass, and several umbrellas opened out on the pavement. "Even so, Mrs. Parrish, and it's out of friendship towards your husband that I'm telling you this. Timothy Albright is not an honourable man."

"What makes you say that?" Teresa glanced across at Farley again, but seeing that his face had closed off to all inquiry, she sighed and changed the subject. "Are you going back to Birmingham?"

"Well, I don't see what else I can do. Your husband seems fixed on not going. That is, you heard us talking about the commemoration ceremony?" He glanced towards her and nodded, as though he had confirmed it to himself. "Parrish has got it into his head that he doesn't deserve the honour, and that's that. Of course, I don't know *how* he got that into his head. The only thing I can think of is that he's ashamed he was sent home shell-shocked and had to leave the fighting behind. As though a thing like that could be anyone's fault. You can leave me off here."

The traffic lights in front of them had just turned red, and the train station was only a short walk away. Farley sprung open the car door, stepping out, and Teresa, all in a rush, said, "Do you think anyone can make him change his mind?"

Farley peered back in the car door at her, and something in his sharp face softened. "Maybe *you* can do it." A car horn blew behind them as the lights changed again, and he waved her off.

The traffic coming home was so heavy that Mrs. Parrish was back by the time Teresa returned. She was sorting through the bags of groceries in the kitchen, and she did her usual routine of refusing to let Teresa help her put away any of it. "No, no, my dear, I'm quite all right!" Then, when Teresa was out of the kitchen and halfway down the hall, she called out, "Whatever did you need the car for?"

Reluctantly, Teresa doubled back to stand on the threshold of the kitchen. "I'm sorry, I wasn't sure about borrowing it without asking, but Luke seemed to think it was all right."

"Luke?" Mrs. Parrish's pencilled eyebrows had risen almost to her hairline.

"Yes, I was dropping a friend of his to the train station just now."

"Luke doesn't have any friends." Her mother-in-law shook her head as she returned to unpacking her bags, as though the matter had been settled. But Teresa lingered where she was, watching her, and there was an edge to her voice when she spoke next.

"Luke has quite a few friends in the world, Mrs. Parrish, people who think well of him, who are hoping and praying for him to get better."

"Get better?" Mrs. Parrish looked up at Teresa again in disbelief. "Oh, my dear, do you really still think that's going to happen?" As Teresa was silent, she went on, "Tell me, did you only marry my son in the hopes that he'd 'get better'?"

"I love Luke," said Teresa firmly. "I love him whether or not he gets better. But I'm not just about to give up."

"So, you think that's what *I've* done? That I've given up on my own boy?"

"I never said that, Mrs...."

"Do you know," Mrs. Parrish interrupted. "I can't imagine where all this formality has come from. 'Mrs. Parrish' this and 'Mrs. Parrish' that. My dear Teresa." She pronounced the name as though it stuck in her teeth. "You're a part of this family now. You may call me by my Christian name, and I shall call you by yours. We'd better get comfortable with each other, after all, since you're going to be here for a long time."

She was staring hard at Teresa now. It was almost as if she expected Teresa to contradict her. Instead, Teresa looked right back and said, hearing her own voice as though from a great distance, "Very well, Joanna. And since I'm going to be here for a long time, I'd like to have more of a share in the housework. I'd like to cook at least three meals a week. I'd like to start buying our main groceries from Kathleen and Brian's shop. And I'd like you to stop coming to Luke's hospital appointments every month."

Mrs. Parrish blinked and looked back down at her bag of shopping. She was clutching a tub of margarine in one hand, and she stared at it now as though she didn't know what to do with it. After a moment, she said, in a strained voice, "We shall talk about all that some other time."

"*I* think we should talk about it now," said Teresa. But her mother-in-law, rather than responding, just lifted her head again and looked past her. Teresa turned to follow her gaze, and saw that, quiet as a mouse, Luke had come down the stairs and was standing in the hall behind them. He looked pained. Then again, he looked pained most of the time, so how could she say that it was any worse now than it had been before? She couldn't tell.

"I'm going for my walk," Luke said, and Teresa nodded so quickly that she felt a strain in the muscles of her neck. Luke, when he was feeling up to it, liked to go around the Common in the evenings. Of course, he didn't normally go alone. But would he want her with him now, after everything that had happened today? After he had witnessed her eavesdropping on him and his friend and then overheard her disrespecting his mother?

"Do you? Can I?" she stammered, as Luke watched her quietly. Finally, when it became clear that she wasn't able to get a complete question out, he said, in slightly louder tones,

"Mum, Teresa and I are going for a walk."

"All right, dear," came Mrs. Parrish's voice. Teresa couldn't bear to look at her now, and she stared furiously at the ground. "Be sure to bring an umbrella. I don't want you catching cold!"

They brought an umbrella but couldn't use it in the end. The wind was gusting too strongly and kept turning it inside out. That might have had something to do with Teresa's clumsiness too. Though she was normally deft enough with that kind of thing, but she stood for what felt like five minutes at the entrance to Hearsall Common, wrestling with the apparatus.

"It's all right," said Luke eventually. He almost looked sorry for her. "We don't really need it."

Teresa relented. It was true. The rain coming down from the wintry sky was only enough to drizzle their faces. But still, she tied Luke's scarf more securely and tucked her arm through his as they came into the park. He let her do all of that, which was an encouraging sign.

It was still light, and there were several other people out walking, including a few neighbours, who greeted them as they passed. After the third such greeting, Luke directed them to a more solitary path, one which sloped upwards and brought them through some sad-looking trees. The ground underfoot was slippery with mud, and Teresa placed her feet carefully, wondering if her husband had really chosen the most unpleasant walk possible just to avoid a few hellos. But when they were clear of the trees and a part of the city came into view below, she understood that there was a bit more to it than that.

Luke removed his arm from hers. He shifted his footing and looked towards the spire of the ruined cathedral. Amid the messy scaffolding and cranes that dotted the skyline, it looked rather noble. But Teresa found she could not look at it for very long.

"They're going to build a new one beside it," she said to her husband, though she wasn't sure if he was listening. She was never really sure if he was listening. "A new cathedral. They're making plans now."

"I wish they'd leave it be," said Luke, quietly. His words were thrown away by the wind so that Teresa barely heard them. She took a step closer, so that they were standing shoulder to shoulder.

"Well, where do you expect the people to go and pray? There's no roof."

"They can pray in the open air."

"Not on a day like today."

"I could do it." Luke looked towards her. Teresa was almost smiling now. The conversation reminded her of some the odd arguments they used to have, before the war.

"Well, most people aren't as tough as you."

"I'm not tough." His words were clearer now, and he was speaking a little faster. "You know, sometimes I dream I'm back there, back in the East, and then I wake up and I'm *here* and it's cold and wet and miserable. And I think I wouldn't mind going back."

He was looking at her again, with a wary expression, as though he expected her to be shocked by his words. But Teresa wasn't shocked. She breathed in and took the plunge. "Are you sure there isn't another reason for that?"

Her voice had been gentle, but Luke flinched as though she had shouted the question. Figuring she might as well go on, Teresa said, "Your friend, Farley –"

"Not him again," said Luke.

Teresa persisted. "He thinks that, because you were sent home after you were shell-shocked, you feel guilty, that you think you don't deserve-"

"You shouldn't talk about things you don't understand." Luke rounded on her.

"It wasn't *me* who said it," said Teresa, stung. "It was Farley."

"He doesn't understand either. He thinks I'm sore about being sent home? It's not like they were ever going to let me stay. Were they supposed to put me firing twenty-five pounder guns when I didn't even know that two plus two was four? My mind was gone. I don't remember *anything* from back then. I've said it over and over, but no one ever seems to believe me!"

Luke's voice had risen as he spoke, carrying across the Common, and Teresa saw a few pedestrians on other paths glance over at them. Very lightly, she put a hand to Luke's sleeve. He didn't seem to notice it. "It's all right," she said, quickly. "I believe you. I do. And we don't have to talk about this now."

"You're the one who brought it up!"

"Well, I shouldn't have!" Tears sprang into Teresa's eyes. "You're right, I don't know anything. Can we just go home?"

Luke inhaled deeply. He put a hand up to the bridge of his nose, dislodging her own hand so that it fell away. "I wish people would just *ask*." Turning to her, as though with a renewed effort, "I wish you would just ask if you wanted to know something."

Teresa felt like a bubble was growing in her chest, fit to burst at any minute. "What do you think we've been doing these past few months, Luke? Why do you think Mr. Albright and I kept trying all those different things with you? We wanted you to be able to talk. We wanted you to feel safe to answer whatever questions—"

"I *did* answer your questions," Luke said, and his voice broke very slightly, so that Teresa became terrified. She had never seen Luke cry before. Was she about to see it now? Was she going to have to stand here and watch him cry, knowing that it was her fault, knowing that she, with her lack of all that patience and care and kindness that a wife was supposed to have, had reduced him to that state? Luke went on, in a steadier voice, "I told you I didn't remember what happened. I told you, over and over. Because the last thing I remember is the Japanese coming over the hill to attack our camp: I don't remember the shell exploding, I don't remember how I felt or the pain or anything like that, I don't remember what came after for months and months and I don't think I ever will. But that's not the *only thing*," He sighed, " that made me like this." He flapped his arms, looking down at himself. "I know I'm not myself anymore: I know I came back wrong. But it's not what you think, what everyone thinks. It's not…"

Teresa was rubbing his back now, tracing comforting circles between his shoulder blades. They spent a minute or two like that, in a silence that she did not really understand, until Luke seemed to come to himself again. He glanced around at Teresa, the distance in his eyes turning to focus. He watched the tears slipping down her face. He asked, "Did you go through my letters, in the trunk? To get Farley's address?"

She nodded, lifted her right sleeve to her face to dry the tears, but they kept coming. She turned away, to fix her eyes on what she hated, the ruin of the cathedral, the ruin of her city, because at least it was better than seeing the disappointed look in Luke's eyes.

"Why didn't you just ask me why I never wrote back to him? I would have told you. I can't stand to write to him. He was captured by the Japanese in '42. You know that probably, from Reverend Albright, while we were retreating from Burma. Farley left our troop in the morning, to scout out a new location to set up our guns. We were supposed to wait for him across the river. But we had no boat to cross it. This villager with a hay cart came up, only he wasn't really a villager at all. He was a Japanese soldier, and he was hiding a machine gun in the hay. Everyone died except for me."

Teresa had gone cold, very, very cold. She kept staring at the cathedral, but she couldn't see it anymore. Instead, she could see the scene Luke was describing. She could almost hear the staccato of machine gun fire in her ears and the screams of the men.

"I played dead. I was covered in blood, anyway. There was blood everywhere, and they left me. They must have found Farley on his way back to us and taken him prisoner. Some villagers found me later, real villagers, though I suppose I wouldn't have known the difference at that stage. They hid me in their house overnight, until the Japanese moved on to the next village. They risked their lives for me, and I never even found out their names. I don't even know what happened to them after I left that place. Maybe they were found out and punished."

Somewhere through his story, Teresa had stopped rubbing his back, maybe because the gesture felt futile, maybe because she couldn't focus her attention on anything else but the terrible things he was telling her.

"That's why Farley calls me Lucky," Luke said. "Because I'm the only man who survived that surprise attack. I don't want a medal. I want to forget that day. I want, just for once, to go to sleep and not hear those men screaming. You're shivering."

Startled, Teresa looked around as Luke unwound the scarf from around his neck. She began to protest, but he unfolded it to its full width and put it around her shoulders, over her thin coat. And then he said, quietly, "I'm tired." He looked it, too. She had never heard him say so much before.

"Luke," said Teresa. Sick with worry and guilt, she could barely speak. "Luke, I'm sorry." And there it was again, the futility of everything she offered him, unwanted touches and empty apologies.

"Just ask me next time," he said, and then they walked home in utter silence.

NO REST FOR THE WICKED

Maggie Henshall had kept house for the Reverend Albright ever since he had first moved to Coventry twelve years before, and she had never seen him turn away anyone who had come to his door seeking help.

Yet there he was, the thin, haunted-looking stranger, waiting on the doorstep, and Mr. Albright was insisting that she go out and tell him that her master was not at home. Mrs. Henshall had a good view of the man from the window of the study, whose blind she could manipulate in such a way as allowed her to see without being seen. The stranger had a military bearing, though he was dressed in a rumpled suit, and his troubles seemed to hang heavy on his brow.

"I'm sure he *is* troubled," said Mr. Albright, when she gave voice to that last observation. "And I'm also sure that there's no way on this earth that I can help him. I have a pretty good idea what he's looking for, and it's not something I can give."

Mrs. Henshall was curious, very curious, but she was also very aware that lately she was gaining a reputation as something of a gossip. Mr. Albright had chided her just yesterday for this tendency, because the rumours about his relationship with Teresa Parrish, after going around the neighbourhood for some days, had circled back to him.

Mrs. Henshall didn't think it was really fair to blame her if a careless remark to her good friend Mrs. Lyndon had ended up being blown out of proportion when passed on to others in the neighbourhood. Neither did she think it was her fault that Joanna Parrish was always trying to find something to justify her grudge against her own daughter-in-law. If Mrs. Parrish wanted to believe that Charlie and Beth Evans's daughter would stray from her shell-shocked husband, and take up with a minister, no less, then she could do so to her heart's content. Mrs. Henshall, for her part, didn't believe it for a second.

Now, whether or not Mr. Albright had gotten too attached to the girl was a slightly trickier question. But in any case, rather than arguing the issue further and opening herself to further criticisms, Mrs. Henshall swallowed her curiosity and went out to talk to the stranger. The man had very pale eyes, she noticed, which watched her, unconvinced, as she made excuses for her master.

"He often goes to Birmingham during the week. He's at a meeting there now."

"I'm from Birmingham, as luck would have it," said the man, who had given his name as Bill Farley, formerly a sergeant in the 28th Field Regiment. "If you give me an address for the minister, maybe I can call on him there instead."

"Oh, well, He never stays the night there, you see, and he's at meetings all day. I don't know when he'd find the time, between that and getting his train home," hedged Mrs. Henshall, while Farley blinked his disconcerting eyes at her.

"So, he won't see me, then, and that's that."

"Well, I never said... – of course he wouldn't..."

Farley just walked away into the darkening street, not bothering to wait until she had finished talking. No manners, but then, a lot of these military men were the same, reflected Mrs. Henshall. They couldn't all be like Mr. Albright, who had been to hell and back and still knew the appropriate amount of time to spend in someone's house on a morning call. Why, Luke Parrish had never had any manners at all, and getting shell-shocked had only made matters worse. Mrs. Henshall shook her head with regret as she went back inside. The boy was nothing like his father, who had had a smile for everyone even during the darkest days of the war, even when he himself was getting sicker by the day.

"You must think I'm cruel to close my door to a man in need, " said Mr. Albright, interrupting her reverie as she cleared away the tea things. He was seated right at the edge of his chair, watching her movements.

Mrs. Henshall, though she still could not get the man's pale eyes out of her head, was feeling somewhat less sympathetic to him now, and responded easily enough, "Maybe that man shouldn't have come calling so late on a Monday evening, then, if he needed help so badly. Even saints have to close their doors sometimes."

Mr. Albright laughed at this, a hoarse, startled laugh. "I'm no saint, Margaret. But thank you."

The rain, which had been only a drizzle when Luke and Teresa walked through the Common, grew heavier at nightfall and lasted until morning. By then there was talk of flooding in some parts of the city, and the scaffolding on Wragby Row groaned and creaked with the wind. Nonetheless, Teresa set out early, clad in her mackintosh, for Kathleen and Brian's shop. She didn't take the car because of the inevitable conversation that would ensue with Mrs. Parrish. Although she knew that eventually she would have to talk to her mother-in-law again, she couldn't face doing it at that hour of the morning.

At any rate, the weather had something of a soothing effect on her nerves. She had barely slept last night, plagued by short, repetitive dreams in which she was forever getting up to find Luke's bed empty, and asking Mrs. Parrish where he had gone only to be greeted with a blank stare. When Teresa actually did check his room the following morning, peering around the door, she saw his auburn head on the pillows and quickly shut the door again.

It was some relief to know that her actions had not driven him away. But though a part of her wanted to stay and ensure that did not happen, another part of her shrank from the prospect of spending any more time than she had to in that dark, dingy house. As long as she had been able to think of herself as a good wife, however long she had had to stay in that house had not mattered; it had all been part of her 'duty'. But now it was clear that what she did made no difference. Her duty meant nothing anymore because she was not, in fact, a good wife. It didn't matter how much Mr. Albright waxed philosophical about lack of understanding being understanding in itself because in the end, it just wasn't true. Teresa didn't understand Luke, and that meant she couldn't help him.

So now, ready to do the hardest thing of all and admit that her sister had been right when she had said that Teresa knew nothing about marriage, Teresa drew up the doorway of Burneys' Grocery. Kathleen and Brian lived in the rooms upstairs, and she found herself looking up now at the window with the lace curtain that had belonged to her old room. She had weathered the whole war looking out through that window. Back then she had thought that there could be nothing duller and more colourless than the lives that the Burneys led, lives that revolved around holidays to Blackpool and tea rationing and the delivery of onions. But a life with no point to it at all, a life that she was not fit for, well, that was rather worse, wasn't it?

Teresa stepped into the shop intending to have a good cry on Kathleen's shoulder and found instead an unfamiliar girl behind the counter. The girl was leaning on her elbows and chewing on something as she read a magazine. On seeing that she had a customer, she turned another page in the magazine unabashedly and said out of the corner of her mouth, "All right, Auntie Tess?"

Teresa just stared at her. "Who are you? And where's Kath?"

Brian emerged from the aisles before the girl could reply and snatched the magazine out of her hands. "What did I just tell you? You can read that on your own time." He turned his gaze to Teresa, giving a weak smile. "You remember my niece, Debbie, from Dewsbury?"

Teresa did not, in fact, remember Debbie, who was all grown up since she had last seen her, and the knowledge that she was Brian's niece did not make her presence in the shop any less confusing. "Where's Kathleen?" she said again, a little shakily.

"She didn't want me to tell you. Said you had enough to worry about. She..." Brian grimaced as he came back behind the counter. "She had a fall yesterday."

"A fall?" Teresa repeated. To her, falls were something that only happened to older people. Not to her sister, who, at thirty-seven, could certainly not be considered old. She looked between Brian and Debbie frantically. "How..."

"Auntie Kathleen's worn out," said Debbie. Pointing at Teresa, "Because *you* went and got married. And there's been no one to pick up the slack here."

"I..." But whatever defence Teresa had been about to make got stuck in her throat, as in her head she replayed all the times she'd gone to the shop over the past few months. She focused in now on the weary set of Kathleen's mouth during those times, the way her hand always went to her lower back when she was walking around. And still, day after day, Teresa had talked and talked to her about Luke's recovery, never asking how she was getting on.

She must have gone pale, because Brian put out a hand to her arm, and even Debbie looked a bit guilty. "Never mind what the girl says, Tess," her brother-in-law said quickly. "We've been managing fine just the two of us. I called in Debbie to help out a bit while I'm gone on deliveries and such, until Kath's out of the hospital. Tess, don't look like that."

"I'm all right," said Teresa, and her voice sounded unnaturally high to her own ears. But she was looking now at the shadows under Brian's eyes. "I'll be all right, once I've seen her."

When Luke awoke to lashing rain, his mother told him that Teresa had set out early to call on Mr. Albright. This seemed natural enough, until Mr. Albright himself showed up around noon looking for Teresa. Judging by what he said, there had been no visit from her at all.

"Well, I didn't actually ask her where she was going," said Mrs. Parrish, crossly, when thus contradicted. She had invited the minister to stay for a cup of tea, and though the smell of roast beef was slowly filling the house from the kitchen, she was, so far, maintaining the pretence that they were in the habit of dining at a later, more fashionable hour. "I just couldn't think of anywhere else where she might have been headed. She doesn't have many friends besides you, you know, Mr. Albright."

Luke's stomach was rumbling with hunger, but, with an effort, he roused himself to address the situation at hand. "What about her sister's shop?"

"I called in there on my way here," said Mr. Albright, and they both looked at him in surprise. He looked unabashed at their attention as he reached for another biscuit. "There was a girl behind the counter I didn't recognise, and no sign of anyone else."

"Hmph," said Mrs. Parrish, after a moment's hesitation. "Well, I suppose that's strange. I hope she shall ring if she's going to be delayed any longer. I shouldn't like to keep you waiting here, Mr. Albright." She sent a pointed look to her son, but Luke, who had been thinking of his dinner moments before, now had his thoughts fixed in quite another direction, and his gaze fixed on the minister.

Luke had never paid much attention to gossip before. He had been aware for some time of the rumours about his wife and Mr. Albright, simply because it was impossible to stir a foot in the neighbourhood and not be exposed to them, but Luke also knew how quickly stories got out of hand in this place. He remembered a few instances before the war when his own name had been attached to that of a neighbourhood girl, and the inconvenience that such rumours had brought, for they had only ever been that, just rumours. Luke's policy, then and now, had always been to ignore and deflect. It was all so trivial, anyway, when you looked at what had gone on in the world over the last few years.

So, Luke had given no credence to the gossip about Teresa and the Reverend Albright, and had not for a single second doubted his wife's loyalty to him. There was no mistaking those steady, warm blue eyes. Every time his thoughts even tended towards questioning her, he would remember the way she had looked at him on the train home from their honeymoon, and he would hear again the utter sincerity in her voice as she declared that she *was* happy because she was with *him,* as though those were two facts that could not possibly be separated from one another.

The sensation in Luke's chest now as he looked towards Mr. Albright was therefore difficult to explain. It was a kind of twisting, clenching sensation that suggested he disliked the man, even though he was sure that Albright had done nothing to warrant such dislike. The man's eyes softened whenever he mentioned Teresa's name, but then again, he *was* fond of her, and Luke was no stranger to that fact. It did seem strange that he had taken such pains to locate her, including visiting her sister's shop, but as he had explained to Luke and his mother when he first arrived at the house, Teresa had missed their appointment yesterday and he had something of importance to tell her.

It was none of Luke's business, of course, what that something was. Just in the same way as he was aware of the rumours, he was aware that though Teresa and Mr. Albright's friendship seemed to have originated in a mutual interest in him, it had now extended far beyond that. Luke told himself that he was just as happy to fall by the wayside, if it meant that he would be left alone from now on. He wanted no more interfering. He wanted no more hopeful looks in Teresa's eyes when she heard of some new 'miracle' treatment. All the same, he just wished

–

Well, he wished she would finish up whatever it was she was doing and hurry home, because every time he heard footsteps on the pavement outside, he thought it was her, and the longer he sat here, the more these strange feelings were going to swirl around within him.

Mum excused herself to go and check on the progress of the roast, surreptitiously, of course, which left Luke and Mr. Albright alone. Luke had been watching Mr. Albright for some time now, and finally the minister returned his gaze. But rather than looking uncertain or disconcerted by Luke's attention, as he had half expected, the older man simply sighed and said, "Well, Luke. It is rather worrisome, isn't it?"

"Teresa can take care of herself," Luke said stiffly.

Mr. Albright opened his mouth as though he were about to protest, but at that moment they heard the sound of high heels on pavement outside, and their heads turned in the direction of the door. A woman passed the parlour window and kept on walking down the street. It was not her, naturally. Luke was annoyed at himself, but he didn't much like the half-smile Mr. Albright gave him after they had realised their mistake; it was a smile that said plainly that they had something in common, that their foolishness revolved around the same pretty girl. And that wasn't right, because Teresa wasn't some girl at a dance that no one had laid claim to yet; she was Luke's wife! Or was that in question now, somehow? He was getting the strangest feeling, from the unflappable manner of Mr. Albright, that it was.

"You're right, of course," said Mr. Albright, and it took Luke a moment to realise that he was responding to his previous remark. "Teresa is perfectly capable of taking care of herself. I find it all too easy to forget that she,– and many other women like her,– was forced to do exactly that when men like you and I were halfway across the world."

"I left the war in '43," said Luke shortly, because there Albright went again, lumping them together as though they'd had the same experiences. "Long before you."

"That was hardly by your own choice." With a dry chuckle, "And my staying in the war was hardly by my own choice either."

Luke shifted in his seat, uncomfortable with the sudden turn in the conversation. He hoped Albright wasn't going to start going on again about being a P.O.W. He had narrowly avoided such a conversation with Farley yesterday, and he didn't feel remotely prepared for it today. But Mr. Albright just coughed and said instead, "I hear you had a visit from an old friend recently."

Luke looked up at the minister. "Teresa told you?"

"Well, when she spoke to my housekeeper on the telephone, she said something about an unexpected guest." Mr. Albright's eyes were suddenly guarded. Instantly Luke sensed that the man knew more, possibly much more, than he was letting on. And then his mind ran on ahead to a possibility that had not occurred to him before, that Teresa's summoning of Bill Farley had been another one of hers and Albright's failed plans to 'cure' Luke.

"It was a man from my old troop," he said, after a minute's consideration. "Teresa didn't tell me before inviting him here. I was taken by surprise."

Mr. Albright was nodding, his hands on his chin. "I can't say that I blame you."

"You knew about it before?" Luke said bluntly.

The minister looked startled but he nodded. "Yes,– I'm afraid I did. I did warn Teresa that it might not be the best idea." And then, as Luke was gearing up to take offence at the blatant admission of what he had suspected, Albright said something which surprised him out of it. "I happen to know the man."

"You know Bill Farley?"

"I met him in Rangoon. We did not..." Albright lowered his hand from his chin and rested it on his thigh instead, with some deliberation. "We did not see eye to eye. I fear that–" He raised his eyes to Luke's again. "I fear that Mr. Farley may have made some unfavourable remarks about me to your wife."

Luke sat quietly, waiting for more. But one minute crawled by and then another, with the minister still watching him anxiously, and at length he realised that the man was waiting for him to respond,– that he was actually looking to him for reassurance about what Teresa might think of him. While he was still getting this straight in his head, Mum came back in.

"Mrs. Parrish," said Mr. Albright, rising to his feet in a graceful movement which belied his short, sturdy form, "I'm keeping you and your son from your dinner. Please, don't let me impose on you any longer."

"You're – you're not... that is, we usually eat much later – but you're welcome to join us..."

"You're very kind, but I have something waiting for me at home. Give my best to your daughter-in-law." Mr. Albright gave a small, old-fashioned bow to Mrs. Parrish and then nodded towards Luke before taking his leave.

"Well, so the minister eats dinner in the middle of the day too," said Mum with some satisfaction, when the two of them had sat down to dinner. Then, with a curious glance towards Luke, "Whatever were you talking about while I was gone? It sounded very serious."

Luke was grateful for the distraction that his beef provided (it was a bit dried out from their long wait, but beef was beef), and fell back on a phrase that he had used many times before. "I don't remember."

The doctor's official diagnosis was not much more complicated than Debbie's had been. Kathleen was worn out and needed rest. When she got out of the hospital in a few days' time, he warned that things could not simply go back to the way they had been.

"I've seen many cases like this over the last few years. Why, we've had the same problem among some of our staff here. Absences due to wartime make people take on a greater workload than is possible for them to handle in the long term."

"But it's not because of the war that there's been no one to help out in the shop," said Teresa, in a low, tremulous voice. "It's because I got married –"

"Will you stop talking nonsense, Tess? This is not your fault." Kathleen began to struggle into a sitting position, so that both Teresa and the doctor had to wrestle her back down. She eventually gave in, but went on glaring at her sister. "I took on too much, that's all, like the doctor said. I'll be more careful."

"That's not good enough," said Teresa faintly. When the doctor had gone, she went on, steadying her voice, "There's nothing for it. I'll start taking some shifts again to give you a break."

"No, Tess, you've got your hands full with Luke and everything –"

"It's not like he's a child who can't be left alone. Mrs. Parrish is around most of the time anyway. And I could just take two or three shifts a week, something like that. How about Saturday and Sunday? That's when it's worst of all, isn't it? I could come in this Saturday."

"Tess, you don't even know what you're saying. You're just in a panic. Brian was too, when I had my fall, but he calmed right down when he could see that I was all right and I'm telling you, Tess, you're making too much of this. Look at me! I'm all right!"

Obediently, Teresa looked at Kathleen, and all she could see was that somehow, at some point in the last few years, her older sister had started to get old. She had crow's feet and a web of grey in her hair, and her hands were sinewy and strained, even as they lay relaxed on the bedclothes. While Teresa was trying to figure out how and when these changes had happened, into her mind, unbidden, flashed a picture of her mother's hands. She thought of how strong they had looked when she made dough, and then she thought of how strange they had looked, with their painted nails, when she and Kathleen had been brought to the morgue to identify their parents' bodies.

"I *want* to do this," she told Kathleen. "I want to help. And anyway, I've been thinking about getting back to work."

Her sister gave her a look which told her that she was entirely unconvinced by this, but before she could argue the point any further, a nurse passing by informed them that visiting hours would be over soon.

"What time is it?" said Teresa, who had not looked at her watch all day. Seeing that it was past two p.m., she bit her lip.

"Go," Kathleen urged her. "They'll be worried about you at home by now. I'm guessing you didn't ring up to tell them where you are."

Teresa hadn't rung the house, but she doubted if Mrs. Parrish would be anything but mildly annoyed at the inconvenience Teresa had caused. All the same, she left, promising her sister that she would visit again the next day.

The rain had eased off, and downstairs, the tiled floor of the hospital lobby gleamed as the sun reflected off wet footprints. As she was making her way along, Teresa was waylaid by Luke's Dr. Jackson.

"Mrs. Parrish! What brings you here?" He was a tall man, even taller than Luke, and had to stoop a little to address her.

"I'm visiting my sister," Teresa explained. "She had a fall yesterday and they say she's suffering from exhaustion."

"Indeed!" Dr. Jackson's tone was the same as if Teresa had just informed him that she enjoyed reading in her spare time. "And how is your husband?"

"He's as well as can be expected, thank you, doctor."

"Have you given any more thought to the treatment I suggested at his last appointment?"

Teresa looked at him in surprise. "Well, no, I haven't, doctor, since my mother-in-law was so against it."

Dr. Jackson sighed, as though he had been expecting this. "Joanna Parrish is a good friend of mine. I attended her husband during his illness, you know. But she can be, well, somewhat old-fashioned in her attitudes. If you're waiting for her to change her mind about what her son needs, you might be waiting a very long time."

"You think that this is what Luke needs, then?" Teresa couldn't help seizing upon the last part of his speech. "Because he doesn't seem to want it. He says that he can't remember a lot of what happened, and that there are other things..." She hesitated. Was it really right to be saying this in the middle of a crowded lobby, with the sunlight streaming in and other people milling around? But her eagerness made her press on, "There are other things in the war, besides his shell-shock, I mean, that haunt him just as much."

"I don't doubt it," said Dr. Jackson. "And as to your husband not wanting it, I can't think of many soldiers who would have actively volunteered to undergo the kind of treatment I'm suggesting. I can, however, think of many soldiers whom it has most definitely benefited. Here." He scribbled something down on a piece of paper and handed it to her. "This is the name and address of the psychiatrist I mentioned to you before. Dr. White has helped many men like your husband. Perhaps you might be able to persuade Luke to go and meet with him, at least."

Teresa thanked him, which he acknowledged with a wave of his hand as he passed on. She put the piece of paper in her pocket and told herself that it would stay there, but several times on the bus home, she found herself taking it out and looking at it. The address was a Birmingham one, but she knew the street fairly well. It was down the road from the university. It would be familiar to Luke too.

Each time her mind started down that route, however, it was quickly called back again by the jolt of the bus, or the loud voice of one of her fellow passengers. And then Teresa would remember what Luke had said to her. *Just ask me next time.* But what if she asked him about this? Would he still see it as her having gone behind his back, conspiring with Dr. Jackson about a miracle cure for him? Was that how he saw her after all?

She didn't know the answer to that, but she didn't care to find out. Teresa folded up the paper and put it back in the pocket of her skirt.

Teresa stepped into the house warily, half-expecting Mrs. Parrish to come barrelling out of the parlour or kitchen and berate her for her absence. When this did not occur, she shook out the drops from her umbrella, which was mostly dried, set it standing at the edge of the banister and went into the kitchen. The table had been cleared and the dishes washed, though they were set in the rack to drip dry. Teresa took off her coat and picked up a tea towel, just for something to do.

She was on the last glass when she heard the umbrella falling in the hall. Instinctively her shoulders tightened, and she turned towards the kitchen door as footsteps approached. When the door opened to admit Luke rather than Mrs. Parrish, she sighed in relief.

He looked relieved, too, to see her, which was strange. Teresa tripped over her tongue several times explaining about Kathleen. When she had reached the end of her explanation, she realised that she still had the glass and tea towel in her hands, and put them down, feeling a little foolish.

Luke had a funny expression on his face, as though he was concentrating very hard on something. "You haven't eaten, then?"

"No, I didn't get the chance. But I'm not very hungry anyway, I've been all..." Teresa flapped a hand to indicate her state of mind, and Luke's eyes followed the movement.

"And your sister?" he said, after a pause that was so long it was almost painful. His eyes returned to Teresa. "She's all right?"

"Yes I – I think so. I hope so." Teresa hesitated, then plunged forward. "I might have to start taking a shift or two at the shop again. At least until they can find someone to take on. But I know they've been trying these past few months and no luck.... I suppose no one wants to work in a shop anymore. They've all gone to the factories or – anyway. Would you mind awfully?"

Luke looked as though he was considering the question very seriously, but then he asked, "Mind what?"

"Me helping out at the shop," said Teresa, patiently. "I'd just do a few days a week, maybe at the weekends."

Luke nodded. "Of course. You should help your sister." He looked up at her again and cleared his throat. "Mum's at a prayer meeting. And the minister was here earlier, looking for you."

"Oh!" Teresa frowned. "I never rescheduled for our meeting yesterday. I'd better ring him now." She made for the door, and Luke moved a fraction to let her pass. Their arms brushed, and Teresa made a face to herself as she walked on, wondering why she felt like she was missing something important. She had her hand on the receiver of her phone when she turned again, to see that Luke was still standing in the threshold of the kitchen, apparently lost in thought. She sighed. "I'm sorry I didn't ring to let you know where I was. I was barely thinking straight this morning when I found out about Kathleen. I was so..."

"You don't need to say sorry," said Luke, turning to face her. And then something remarkable happened. The left corner of his mouth lifted, and he bestowed upon her a half-smile. Teresa nearly dropped the receiver and only barely managed to keep her balance.

Luke had gone back upstairs again by the time she finished her telephone call. But when Teresa went up to her own room and closed the door, she had not been sitting down five minutes when she heard a knock.

"Come in!" she called, while her heart did a funny little twist in her chest. Luke had never visited her room before.

He opened the door slowly and stood in the threshold for a moment. Teresa had shifted her position on the bed so that her feet were on the ground, and now she patted the space beside her, thinking he must want to talk to her about something. Maybe he wanted to talk about Burma again. "Do you want to sit down?"

Luke cleared his throat again and shook his head. He straightened up until he seemed to be standing to attention. "We could go out somewhere, if you want." He spoke so stiffly, like they were strangers, but the words coming out of his mouth were so wonderful that Teresa didn't care. "And you could get something to eat, since you haven't had dinner."

Teresa wanted to just gaze and gaze at him, but she was also slightly afraid that if she made him self-conscious, he would change his mind. She said, lightly, "I can't think of anything else I'm doing."

Luke gave her that half-smile again and went out. When he had closed the door, Teresa fell back on her bed and grinned up at the ceiling.

Luke didn't know what he'd gotten himself into. It was as though, back in Teresa's room, someone else had briefly possessed him and made the suggestion that they go out. Of course, it was the very last thing he wanted to do. He got enough staring and pointing at service every Sunday. In the crowded pub on Fleet Street where they ended up going, it was even worse, because people had no sense of shame about staring. Since they had been loosened up by a few drinks, they had very little shame about anything.

Luke and Teresa weren't drinking. They both had lemonades in front of them, and she was clutching her straw like it was a lifeline, probably because he hadn't said a word since they had sat down here, apart from ordering. But what was he supposed to talk about? He had asked about her sister, and Teresa had said that she was all right. He was most certainly *not* going to ask about Mr. Albright. So, what did that leave?

He cleared his throat, and Teresa looked up hopefully, but on seeing that he was not going to say anything, she put the straw back in her mouth and returned her eyes to the table.

She had dressed up for tonight in a green shantung frock that Luke had never seen her in before. It had a nice collar that showed off her slim neck. He had complimented the dress earlier so he couldn't do so again. It was a pity, really, that he had already used up all the good talking points on the walk here from the house. He ought to have rationed them out and then they wouldn't be caught in such a dead silence as they were now.

"Excuse me a minute," he said to Teresa, rising from his seat, and she half-rose, too.

"Are you all right? Should I–"

"Stay where you are. You don't want to miss your food," he told her. Reluctantly, she sank back down in the chair. He could feel her eyes on his back as he made his way through the pub. But rather than turning towards the bathrooms, he turned to the back door, which led out onto an alley. As he was coming up the alley towards the street, without much idea of where he was going beyond the need to get some fresh air, someone launched themselves at him out of a doorway.

Luke grunted and struggled with the man. It wasn't much of a contest, as after the initial shock had worn off, he realised that the man was skinnier and shorter than him, and by the time a few factory workers who had been smoking outside came up to see if he needed help, Luke had a pretty good idea of who the man was.

"I'm all right," he told the men, and as his would-be attacker, now a safe distance from Luke, wiped his mouth, produced a wobbly grin and pronounced the name "Lucky" in greeting, Luke added, grimly, "I know him."

The factory men retreated and returned to their cigarettes. Luke, meanwhile, took a firm hold of Bill Farley and brought him out to the street, where the light of a streetlamp showed him that the man was still in the same clothes that he had been wearing when he had visited the day before. They were now rumpled and stained, and Farley's eyes were bloodshot.

"What are you doing here, Sarge?" Luke said, quietly, as he kept a hold of the man's collar. "I thought you were back in Birmingham."

"I didn't get the train." Farley wiped his mouth again, this time with his sleeve, and made a feeble attempt to free himself from Luke's grasp. When that didn't work, he began to giggle. "Thought I'd stay and see how you are. How you are. How *are* you, Lucky?" He giggled again.

"You didn't stay to see me," said Luke, who had not missed the hard gleam of something in Farley's eyes: something entirely humourless. "You stayed to see Albright. Didn't you?"

But his words did not have the intended effect on Sergeant Farley. Instead of admitting that what Luke had said was true, his eyes bulged wider, and he lurched forward. The strong scent of whiskey washed over Luke. "Albright, you say? Is he here? Did he send you? Is he…" Farley's eyes rolled in his head as he attempted to look around. When he finally followed the movement by turning his body, he overbalanced and would have hit the ground had Luke not grabbed him by the arms.

"Bill, get a hold of yourself."

Something dawned on Farley's face at those words, and he made a wobbly salute. "Yes, sir!"

"Don't 'yes, sir' me, *you're* the sergeant. You're supposed to give *me* orders," Luke snapped.

"Quite so, Corporal Parrish." Farley coughed and squared his shoulders. "And as your sergeant, I command that you let me go."

"If I let go of you now, you'll fall," Luke pointed out, and Farley made a face but did not dispute the point.

Hearing faint laughter behind him, Luke looked around to see that the factory men, who had now finished their cigarettes, had lingered in the doorway of the pub to watch the exchange. Looking back at Farley, who was now tilting towards Luke's shoulder, he debated within himself for a moment and then beckoned to the men.

"Sorry," he said, "but it looks like I might need your help after all."

Teresa's food arrived shortly after Luke departed the table. It was steak-and-kidney pie and it smelled divine, but she had only taken a few bites when a girl approached her table. "Auntie Tess!"

"Debbie!" Teresa exclaimed, putting down her fork. She had barely recognised the girl under all the lipstick and rouge she was wearing.

"I wasn't going to come up because I'm not supposed to be here," Debbie said in a stage whisper, slipping into Luke's recently vacated seat. "But you looked lonesome, so I thought I'd better say hello. You won't tell Uncle Brian you saw me, will you?"

"That depends," Teresa said, attempting to inject some sternness into her tone. "Are you doing anything he might not approve of?"

"Nothing! I'm just here with some pals. There they are." Debbie pointed out a table of young women, similarly attired and made-up, who were evidently watching them while pretending not to watch them.

"They look a bit older than you," Teresa said, after a moment's pause. "And they can't be very good pals of yours since you've only been here a few days."

"I met them in the shop. It gets so dull there you *have* to talk to people." Debbie, apparently trying to head off Teresa's next remark by turning her inquisitiveness back on her, leaned forward on her elbows and asked confidentially, "Was that your husband, just gone?"

Rather than making the obvious retort – that since she had been sitting with him in a pub, he could hardly be anyone other than her husband – Teresa said, "Yes. That's Luke."

"He passed our table. He looked so *cross.*" Playing with the straw of Luke's half-empty glass of lemonade, Debbie went on, "Uncle Brian says that he was shell-shocked in the war. Is that true?"

"Yes," Teresa said, as she resumed eating pointedly.

"He can't be much fun, then." Still twirling the straw, Debbie appeared to consider. "But then, the minister isn't much fun, either, I'd reckon. Poor Auntie Tess. You should find a *nice* man who makes you laugh."

Teresa nearly choked on her mouthful of pie and had to reach for her glass of lemonade. She drained the whole thing, and once she had swallowed, wiped her mouth with her napkin. Her voice was hoarse from coughing when she spoke again. "What did you just say?"

Debbie was watching her with wide eyes. "It was just a joke."

"Have you heard something?" Teresa demanded.

"I haven't heard anything, Auntie Tess. Don't mind me, Uncle Brian always says I talk a lot of rubbish."

"Then what was that about the minister? 'The minister isn't much fun'? What does *that* mean?" Teresa could feel her own heartbeat, high in her chest. "Debbie? Look at me."

With a sigh, Brian's niece finally relented. "It's just, I heard some people saying that you and the minister, well, that there might be something going on. Of course, I didn't believe it. I was just teasing, Auntie Tess. I thought you must know what people have been saying."

The room was suddenly very hot. "I didn't know," said Teresa, numbly. "Did my brother-in-law tell you this?"

"No, of course he didn't. He wouldn't repeat gossip like that anyway."

"He wouldn't *repeat* it. But he knows about it?" Teresa stared at Debbie, who was now squirming in her seat and avoiding her gaze.

"I don't know if he knows or not. Listen, Auntie Tess, there's no need to get so upset. People talk. It's the same back home. I'm sure it'll be something else next week."

Teresa just shook her head. She felt like the whole pub, and not just Debbie, was watching, waiting for her reaction. As though to confirm the feeling, she looked up, and saw, at a neighbouring table, a woman's eyes just flickering away from her. Teresa's heart sank.

Then someone cleared his throat behind her. Her head snapping around, Teresa saw a man in factory overalls standing by their table. "Mrs. Parrish?"

"Yes?" she said, a little more sharply than was perhaps necessary. The man, unfazed, said,

"Your husband sent me to fetch you. His friend's had a little too much to drink and he's helping him into a cab."

"His *friend?*" Teresa repeated, with a frown.

"I think I'd better go." Debbie said, sliding out of her seat, and Teresa didn't bother saying goodbye as the girl hurried back to her friends. She just reached for her coat, left a pound note on the table for the bill and followed the man outside.

It took quite a while to find a cabdriver willing to take a man in Farley's state, and even longer to wrestle Farley into the seat. Luke had help from one of the factory men, while the other went into the pub to fetch Teresa. She was pale faced when she joined them, and stared at Farley, who was lolling in the middle seat where he had been placed.

"Sorry about this," Luke told her, and told her about the encounter outside the pub. "He says he never left for Birmingham. He's been here since yesterday, and I don't think he's stopped drinking all that time."

Teresa took this in and gave a slow nod. She then thanked the men who had helped them, who touched their caps in acknowledgement before going away. She got into the seat beside Farley. Luke, instead of going in the front of the cab, took the other side so that the man was propped up between them.

"Where to?" said the driver, warily, as he looked in the rear-view mirror at Farley.

"The train station," said Luke, decisively. There was a late train to Birmingham at eleven p.m. He knew because he had often caught it himself in his university days. But then, as the cab began to move, he looked sidelong at Farley. The man was breathing shallowly, with his head tilted back, eyes trained on the roof of the car but not really seeing anything. "Actually," said Luke, and both Teresa and the cab driver looked at him. "Can you take us to Kenilworth Road instead?"

He planned it out in his head and explained to Teresa on the way home. They would put the Sarge in Teresa's room, where he could sleep it off, and Teresa could come in with Luke. It would be a bit of a squeeze, of course, in his small bed, but it should be all right. And though Mum would almost certainly not approve of Luke's guest, he couldn't very well leave Farley to his own devices. The man might get himself into some serious trouble. In fact, it was a wonder he hadn't done it already.

Teresa agreed that they couldn't very well leave Farley alone, and said, faintly, that it was a good thing Luke had found him. Then she passed a hand across her eyes as though dashing away a tear, and when Luke asked her what was wrong, she said it was just that she was feeling very sorry for his friend. It seemed a bit of a strange response, but then again, Teresa *was* soft-hearted.

Between the two of them, they managed to get Farley up to Teresa's room without encountering Luke's mother on the way. Luke got some spare clothes and a glass of water and sat with Farley until he was sure the man was sleeping, and lying in a position that would make him less likely to choke if he threw up during the night.

When he got back to his own bedroom, Teresa was sleeping, too. Or, at least, her breathing sounded even, and she didn't respond when Luke called her name. She was lying at the extreme end of the bed with her back to him, though since it was so cramped with the two of them, it was impossible not to brush against her as he got in under the covers.

Luke turned to look at his wife. In the semi-darkness, he could see that she had wrapped her hair in a scarf, and there were a few locks already escaping. He wound one around his finger, and then softly, very softly, touched her shoulder. He said her name once more, just on the off chance that she might have woken up at the touch.

But Teresa went on sleeping, and Luke, after a fashion, followed. There was not the usual struggle, culminating in one side of his mind delivering the decisive blow and the other side surrendering. Instead, he slipped into sleep in a quiet way, lulled by the sound of Teresa's breathing.

Teresa had never been able to stand anyone thinking badly of her, particularly when that bad opinion was unfounded. What was more, she had not yet reached an age where she could recognise that the bad opinions now circulating around town concerning her, just as they had been formed outside of her knowledge, were outside of her power to change. So she spent most of the night staring at the dark ceiling of Luke's room, trying to think her way out of something that she had been unaware was a problem until a few hours ago.

She would have to put an end to her friendship with Mr. Albright. That was the conclusion she kept coming back to. However much he might have helped Luke already (which was difficult to know) or might help him in the future (something which Teresa, knowing both men and having heard about their wartime experiences, had good reason to think was a possibility), she couldn't go on visiting his house and fueling the gossip.

She felt Luke's touches when he came to bed, and heard him call her name, but though her heartbeat picked up, she stayed still and feigned sleep. Debbie's words had taken root deep in her soul. Any closeness she and Luke might have enjoyed that night would have been spoiled by them, and so Teresa could do nothing.

Having snatched a half-hour's sleep here and there, she woke in semi-darkness to the sound of birdsong. Luke was snoring in his bed, and Farley was snoring in his when she stepped in to get her clothes from her room. She dressed in the bathroom, staring at her pale reflection. She had often been told that she had an honest face. How was it, then, that people could look at her, really look at her, and think that she was capable of lying?

The house was dark and quiet as she got into her coat. Mrs. Parrish would be up soon, and Teresa had never been so grateful to have avoided her as she slipped out the front door and into the grey Coventry morning. She had worn good walking shoes because she planned on covering a long distance today. She would be walking to the hospital to see her sister and, on the way, dropping in to Mr. Albright's to tell him what she had decided.

A decision, however, made in the course of a white night soon appeared quite differently in the light of the day. By the time she reached the minister's house, she was debating whether she ought to go in at all. She lingered on the doorstep without seeming to be able to lift her hand to ring the bell. She was about to go away again when out of the corner of her eye she caught a movement in the window adjacent to the door, the twitch of a blind.

Seconds later, the door flew open, and Teresa, expecting to see the housekeeper, saw instead an unusually flustered Mr. Albright. His black hair, normally combed down smoothly over his head, was sticking up in all directions as though he had been running his hands through it, and there was a dark flush in his cheeks as he murmured a greeting to Teresa. He was attempting to tie his cravat and couldn't seem to get the knot right.

"I'm sorry to come so early," said Teresa. What had she been thinking? Was she actually going to be able to say the words to him, insult him by the suggestion of an affair? Scrambling for something else to say, she added, "Were you working on your book?"

"Working?" Mr. Albright looked startled. He finally gave up on the cravat and just threw the end over his shoulder instead. "No, not working. Please come in, Teresa."

She followed him inside and was surprised when he led the way to the study instead of the parlour. Then it occurred to her that it was so early, Mrs. Henshall wouldn't have arrived yet and therefore could not make them tea. She saw, as they came in, papers scattered over Mr. Albright's desk, evidence that he had, indeed, been working and that she *had* disturbed him. "I can come back."

"No, please," said Mr. Albright, as he indicated the chair opposite his desk. He waited until she had sat before taking his seat himself, and he folded his hands together.

A moment's painful silence followed before they both attempted to speak at once.

"You first," he said, with another startled blink at her.

"No, please." Almost miserable with mortification by now, she gestured to him, and he cleared his throat before starting again.

"I'm glad you stopped in, as I was hoping to speak with you about something." He shuffled the papers before continuing. Teresa, glancing at them, saw with surprise that they looked like official documents, rather than rough notes. "You may recently have heard a report concerning myself..."

"So, you've heard the rumours too." Teresa couldn't help interrupting. She was very relieved that she wouldn't have to be the one to break the news. "I only heard last night, and I was so upset I couldn't sleep. I had to come and see you as soon as I could. I don't know what can be done, but all I know is, if we go on as before, things are just going to get worse and worse and..."

"Forgive me. The rumours?" said Mr. Albright, who looked like he was struggling to take in her words.

"About you and me." Teresa could feel herself blushing now, which was just silly since the rumours were preposterous and she and Mr. Albright were good friends and therefore she should have been able to shake off the feeling that, by voicing such rumours out loud, she was crossing some invisible boundary between them.

Mr. Albright's expression cleared, and he leaned back in his seat. "Ah, I wouldn't pay those any heed. People will talk, you know, and they get curious when they see an unmarried man like myself paying particular attention to any woman. Particularly one as well, he indicated her, but did not fill in the missing word, " – as yourself. My being a minister, of course, adds to the scandal in their eyes. But no, I wouldn't pay such gossip any heed if I were you."

Teresa stared at him. "But isn't that what you wanted to talk to me about?"

"I – well – that is, I... There was a different matter that I wished to discuss. But we needn't talk about that now," he added hastily, "As you seem to have taken these rumours more to heart than I anticipated –"

"Of course I've taken them to heart. It's a serious thing to be accused of! And I had to hear it from my brother-in-law's niece."

"That must have been embarrassing," said Mr. Albright, gently. "However –"

"How long have you known?" Teresa demanded.

"I beg your pardon?"

"How long have you known what people were saying about us?" A part of her was quietly appalled that she was actually speaking to a minister like this, but the rest of her was raging, weary. "Because I would have liked to have had some warning."

"I heard about the rumours from my housekeeper the other day. I wouldn't have insulted you by repeating them!"

He had raised his voice a fraction, so Teresa felt justified in rising from her seat. She couldn't stop staring at him, at this man whom she had thought of as a friend, whose eyes were dark with things she didn't understand. Teresa shook her head and took a step back from the desk.

"Teresa." Mr. Albright stood up and came around the desk. He halted a few paces from her, and held up his hands, palms out, in a placating gesture. "I should have told you right away. I suppose the rumours seemed so ridiculous that I didn't imagine anyone would take them seriously. I should have thought of your position. And I suppose I should have…" He rubbed the scar on his temple as he thought for a moment. Then, locking eyes with Teresa again, "I've enjoyed your friendship these past few months. Perhaps more than you know. But it seems I should have thought more of outward appearances."

Teresa tried to glare at him, but she could already feel the anger leaking out of her body. It was remarkable, really.; Here was this man, shorter than her, quite ordinary-looking, and with a few quiet words he could make her feel just how enormous and all-encompassing his presence was. What could Bill Farley have meant when he had warned her about him? How could she mistrust a man whose whole being professed sincerity?

"I've enjoyed our friendship, too," she said, stiffly. Chancing a glance at him, she was almost frightened by the softness of his expression. It brought more words tumbling out of her. "And I don't think you know how much it's meant to *me*. I thought when I got married, I'd never be lonely again. But…"

Teresa stopped, feeling she couldn't say any more without being openly disloyal. But Mr. Albright was nodding his head, and he didn't look shocked. He said, slowly, "When I saw you for the first time that Sunday, standing beside your husband, I just thought to myself, 'There's a nice couple'. But then, as I got to know you, I began to see what a difficult path you had chosen for yourself. Luke Parrish is a good man, but anyone can see that he has things on his mind. And sometimes you can't follow him where he goes. Is that true?"

Teresa nodded and couldn't help the sob that escaped her as she said, "But I do love him."

"Anyone can see that, too." Mr. Albright smiled at her, such a sad smile that it made Teresa want, inexplicably, to comfort him, even though she was the one crying. She took a step closer and said, fervently, "I *wish* people didn't have to gossip."

"I *wish* people didn't have to gossip."

"But that is what people do."

"I wish they didn't have to spoil things," Teresa went on, and choked out her next sentence. "Because you know I can't visit you like this anymore."

"I know. Or rather, I guessed that was what you were going to say." Mr. Albright reached out and took her hand and held it for so long that Teresa looked up and stared at him. At length he blinked as though coming out of a trance. "Goodbye then, Mrs. Parrish."

He let go of her hand, but Teresa didn't move. An awful realisation was crashing over her. Rapidly, she began counting up in her head all the times that she had laughed at his jokes, all the times that he had driven her home and they had lingered in his car, talking about things she couldn't remember, all the times that she had come home smiling after having met him. She felt frozen with horror as it occurred to her that, perhaps, the idea of there being something between them wasn't so preposterous after all.

"Teresa?" Tim was looking at her with concern. Tim. She could call him that in her head now, because there was no hiding anymore. Teresa kept crying, kept her face turned to the side as she moved forward and threw her arms around him.

He stood still, startled, and it was only when he returned her embrace that she was able to breathe again. He breathed out, too, a great, shuddering sigh that rustled her hair, and his arms went around her. He held her tightly against him, and Teresa rested her head against his shoulder and stared at the bookshelf in the corner of the room and felt just as if she had been split down the middle, with one side made of pure happiness and the other side pure misery.

She had not been held like this in a long time. In fact, she had never been held like this, and as, after a few minutes, they moved a little apart until they were able to look at one another properly, she could see that Tim's face was only inches away from hers. She could have kissed him if she wanted to. And she *did* want to. That realisation was even worse than the one that had come before. His eyes were paler now, very green and very wide. Teresa moved in a fraction, and then wrenched herself away from him with a gasp.

"Teresa…" He followed her out to the hallway. She was almost running, tripping over her own feet, tears running down his face. "I'm sorry." As though he had something to be sorry for. As though that, just now, hadn't been all her.

"I can't see you again," she said without turning. Her voice was all mixed up from crying: it went high and low and all over the place in just a few words. "I *can't*." She fumbled with the doorhandle and pushed out into the street, feeling the cold air hit her face with relief. He did not follow her any further.

It wasn't that Mrs. Parrish didn't believe what her son told her, about Teresa's sister being ill. Of course, she knew that must have been true. She just didn't think that was all there was to it. She woke up that morning to a great deal of surprises, not least of which was the stranger sleeping in Lily's room, the stranger whom Luke claimed was his friend, and whose presence he attempted to explain over breakfast. Luke attempting to explain anything was remarkable enough in itself. Then there was the fact of the explanation, that he and Teresa had gone out the night before while Mrs. Parrish was at her prayer meeting. *Gone out?* Her son didn't just *go out.* She gazed at Luke as he talked and knew in her bones that something strange was going on, and that there was more to her daughter-in-law's absence that morning than a mere sick relative.

Mrs. Parrish had always prided herself on her intuition, which now prompted her to get up halfway through breakfast, without so much as clearing away the things first, and drive to Mr. Albright's house. She felt a little foolish, of course, when she got there to see that the blinds were still down over the windows, and that Maggie Henshall's car was not in the driveway. The housekeeper had evidently not arrived yet. Mrs. Parrish lingered a few minutes on the pavement, walking back and forth past the windows without any particular aim. She was beginning to talk herself out of her suspicions when her persistence was rewarded. Peering in the window of Mr. Albright's study, she saw that the edge of the blind had been partly caught on a framed photograph on the windowsill, leaving a small gap to see through.

And Mrs. Parrish *did* see. She saw her daughter-in-law and Mr. Albright, talking, just talking, but standing *very* close together. They were standing rather closer than Mrs. Parrish would have thought necessary for normal conversation. At length, Mr. Albright took Teresa's hand (Mrs. Parrish must have been watching from the street for a few minutes by then and had already received some strange looks from passers-by) and held it for a long time. After he had dropped it, the girl launched herself at him, truly. He didn't push her away, either, but clung to her. Mrs. Parrish could scarcely believe her eyes, or her luck.

It was something to have one's suspicions confirmed, but Joanna Parrish was a woman of some delicacy, and being rather afraid of what she might see next if she continued to watch, she turned her eyes away from the embrace, and took a step back from the window. She therefore had no warning when Teresa burst out the front door of the house a minute later, and had the girl not been blinded by her own tears, she would certainly have seen her mother-in-law waiting outside the house. It would have been satisfying to see the deceitful little thing caught red-handed, of course, but it would not have been exactly pleasant, and so it was probably for the best that no confrontation ensued. *Time enough for that later*, Mrs. Parrish reminded herself. For now, she could press home her advantage in another way.

With no housekeeper present to answer the door and announce her, Mrs. Parrish figured she might as well just let herself in, and she did precisely that. To her credit, she *did* knock lightly on the door of the study, which stood ajar, before pushing it open.

Timothy Albright was standing with one hand leaning on the desk, and the position looked strained, as though it were the only thing keeping him upright. His other hand he kept passing over his face, to rub his eyes and then his mouth and then his jaw. His breathing sounded shallow and panicked.

Mrs. Parrish announced her presence with a cough. His whole body jerked in alarm as he looked up, and then he muttered something under his breath that might have been a curse. Mrs. Parrish would have believed anything of the minister after what she had just witnessed.

"I'm sorry to disturb you like this, Mr. Albright," she said, in as gentle a tone as she could muster. "But I was looking for Teresa. We missed her this morning, you see." Affecting bewilderment, she continued. "And she just ran past me in the street, in an absolute daze, poor child. Has something happened?"

Mr. Albright sighed and put a hand to the back of the chair beside him, slowly lowering himself into it. "It must be because of her sister," he said, without looking at Mrs. Parrish. "You've heard she's in the hospital?"

"Yes, my son told me." Mrs. Parrish tried for a fraction of a second to remember Teresa's sister's name, and then gave up. "Poor woman. I'm sure it must be very distressing for Teresa. That was why I came looking for her, to tell you the whole truth, Mr. Albright." She took a step towards the desk and did not take her eyes off the minister's face as she spoke, to make sure that her words landed. "I wanted to make sure she knows that she has someone to confide in, if she wishes. One woman to another."

There was a silence, broken only by the sound of the ticking clock on the mantlepiece. Then Mr. Albright, with one hand on his forehead, peered up at Mrs. Parrish at last and said, carefully, "That's very kind of you, Mrs. Parrish." He indicated the chair opposite him with his free hand. "Won't you sit down?"

She took another few steps, until she came level with the chair he had offered but remained standing. "Actually, Mr. Albright…"

"Yes, Mrs. Parrish?" He sounded weary rather than fearful. It wasn't the exact effect she had been hoping for, but it was close enough.

"I *haven't* told you the whole truth. Teresa did see me just now, in the street. And she told me something rather distressing. She told me that you tried to kiss her." Mrs. Parrish watched as Mr. Albright covered his eyes with his hand again. "But that can't be true, can it? The poor thing must be confused. You couldn't have tried to kiss a married woman."

Mr. Albright breathed in sharply through his nose, and said, his words slightly muffled by his hand, "I did."

"You did?" Mrs. Parrish didn't have to pretend to be shocked that he had actually admitted it.

"I did," said Mr. Albright. "And it was very wrong of me." He removed his hand from his eyes and brought it down to the desk, tapping his fingers on the wood. His eyes were still trained on the surface of the desk as he said, "But I also know for a fact that Teresa didn't say anything of the sort to you. Why would she confide in someone who has done nothing but persecute her since she married her son?" He raised his eyes to Mrs. Parrish's. She'd always thought the man had the most unpleasant eyes, deep-set and muddy green. "Which means that you must have found this out some other way. By spying, perhaps?" He glanced at the window, whose blind was still snagged on the photo frame.

The infuriating thing was that Mrs. Parrish could feel herself blushing, despite the fact that the minister was evidently the one in the wrong. His version of how she had found out, however true it might be, just sounded so much less dignified. *Spying.* She tried to steer the conversation away. "That girl accused *me* of persecuting her?"

"She didn't have to. I could see it for myself. That first evening, when I visited, she made a mistake with the cake, and you took her aside. You berated her most unkindly." Mr. Albright smiled grimly as Mrs. Parrish opened her mouth to protest this fact. "Your house has thin walls, Mrs. Parrish. Did you think I wouldn't hear what was going on? Even your son must have noticed."

"Don't bring Luke into this." Mrs. Parrish could feel her face getting hotter and hotter. "I may have been a little impatient with Teresa that evening. I don't remember the details now. We do have little disagreements from time to time, but I'm sure she doesn't take such things to heart. I'm sure she knows that I have nothing but affection for her. And if, now and then, I try to guide her behaviour or make a suggestion that might help her improve... well, since the girl has no mother of her own, I'm sure you can understand that."

"Better to have no mother, I should think, than someone fitting your definition of the role." With her increasing agitation, Mr. Albright just seemed to be getting calmer and calmer. "You've said not to bring your son into this, but I cannot see any other way to explain your treatment of Teresa. It's not just snobbery because her family are shop people. It's not just a belief that, in your words, there are things she needs to 'improve.' No, it goes beyond that, doesn't it? You hate her. You really hate her."

Mrs. Parrish was silent. She could feel a pulse throbbing in her neck. Mr. Albright studied her, and slowly rose to his feet, the papers on his desk fluttering with the movement. "You hate her because you used to be the only person Luke needed. Then they got married, and instead of being glad that Luke had someone else to take care of him, you were furious, weren't you? Your son is not an easy man to live with, but you've never had any compassion for Teresa's position."

"Don't tell me I have no compassion," Mrs. Parrish spat. "I was made of compassion, at the start. I was worn down, just as you would have been too, if you'd had to live with the girl and watch her blunder her way through the smallest task. She hasn't the slightest idea what my son needs. She never has. She didn't know what she was getting herself into when she married him, and now I'm going to give her the chance to get out of it!"

She put a hand to her mouth. She hadn't meant to say the last part out loud, but there it was, and it was too late to take it back. Defiantly, she looked at Mr. Albright, who was staring at her. "Well? Don't look so shocked. You know it's impossible for things to continue between her and my son, now that I've seen – now that I know what I know. And since theirs hasn't exactly been a *traditional marriage*, it shouldn't be too hard to secure an annulment."

"An annulment?" Mr. Albright repeated.

"Yes, an annulment. Why, you look as if you never heard the word before." Mrs. Parrish folded her arms, unable to hide her satisfaction at the upper hand she had gained. "I can keep a secret when I'm required to, you know, Mr. Albright. And I would hate for your reputation to be spoiled by such a slight indiscretion." She watched him. "If you and Teresa can be patient, perhaps in time you can even get married without scandal."

He was almost smiling now. For a moment, he looked transfixed by the possibility of marrying Teresa. Mrs. Parrish couldn't imagine where the great attraction lay, but that was neither here nor there. At any rate, Mr. Albright began to shake his head, slowly and sorrowfully. "It's impossible," he said quietly. "I couldn't marry her. Even if she didn't love Luke, maybe…" He looked up at Mrs. Parrish with a sudden decision. "But she does. She does love your son. Today was a mistake, and you can't punish her for it."

"I don't see what I'm suggesting as punishment. I see it as setting her free. I see it as the *compassionate* thing to do."

"She wants to be with Luke! And if you truly want what's best for your son, Mrs. Parrish, you'll let *him* decide what to do about what happened today. You'll let Teresa tell him herself and seek forgiveness –"

"Luke can't decide anything for himself," Mrs. Parrish snapped. "So, it falls to me. As for you, Mr. Albright, you have two choices. Do you want everyone to know about what happened today, or do you want to go on doing the work that you do? Such important work it is, too, Mr.

Albright, I shouldn't want you to abandon it and let things between my son and his wife take their natural course?"

Mr. Albright had gone pale. With one hand, he shuffled the papers on his desk. "You're threatening me." He gave a small, bitter half-smile as he said, "But I should think you, of all people, Mrs. Parrish, would understand that people sometimes make mistakes. Even married people. Even people whose husbands are ill and depending on them." He looked at her, coldly and deliberately. "Even you, Mrs. Parrish, as your husband lay dying in Coventry General five years ago."

Mrs. Parrish's cheeks had been on fire a few minutes before. Now her whole body underwent a temperature change, and she felt she became pure ice. She stared at Mr. Albright from the protection of her cold shell and said in a voice that sounded far away to her own ears, "I don't know what you're talking about."

"I think you do, Mrs. Parrish," Mr. Albright said, sadly. "I think you know very well what I am talking about."

After Mum had stormed away on some mysterious errand, Luke went up to check on Farley. He had brought him one of his own shirts and a pair of trousers, and he was about to go away again when his friend croaked a greeting. "Lucky."

"You're awake," said Luke, turning back to look at Bill. Gesturing to the chair where he had put the clothes, "You can wear those. Teresa said your suit had to be washed."

"Thank you," said Farley uncertainly, as he got into a sitting position. His jaw was dark with stubble, and his eyes still bloodshot. Whatever colour there was in his cheeks appeared to have struggled to get there, and it was spread out in blotches over his pale skin. He looked around him and asked, "Where am I? Is this your house?"

"You don't remember?" said Luke, wearily. "I ran into you last night in town. You could barely stand. Teresa and I brought you home."

"Ah," said Farley, looking down at the bedclothes. "Well, I'm sorry to have been trouble to you." He glanced at the spare clothes on the chair, and he shifted one pyjama-clad leg out of bed. "I won't impose on you any longer. Tell your wife thank you from me and –"

"Just a minute," said Luke, and Farley glanced back at him, with a look that was almost hunted. "Well. You'll want to eat something first, before you go, won't you?"

The breakfast things were still laid out downstairs, and Luke poured his friend the rest of the coffee in the pot, sensing his eyes on him as he did so. Without returning his gaze, he said, "Why do you want to see Albright, anyway?"

"What?" said Farley, as he took the cup. Luke sat down opposite him, handed him a slice of cold toast and took one himself. He had a sudden flash of memory of them sitting opposite each other just like this, eating bully beef in their tent while the ground beneath them shook with the reverberations of Japanese guns.

"Albright, Albright. You wouldn't shut up about him yesterday. When you were making any sense at all, that is. The rest of the time…" Luke bit into his toast and looked up at Farley, who was sipping his coffee very gingerly, as though he expected to be sick any minute. "Is he why you haven't gone home?"

His friend made a face and put down his cup. "Not the only reason." Luke waited. "There's no home to go back to. The missus… she's had enough of me."

"She's left you?"

"More like made me leave her. Threw me out. Told me not to come back."

There was a silence. Luke's heart had sunk at his friend's words, the surge of sympathy so strong it was almost alarming. He swallowed the last of his toast and said, finally, "And Albright? What's he got to do with it?"

"Nothing," said Farley, staring off past Luke's shoulder. "Just want to talk to him." Then he seemed to rouse himself, and met Luke's gaze, his tone becoming matter-of-fact. "But he won't see me. Sent his housekeeper to fob me off the other day when I called."

"Is it about Rangoon?" Luke couldn't help asking. "You were in the same camp together, weren't you? Did something happen –"

His friend gave him a look, and out of respect for his friend's former authority, Luke broke off the questioning. He kicked the chair leg with his shoe a few times and then said, "You should forget about Albright. Go back to Lizzy, try to make it right with her."

"There's no making it right," Farley said, vaguely, and then he gave an awful smile. "She won't see me. Albright won't see me. *You* won't see me. I've nowhere to go."

"I'm here now, aren't I?" Luke pointed out.

"And you're counting the minutes till I leave."

"Stop that." Luke leaned back in his chair, suddenly unable to look Farley in the eye. "Stop feeling sorry for yourself. It'll get you nowhere."

"I'm not trying to get anywhere. Not anymore."

"Well, I'm going to bring you to the station in a while. That counts as somewhere, doesn't it? And I'm making sure you get on that train this time."

He expected Farley to protest, but his friend just shrugged and took another sip of his coffee, as though it were all the same to him whether he was in Birmingham or Coventry.

Luke watched him carefully until they had finished up eating, and then he went upstairs to check that Farley hadn't left anything behind in Teresa's room.

"Where did you put the pyjamas I lent you?" he called down the stairs.

"In one of the drawers, I think. I don't remember." Farley was standing in the hall. He cut a pretty pathetic figure, with his too-big shirt and slumped shoulders. Luke sighed and went back into the boxroom. He rummaged through the chest and found the pyjamas in the bottom one, on top of one of Teresa's skirts. As he was taking them out, the skirt moved a bit, and a piece of paper came loose from one of the pockets. Luke put down the pyjamas and looked at the paper.

On it was written, in handwriting Luke thought he recognised: *Dr. Edgar White, psychiatrist and psychoanalytic therapist*, and under it the address of his practice. It was in Birmingham. Luke frowned down at the piece of paper for so long that Farley shouted up to ask him if he was all right.

"I'm fine. Fine." Luke came to the top of the stairs again, a bit dazed. "Listen, Sarge, change of plan. I'm coming with you to Birmingham."

"What's wrong?" said Kathleen, for the third time, and Teresa halted. She had been reading aloud from *Gone with the Wind*, but she got the feeling now that her sister was less interested in the exploits of Scarlett O'Hara than in discerning Teresa's mood. She put down the book, marking their place with her thumb as she looked up at Kathleen.

"Nothing. Really. I'm just tired from last night. I told you about Luke's friend and having to bring him home."

"You told me, yes." Kathleen shifted on her pillows restlessly. "Debbie's been to see me this morning. She left just before you came, actually. Had to get back to the shop."

"Oh." Teresa looked down.

"She thinks she might have upset you when you met last night." Kathleen was looking at her kindly, Teresa could tell, so kindly that she knew she would lose what little control she had left if she met her gaze. "She said something silly about the minister."

A tear splashed onto the cover of *Gone with the Wind*, and Teresa quickly wiped her cheek.

"Tess," said Kathleen, and her voice was so quiet that it was almost drowned out by the din of the hospital ward, but it was all she had to say. Teresa craned her neck to look up at the ceiling and blinked away the fresh tears that were welling up in her eyes.

"I can't – I mean, *you're* the one who's sick, I can't come in here and just –"

"Tess." Her older sister's voice was a bit louder this time, and more insistent. At last, Teresa met her gaze.

"I think I might be in love," she said, miserably.

"With Luke? And you've only just realised this?" Shaking her head, Kathleen settled back against her pillows, but Teresa kept staring at her.

"Do you think it's possible to be in love with two people at the same time?"

"I wouldn't know," said Kathleen, warily. Tilting her head towards her sister, she added, "You don't mean the minister?"

Teresa nodded, and Kathleen squeezed her eyes shut. "Oh, Tess. Oh, Tess, no."

SETTLING OLD SCORES

*L*uke had not used the telephone in his house in years. It took him a minute or two to remember how to dial, and it didn't help that Sarge was hovering in the hallway watching him.

"What are you doing?" Farley asked. Luke, who had just brought the receiver to his ear, made an impatient gesture at his friend and listened as the operator put him through. His heart began to beat faster and faster as a female voice on the other end of the line said,

"Good morning, Dr. White's office?"

"Hello?" Luke's voice was hoarse, too hoarse to be understood. He cleared his throat and tried again. "Hello."

"Hello, how can I help you, sir?"

"I'd like to – er –" Luke glanced at the name on the piece of paper, clearly written in Dr. Jackson's handwriting.

Then he caught Farley's eye and instantly regretted it. The intensity of his friend's pale-eyed gaze almost made him lose his nerve. It was another minute before he could get out the words. The voice on the other end of the line waited patiently. "My doctor referred me to Dr. White. I'd like to make an appointment, for today if that's possible."

Dr. White's secretary inquired as to the name of Luke's doctor, informed him that there was indeed a free slot today between twelve and one p.m., and said a cheery goodbye before hanging up. The whole exchange could not have taken longer than three minutes, but as he slowly put down the receiver, Luke felt just as exhausted as if he had been standing there for hours and hours. His hand was sweating and trembling slightly. Reluctantly, he met Farley's gaze again, only to say curtly, "Let's go."

Since Luke couldn't drive, they were forced to walk to the station, and this gave his friend plenty of time to interrogate him. "That's why you're coming to Birmingham, then?" Farley asked, with barely concealed anger, as they were passing the gates of the Common. "To have your head examined? Tell me, was this your idea or your wife's?"

"It's none of your business," said Luke, glancing at Farley. "And it was my idea."

"I don't believe you. Look at you, man. You're shaking." Farley reached out to touch Luke's arm. Luke shook him off and quickened his pace. "You know what this doctor's going to do, don't you? He's going to ask you questions and write your answers down in a little notebook, and then he's going to stuff you full of meds and send you away again, and you'll be just the same as before, only –"

Luke made a sharp turn to cross the street before the traffic lights. Farley followed and dodged an oncoming car. "Only," he went on, jogging by Luke's side as car horns blared behind them. "Only now you'll be even worse, because you won't be able to do a thing without your meds. That's how they get you, you see. *That's* why I don't trust 'em, not a single one of 'em –"

"I'm already on meds," Luke said, wearily. His friend, cut-off mid tirade, opened his mouth and closed it again, staring at him. "They are supposed to help me sleep."

"To help you *sleep*?"

"I get nightmares."

"Well, we all get nightmares, Lucky. I don't think I've had a decent night's sleep in years. You ask any man who saw the things we saw, and he'll say the same thing. You don't need some quack to tell you why that is –"

"I don't know what I need," Luke said, looking straight ahead. "All I know is, she wants me to do this, so I'm going to do this for her."

"Ah, so it *was* her idea." Farley sighed. "Your wife, Parrish, if you don't mind me saying –"

"I *do* mind," Luke said, but Sarge just ignored him, as he always had done when he wanted to get a point across.

"Well, she's nice and pretty and all that, but she's so young. She can't be more than twenty-two, twenty-three. Do you really expect her to understand what it was like for you, for us, out there?"

"She's been through more than you know." As Farley subsided into silence, Luke glanced at him. "You're right, though. She *is* young. And she should be married to someone who can show her a good time, not someone like..." He trailed off, unable even to put into words the depth of his unsuitability.

"No one forced her to marry you." A definite note of bitterness had entered Farley's voice, and Luke got the feeling they weren't just talking about his own situation anymore. "No one forced her to say the words. Maybe she thought it would be different, better, I don't know. But you can't help that."

They were quiet for a while, each lost in his own thoughts. Luke had brought his watch and checked it now and then to see that they were making good time. The train that he was hoping to get would leave the platform at quarter to ten. It was twenty to by the time they reached the station, but Farley, instead of matching Luke's haste, slackened his pace and finally said, as casually as though it were a fact that had been settled long ago, "I'm not going, Lucky."

"You're not?" Luke gazed at his friend in weariness and dismay. "I've got my appointment at twelve, and you're going to make things right with Lizzy. We agreed –"

"We never agreed on anything, Parrish." With a glance at the door of the ticket office, Farley said, "You should go now, while you can still make it. Don't worry about me."

"There's another train to Birmingham in half an hour," Luke said, exasperated. "We can get that one instead."

"I'd like to thank you." Farley stretched out a hand, which Luke ignored. "I'm fortunate that you found me last night." Holding his gaze, he continued, "And I'm glad I got to speak with you properly, Lucky."

"Why are you talking like this?" Luke followed his friend back down the steps and a little way down the street. Dodging a couple bearing suitcases, he hurried to catch up with Farley again. "You're going to go to Albright's house again, aren't you? Why do you need to see him so badly?"

"Get your train," said Farley, without looking around, but Luke shook his head and folded his arms.

"He won't see you. If he wouldn't see you last time, what makes now so different?"

"Nothing," said Bill Farley, at last pinning Luke with his pale-eyed gaze. "Nothing at all. I've just got to try. It's just something I've got to do."

It was a marvel to Teresa that people could just go about their daily business and pass her by without knowing that the very fabric of her life had just changed. By admitting to her sister that she loved Mr. Albright, she had voiced the unthinkable. And now, while in her mind she was jumping to various possibilities, the hospital continued to function around her. Families waited on chairs and patients were wheeled around and doctors consulted with one another in the corridors.

She thought about carrying on her friendship with Mr. Albright, and how, with a little self-control on both of their parts, they might stop themselves from taking it any further. That way, she could go on seeing him every day while knowing that she was doing nothing wrong. But then her mind leapt on. one kiss, one touch, and their friendship would turn into something else entirely. It had nearly done so this morning, and she had wanted it to. Her mind went to the next natural conclusion. They would have to part ways. She would have to see him one more time, of course, just so that she could thank him for his friendship and explain to him that it was not his fault and –

They could run away together, she and Mr. Albright. This possibility stopped Teresa in her tracks, right down the corridor from the ward that she had just left, where her sister had sent her on her way with some very stern advice. *Don't see him again. And whatever you do, don't tell Luke. You've done nothing wrong – yet.* Teresa ignored this now as she had ignored it then and carried on with the daydream. She and Tim could run away together, get out of England and go somewhere they weren't known. They'd spend their days together quietly, just as they had always done when she had come to visit him at his house. He would work on his book and perhaps she could help him, too. She could pass him sheets of paper for his typewriter and lean over his shoulder to advise him on some phrase. And –

Teresa reached the end of the corridor and came face to face with Luke's doctor.

"Mrs. Parrish! We meet again." Dr. Jackson had a chart in his hand and was smiling at her. "I must congratulate you."

"Congratulate me?" said Teresa.

"Yes, I just heard from Dr. White that Luke has scheduled an appointment with him today. I had told him a little bit about your husband's history, you see, and he is naturally curious to meet him, but we both thought it might take a little more persuading. I will not interrogate you as to your methods, Mrs. Parrish, only congratulate you for their success."

"Luke's seeing Dr. White?" said Teresa, staring at the doctor. "But how did he... I had nothing to do with that."

"Come now, Mrs. Parrish, you must take at least a little credit." Dr. Jackson patted her on the shoulder, already distracted by an item on his chart. "Well! I must be going. I shall see you at Luke's next appointment."

Teresa put a hand to her head, where she was beginning to feel the first, faint throbs of a headache. She tried to process everything the doctor had just said. Luke knew about Dr. White, somehow. He must have found the piece of paper Dr. Jackson had given her before. Luke must have thought that she had been waiting for the right moment to talk to him about it, when, in reality, she had never had any intention of telling him. She didn't want to be accused of interfering again.

He had decided to go, and he had made arrangements, without telling anyone. Did that mean what she thought it meant? Was it a hopeful sign? Teresa didn't feel in the least bit hopeful, but that might have had more to do with what had just been running through her head a few minutes before. Here was Luke, following through on something that he thought she wanted him to do, and here was Teresa, daydreaming about running away with Mr. Albright.

Mrs. Henshall was late to work that morning, due to an illness in her family. It was around half past eleven when she reached Mr. Albright's house, and so Mrs. Henshall was disturbed to find that her absence had not even been noted. The minister was in his study as usual, but he was evidently not himself. Mrs. Henshall had never known a man who took better care of his appearance, but this morning Mr. Albright's hair was dishevelled, he hadn't shaved, and he hadn't even a cravat on. He was scribbling feverishly as his housekeeper came in, and didn't even look up as he said,

"Mrs. Henshall,– good morning. I was about to ring, to tell you to take the day off."

"The day off, sir?" Mrs. Henshall wouldn't have been so surprised if the place had looked remotely clean, but it didn't. She had seen muddy footprints on the hall floor as she was coming in, and there were papers strewn all over Mr. Albright's desk. The fire hadn't even been lit. She pointed all of these things out, but Mr. Albright just made a distressed noise and held up a hand, poised beside his left temple, as though he were about to swat some non-existent fly. With his other hand, he kept writing.

"Mrs. Henshall, I am asking you to take the day off, please. There are some things I need to look into, some matters that need my attention."

"I don't think you're quite well, sir," said Mrs. Henshall, staying where she was as she stared at him. "I think you ought to see a doctor."

"I don't need a doctor," Mr. Albright burst out, and then the hand he had been holding by his left temple came down again, to pinch the bridge of his nose as he closed his eyes. "I'm sorry, Margaret. I didn't mean to snap."

"No need to apologise, sir," she said coolly. "I understand when I'm not wanted."

Fuming, she left the study and passed down the hallway. She hadn't even removed her coat or put down her bag. As she stepped out of the front door, she came face to face with the pale-eyed man from the other day, who had just lifted his hand to knock on the door. He looked neater than he had the day before, though the clothes he was wearing were evidently too big for him.

"You!" exclaimed Mrs. Henshall, and then, instinctively, she moved to block his way in. "The minister's not home."

The man, whose name she remembered was Farley, regarded her with equanimity. "That's funny, because I think I just saw him through there." He pointed to the study window without taking his eyes off Mrs. Henshall.

"I'm sure you know it's not polite to go looking through people's windows," she told him.

"It's not polite to lie, either. Let me see him, please."

Mrs. Henshall wasn't going to budge, but then she heard the minister come out into the hall behind her and say wearily, "It's all right, Margaret. Let him in."

"Very well, then," she said, shifting to let the man pass, her eyes darting from the minister to Farley and then back again. "Very well! Since you don't seem to need me, Mr. Albright, I'll be going."

"Goodbye, Margaret," said Mr. Albright, with a glance at her that was half-affectionate, half-exasperated. Then he looked to Farley and gestured for him to follow. The door closed, and Mrs. Henshall saw no more.

It was all very strange. Strange, too, was what Mrs. Henshall saw on her way back to the car. Leaning against a gate a few houses down from the minister's, with his hands in his pockets, was Luke Parrish. She called out his name, but he didn't see her. It looked as though he was waiting for someone. Waiting for that man, Farley? Mrs. Henshall hoped not. She didn't like to think of young Luke being mixed up with someone as unpleasant as that man.

As she drove back through the town, Mrs. Henshall's mind was troubled with all the things she had seen and heard, but she had no way of knowing just how significant those things would soon become, and how often she would soon be called upon to revisit her memory of all that had passed in the space of just a few minutes.

A part of Teresa had been hoping that Dr. Jackson was mistaken, but sure enough, when she got home, it was just Mrs. Parrish awaiting her. It was then necessary to explain to her mother-in-law where she thought Luke had gone, and why. Mrs. Parrish heard it all in cold silence. When Teresa had finished talking, the older woman took a few steps down the hall and then turned again to face her.

"You sent him to Birmingham to see a psychiatrist?"

"I told you, Mrs. Parrish, I didn't *send* him. I didn't even know he was going. Dr. Jackson gave me the name, but I wasn't going to do anything about it."

"I'll kill him," said Mrs. Parrish under her breath, and Teresa wasn't sure if she meant Luke or Dr. Jackson, but when her mother-in-law looked back at her a moment later, the look in her eyes told Teresa that her murderous inclination might have just been redirected at her instead. Mrs. Parrish repeated, "You sent my son to Birmingham? Alone?"

"I didn't send him." Teresa sighed and gave up trying to contradict her. "He's not alone. His friend will be with him. At least, I think –"

"Who is this friend I keep hearing about?" Mrs. Parrish passed into the kitchen, at an agitated pace, and Teresa followed, a few steps behind. "This friend who, according to my son, actually slept in this house last night. Who *is* he, Teresa? Because I'm sure, in the last three years since Luke was sent home from the front, that I've never laid eyes on any friend of his. They all deserted him after his accident."

"They were still fighting overseas, Mrs. Parrish! How could they have visited him then? And this man, his old sergeant, Farley, was taken prisoner."

"The fighting's been over for more than six months now. That's no excuse."

"Yes, but Luke has been throwing away the letters people wrote to him. I was the one who wrote to Bill Farley and got him to visit. I thought Luke needed someone, and I was right, Mrs. Parrish, and now I know that it's not just Luke who needs Farley; Farley needs *him*, too. He..." Teresa trailed off, and wondered, not for the first time, how it was that her mother-in-law could do this to her, how she had the power to reduce Teresa to someone whose spine was made of jelly, someone who was too scared to utter the truth. Teresa *hated* her, she realised just then. She didn't hate Mrs. Parrish, but rather the person she became when she was with her.

"If Luke has been throwing away the letters that this person sent him," her mother-in-law said, advancing towards Teresa, "then I'd like to know what right you thought you had to interfere like that. You think this man is helping Luke? What if being around someone else who remembers all those things actually makes my son worse? What will you do then, Teresa?"

"I don't *know*," Teresa burst out. Mrs. Parrish was now standing mere inches away from her and she could barely breathe. "But at least I'm doing something. At least I'm trying! What have you done for Luke, besides treat him like a child? You might think you're protecting him, but you're making him miserable! He was *miserable* before he married me! And you – it's not often he speaks but when he does you don't even listen to what he says, you act like he's an embarrassment."

Teresa paused for breath, and then, meeting Mrs. Parrish's gaze, found there was another reason why she could not go on. There were tears in the other woman's eyes. They stared at each other for a long moment, and then Mrs. Parrish blinked the tears away and smiled tightly.

"You're right, my dear," she said, with deadly quiet. "You're absolutely right. Luke *was* miserable before he married you, and now he's still miserable. Wives are supposed to make their husbands happy. They're supposed to be loyal and *true*. What are you, Teresa? What are you, exactly?"

There was something in the way Mrs. Parrish uttered the question that made Teresa's blood run cold. For a second, she was frozen, thinking that her mother-in-law must know what had happened that morning and then wondering how she could possibly have found out besides Tim telling her – and Tim would never have told her, of that much Teresa was sure, which left a question.

It was only for a second that she was frozen like this, but the momentary paralysis was sufficient for Mrs. Parrish to shoulder her way past her and out through the hall again. She seized up her coat and hat, and by the time

Teresa had recovered herself enough to shout, almost scream after her that she *had* been true, that she *had* been loyal, that, unlike Mrs. Parrish, she *hadn't* given up on Luke, and that had to count for something – the only response she received was the slamming of the front door.

Luke felt very conspicuous just standing on the street waiting for the Sarge to finish up whatever mysterious business he had with the minister. The December air was raw and uncompromising, all the more so for the clear skies overhead, and he had forgotten to bring gloves. Had Teresa been there when he was leaving the house, she would have made sure he was wearing them. That was yet another example of how Teresa had, over the course of the last few months, made herself indispensable to Luke, and had done so in such a quiet way that he was only now realising it.

Luke shoved his freezing hands in his pockets and put his back to a gate. He had no watch, and therefore no way of determining whether it had been five minutes or half an hour since Farley had walked up to the minister's house. There was a watch at home, his old army-issue watch, buried somewhere in the trunk where he kept all those things that he never wanted to look at again. He should start wearing it again, Luke reflected, and then, a moment later, found himself surprised at the thought, as though it had come from something outside of him.

One thing Luke was also becoming painfully aware of, the longer he stood there in the cold waiting for his friend, was that his appointment time must be creeping nearer and nearer, and that quite soon, he would not just be late but would have consciously, wilfully missed it. This fact didn't bother Luke as much as the unmistakable relief he felt in contemplating his failure, relief that he would not have to sit in front of a stranger for an hour and bare his soul, relief that, as bad as things in his own head sometimes got, he would not have to stir out of that familiar, safe place. There was no way he could have gone on to Birmingham without Farley, knowing the state that his friend was in, or was likely to get himself into, if left to his own devices again. The choice had been clear.

What was less clear was why, given the relief that Luke felt, he had even made the appointment in the first place. It must be as Farley had said. Teresa must have manipulated him into taking that step. Of course, she had never mentioned the psychiatrist to him, and Luke didn't even know how long she had been carrying around that piece of paper. Maybe, after what he said to her the last time she had tried to interfere, she had known better than to apply direct methods of persuasion. Maybe that was why her behaviour had changed over the last few days, and she had become absent and distracted in a way she had never been before. Maybe her sister being sick *was* just an excuse, and really –

Luke stopped that last thought before it could get any further. It sounded more like something his mother would have come up with. For his part, he knew that Teresa was incapable of lying, especially about something like that. It was just that, well, Teresa was one of those people who made you feel as though you were the only person who had a claim on her. When those steady blue eyes gazed at you, it was impossible to imagine that they ever looked at anyone else. Truth be told, though Luke was a little ashamed to admit this, he had actually forgotten that Teresa's sister existed until yesterday. For once, that alive concern in her eyes hadn't been for him but someone else, which had made him feel strange.

Farley came upon him so suddenly that Luke almost missed him. Too wrapped up in trying to clear up the mess that was his own head, he hadn't noticed his friend leaving the house, and the next minute Farley was hurrying past him, head down and shoulders hunched. Luke jolted to alertness and ran to catch up with him.

"Sarge, what happened?" His friend just walked faster. "Bill, tell me, did he see you? Did you get to talk to him?"

Farley didn't even seem to hear him, but when they were passing an alleyway beside a bombed-out house, he stumbled to a stop and Luke, getting a full view of his friend's face for the first time, saw that it was alarmingly drained of colour. He started forward just as Farley braced a hand on what remained of the brick wall, doubled over, and threw up.

It seemed to go for an awfully long time, the throwing-up business, that was. Luke ineffectually patted Farley's back every now and then, and mumbled something like, "It's all right," or, "Get it all out, there you are." This was a busy street, and Luke felt the gazes of passers-by burn through them. Every time someone stared at them, he wanted to run after them and explain the situation.

He knew he would get no answers out of Farley in his current state, and so didn't get into interrogations once his friend had finished emptying the contents of his stomach. He just put an arm around Farley's shoulders and got him out of the cold air, into the nearest building, which turned out to be a pub Luke had often visited before the war. Back then he had liked it for its dark corners and smell of smoke. He liked it even more now, and he found his fingers itching towards cigarettes that were not there.

The Sarge had some in his pocket, as it turned out, and Luke found himself smoking for the first time in years. He hadn't wanted to since his accident, and he hadn't imagined ever wanting to again, but as his gaze met Farley's through the cloud of smoke that rose up between them, he felt glad, glad that they did not need words to understand one another, glad that there were other ways of communicating with a person that did not necessitate the daily struggle that was speech. Luke asked, with his eyes, what had happened at the minister's house. Farley answered, with a shake of the head, that he couldn't or didn't want to say.

It had been a long time since Teresa had been alone in the house. She wondered, in fact, if she had actually been left alone there at all since she had moved in. Even when Mrs. Parrish was out, Luke was a constant presence, usually upstairs, shut in his room, but now he was gone, and his mother was gone, and Teresa, eating lunch on her own, couldn't help but feel that she had driven them out.

The distant sound of drilling reminded her of the construction still going on in the neighbourhood, and Teresa, walking around aimlessly after she had cleared away her plate, began to notice that their house could do with a bit of renovation, too. The walls were too thin, for one thing, she could clearly hear Mrs. Lyndon listening to the BBC next door when she stood in the hallway. She could almost make out the words that the broadcaster was saying. That was probably why it got so cold here, too; there was no insulation. Teresa mentally noted that down and moved on to the next item.

The ceiling in the parlour was sagging in one spot, and the paint there looked darker than the paint on the rest of the ceiling, which might have been the effect of damp. Out in the hallway again, standing in the semi-darkness, she tried the light switch on an impulse, and no light came on. She tried changing the bulb, but the fixture still didn't work. Teresa, shaking her head, dragged the chair she had been standing on back into the kitchen, and wondered how long that light had been broken. She wondered how long they had all three of them been stumbling through that hallway, never questioning why it was dark in the first place.

She wasn't entirely sure why, when she had finished surveying what was wrong with the house, she dialled Mr. Albright's number on the telephone. She just felt she wanted to tell someone what she had discovered. Perhaps the need to hear a kindly voice on the other end of the line outweighed the concerns she would otherwise have had about making that move, so soon after telling Mr. Albright she couldn't see him again. In different circumstances, after all, she would have come to Mr. Albright with her guilty conscience and sought his advice as to what she ought to do about her marriage. And even though seeking his advice now was impossible, Teresa could think of no one else in her life who might offer her what she so sorely needed at that moment: comfort.

She dialled and listened to the phone ring out. As she did so, she mentally calculated how long it might take Mr. Albright to get up and answer. Perhaps he was in his study, engrossed in some work. Perhaps he would look up at the sound, sense that it was Teresa, and show wisdom enough for the both of them by not answering. Perhaps Mrs. Henshall was cleaning one of the upstairs rooms as she often did at this time of day, and would come clattering down the steps, sighing heavily and shaking her shoulders as she went to lift the receiver and utter a begrudging, "Hello?"

But no "Hello" came. The telephone just kept ringing and ringing, and after a time, it started to sound a little desolate. When it cut off Teresa hung up reluctantly, and then all but snatched the telephone off the hook as it started ringing. "Hello?" she said breathlessly.

It was an unfamiliar voice at the other end of the line, young, female and slightly impatient. "Hello, I'm from Dr. White's office. I was hoping to speak to Mr. Luke Parrish. I tried this number a moment ago, but the line was engaged."

"Oh, yes, I was trying to ring someone. I'm sorry." Teresa could feel her face getting hot. The secretary on the other end of the line was silent. "Luke's not here, but I can take a message if you like. I'm his wife." She added that last bit as though it were an afterthought.

"Thank you, Mrs. Parrish. I was wondering, since your husband didn't show up for his appointment with us today, if he'd like to reschedule –"

"He never showed up?"

"No, Mrs. Parrish, I'm afraid he didn't. He made the appointment with me just this morning, so it's possible he changed his mind. It's not unusual, considering the nature of Dr. White's work, for clients to change their minds."

"Something's happened," Teresa muttered to herself.

"I beg your pardon, Mrs. Parrish?"

"I'm sorry," Teresa said, thickly, for there were tears of panic forming in her eyes now. "I'll have to – I'll ring you back." She slammed down the receiver and stood for a long moment in the hallway, her head bowed. Then, as though it had received an electric shock, her body jerked into awareness, and she grabbed her coat and hat and headed out the door.

The Common was the first place she searched, since she knew Luke liked to walk there, but it was deserted. The few walkers that she spotted skirted the edges of the park in their promenade to avoid the mud and were bundled up against the cold with scarves and gloves. Teresa suddenly wondered if Luke had remembered to bring his gloves when he had left that morning. She hoped that he had. Doubling back to the house, she got into the car and drove to the chapel. Every time she had to stop at a traffic light, she nearly cried in dismay. In her mind's eye, she kept seeing Luke stepping off the train at Birmingham station and just *disappearing* into the crowd. Sometimes the image varied, and she saw him collapsed on the side of the road instead, or wandering some street, pale and disoriented, asking for directions from strangers who would not speak to him. Teresa clutched at her own throat and choked out a cry as the traffic lights changed again.

It had occurred to her, of course, that she might see Mr. Albright at the chapel. It had to be four by now, and he would be preparing for evening service. Teresa did not hesitate, however, as she stepped over the threshold of the church. If Luke, for whatever reason, had not wanted to return home, she thought he might have come here. Maybe he had even come to Mr. Albright for help. She had no idea what she would do if that were the case, but the question did not occupy her for long, anyway, because as she walked up the aisle past empty pews, neither Luke nor Mr. Albright was anywhere to be seen. As she approached the altar, she saw instead the sexton and Mr. Albright's housekeeper standing off to the side, evidently trying to have a private conversation while not seeming to realise that their voices were echoing all over the church.

Teresa caught a few words, particularly on Mrs. Henshall's side, as her voice was higher in pitch and pinched with worry. "He did! He sent me home!" Teresa heard the woman insisting, and then, as the sexton rumbled something, Mrs. Henshall interrupted, "I'm telling you, he needs to see a doctor!"

Then the sexton spotted Teresa and cleared his throat. He moved away to continue lighting candles around the altar, while Mrs. Henshall turned slowly to look at the new arrival.

"I couldn't help overhearing," said Teresa, as gently as she could, because the expression on Mrs. Henshall's face suggested that the woman might spook at any moment. "Is everything all right?"

Mrs. Henshall seemed to struggle for a moment to answer the question, and finally said, "No. It's *not* all right."

"Is it the minister?" Teresa persisted. "Is he ill?"

"I don't know *what* he is. All I know is he'd normally be here at this time. I had a funny feeling, so I thought I'd come and check." Mrs. Henshall looked towards the door of the church, and then shook her head. She did not appear to want to meet Teresa's gaze. "He'll say I'm being silly and interfering, of course, but I've worked for him for twelve years and he's never turned me away before."

"Turned you away?"

Mrs. Henshall, now staring down at the tiled floor, explained how she had been late to work that morning, how Mr. Albright had told her when she arrived that her services were not required, and how she had spent the rest of the ensuing day worrying about him. Finally, she looked up at Teresa and wound up her explanation with, "Maybe you can ask your husband if he knows what's the matter with him."

"My husband?" Teresa's heart gave a painful squeeze.

"Yes, I saw him outside the minister's house as I was leaving. I'm *sure* of it. And I'm sure he was waiting for that man."

"That man? You mean Mr. Farley?"

"So, you know him, too." Mrs. Henshall nodded as though confirming something to herself. "Well, then, it looks like I'm the only one who's been kept in the dark. I suppose Mr. Albright thinks I'm a silly old gossip and that's why he hasn't said anything to me." With another sigh, she made as if to move away.

Teresa shook her head as though to clear it and put out a hand. "Wait." The housekeeper turned back. "I know no more than you do, Mrs. Henshall. I came here to look for my husband, because I'm worried about him." The words were not coming easily; they felt as though they were sticking in her throat, but she went on, because she could see no alternative, to suggest that they look for the men together. That was how, only a few hours after having told Mr. Albright that she would never see him again, Teresa ended up driving herself and Mrs. Henshall to his house.

Even if her whole being had not been on fire with nervous energy by now, half from contemplation of what might have befallen Luke and half from anticipation of seeing Mr. Albright again, Mrs. Henshall's company would have pushed her over the edge. The woman kept up a constant stream of anxious chatter on the way to the house, listing all the jobs she would have to do when Mr. Albright allowed her to return to her work, scrubbing the staircase, clearing out the grate, making beds, and so on, and then moving on to speculate about what might be ailing the man.

"Curtains still closed," noted Mrs. Henshall as they passed the study window, with a shake of the head. "I swear, that man never even notices those things. I've told him off, often enough, for working in the dark. One of these days, he's going to ruin his eyes."

"Do you have a key?" said Teresa, but the housekeeper just shook her head.

"It's never locked." She opened the front door and led them inside, calling out for her master as she went. Teresa started to feel sick as they came up to the half-open door of the study. There was just something about the silence of the place, thick and coiling and *waiting*. When Mrs. Henshall, who was a little way ahead of her, pushed the door to and screamed, the odd thing was that Teresa was barely surprised. Something horrible had happened. That much had been clear from the moment they stepped over the threshold.

She was not prepared, however, for the sight of Mr. Albright face-down on the floor of his study, the back of his dark head matted with blood, one hand limp on the carpet and the other buried underneath him. There was no earthly way that she could have been prepared.

"You're going to be all right," she whispered to Mr. Albright, but it felt wrong talking to the back of his head. His kind eyes should have been fixed on her, his head tilted to the side and his fussy hands brushing non-existent crumbs off his trouser legs. The blood had trickled down from the nape of his neck to the back of his white shirt, staining it red. That seemed wrong, too. Tim would be so annoyed that his shirt had been ruined.

Mrs. Henshall was crying now as she rang for an ambulance. Teresa had dropped to her knees, and from this new perspective she could see that there was even more blood than she had thought at first. The carpet around Mr. Albright was dark with it. No, she corrected herself, not Mr. Albright, not anymore. Mr. Albright's body.

A GUILTY CONSCIENCE

*L*uke walked his friend to Station Square for the second time that day, determined on this occasion that he would see him onto the actual train. He would buy a ticket to Birmingham himself if that was what it took. He had no more understanding of what was going on in Farley's head than he had had that morning. Whatever had happened at Mr. Albright's house, Bill Farley would not tell Luke, but he did say something which caught Luke's attention as they were queuing at the turnstile.

It was a quarter to five, close to rush hour, and the station was almost impossible to navigate with the crowds. Luke, after getting an elbow to the face, found his resolve was beginning to weaken, and finally he said to Farley, raising his voice over the din, "If I leave you here, will you swear to get on that train?"

Farley turned to look at him. "I will. This time."

"And you won't come back to try and see Albright again?"

Farley's pale eyes glittered with an odd certainty as he said, "I won't, Lucky. That's all over now."

"What do you mean, it's all over?" Luke asked, the last part of the question coming out jerkily as someone in the queue jostled him. Farley put out a hand to steady his friend.

"I'm going to do as you said, Lucky. Make another go of it with Liz. See the kids again."

"That's good. Good for you, Sarge." Luke attempted a smile, and his friend attempted one too. And then, with a parting pat on the arm, Farley let go and went on. Luke watched him until he had got to the other end of the turnstile. His friend walked more slowly than the others around him, his head down and every second step stumbling. He did not have a soldier's walk anymore. He had, Luke realised with a pang, the walk of a drunk.

To get home, since he had no car and his legs were burning from all the unexpected exercise they had received that day, Luke did something he had not done in years and got on the bus.

He was expecting people to look at him oddly, at least, but the conductor barely spared him a glance as he handed him his ticket, and Luke went and sat down like everyone else. A girl even smiled at him from across the aisle.

Beyond the rattling motion of the bus working its way into his sensitive head, the journey was pleasant enough. Luke disembarked at the Common, and, on an impulse, walked through it to get to his neighbourhood. His shoes were caked with mud by the time he reached the house, but he felt refreshed, restored.

There was no one at home. Luke called up the stairs a few times, but his voice just echoed weirdly in the empty space. There was no smell of cooking in the kitchen when he went through, and no sign that anyone had been in the parlour all day. There were, however, little bits of disorder that greeted his eyes as he came back into the hall. The telephone receiver was hanging off the hook, the umbrella had been knocked to the floor, presumably by someone leaving the house in a hurry. Luke then heard the voices through the wall that separated their house from next door. He thought at first that it was just Mrs. Lyndon's wireless, as usual, but the voices he could hear were too irregular for that. They rose and fell, and one of them sounded as though it might be crying. Luke listened for a minute more and then ventured outside.

Mrs. Lyndon's front door stood ajar. Luke knocked, tentatively, and then knocked again when no one answered. Finally, he pushed it open, and came face to face with his mother.

"Oh, my dear!" exclaimed Mrs. Parrish. "You've got no coat, or gloves! What on earth are you doing out in the cold?"

"I heard voices" Luke started, as his mother seized his elbow and pulled him inside. "Is everything all right?"

"It's Mr. Albright," Mrs. Parrish said grimly. "He was attacked in his house earlier. I'm afraid he was killed, Luke. Maggie Henshall just telephoned to tell us."

Luke just blinked. As they entered the kitchen, he saw Mrs. Lyndon in her rocking chair, snuffling over her handkerchief. "Such a good man," she was mumbling.

"Yes, he *was* a good man," said Mrs. Parrish, coming around the back of the rocking chair to squeeze her neighbour on the shoulder. "And they'd better catch whoever did this." She glanced up at Luke, and said, with just the slightest edge to her voice, "What is it, dear? You've gone pale."

"I think I might know what happened," said Luke miserably.

Mrs. Lyndon roused herself from her crying for a moment, blinking at him curiously, but Mrs. Parrish got there first. "But you were in Birmingham all day, my dear, weren't you? You must have just gotten back. How could you know what happened?"

"I think," Luke went on, confused now by the intensity of his mother's stare, "that my friend Bill Farley-"

"Yes, your friend Farley, the troublemaker, of course," Mrs. Parrish jumped in again. "Why, he might have had something to do with this. Why didn't I think of it before?

We'd better go to the police station at once. Agnes, I hate to leave you alone like this, But you know we must do what we can to help. " She put a hand on the back of her friend's rocking chair again.

"Of course," Mrs. Lyndon said shakily. "I'd come with you if I had the strength. But..." She fell to crying again. Mrs. Parrish gave her a few mechanical pats on the shoulder and then looked back at Luke, the command in her eyes clear. *Let's go.*

Luke couldn't believe his friend's stupidity, but more than that, he couldn't believe his own. He had made no attempt to stop Farley from seeing Albright, despite knowing that his friend had some kind of grudge against the man, despite knowing that Farley had spent the previous night trawling all the pubs in Coventry. Then, when Farley had behaved so strangely after meeting Albright, it had never occurred to Luke to go back and check if the minister was all right. He had just never thought of Farley as violent in that way. Luke reflected bitterly as he sat into the front seat of his mother's car, people could change, and *did* change when Hell had broken them. Surely, he himself was living proof of that.

Mum was quiet for the first few minutes of the drive, as though she was trying to get her thoughts together. Luke could almost hear the gears in her head turning. She had always been a loud thinker. Finally, she burst out, "Mrs. Henshall said on the 'phone that she's sure she saw you waiting outside the minister's house, when that friend of yours went to see him." With a sidelong glance at Luke, "*I'm* the one who spoke to Maggie Henshall. Not Mrs. Lyndon, so no one else has to know. We can just say that Maggie must have been mistaken. We can say you were in Birmingham for the day."

Luke shifted on his seat. "Don't you want to know-?" he began uncomfortably.

"I don't need to know any more than I already do." Confidently, Mum kept one hand on the steering wheel and reached the other to hold Luke's. "*I* know you can't have had anything to do with this. My sweet boy. You wouldn't hurt a fly." Her hand lifted to his cheek, patting his curls. "You were just being a good friend, weren't you? And that man, that horrible man, took advantage of you."

Luke didn't know whether to feel comforted or annoyed. Maybe he was a bit of both. "It wasn't like that, Mum. Farley is- His head's all shaken up. I don't think he could have wanted to hurt Mr. Albright, if not for that. And I should have made sure he didn't get the chance."

"No," said Mrs. Parrish, her hand dropping away and back to the steering wheel again. Her voice was firm. "This is *not* your fault, Luke dear. This is not your fault at all."

When they checked in at the police station and entered the waiting room, Teresa was there alone, biting her nails. She jumped up when she saw Luke and rushed to his side.

"I was so worried about you! Are you all right?"

"Are *you* all right?" he asked her. "I hear you were the one who found him."

"With Mrs. Henshall, yes. It was-" She shook her head, shuddering. Luke watched her as she looked away and thought about the unfairness of it all, why Teresa, of all people, had to be the one to find Mr. Albright. Hadn't she seen enough of that kind of thing in her life? And anyway, this sort of thing wasn't supposed to happen here, at home. Everyone at home was supposed to have been protected from the blood of battle. But here his friend had brought it back into their lives. With that last thought, Luke felt a surge of anger towards Farley.

"Where *is* Maggie?" Mum said sharply. She had been standing aside all this time watching him and Teresa. Now she stepped forward. Teresa blinked, confused by the name for a moment, and then said,

"Mrs. Henshall's answering some questions. They've already talked to me, too."

"And they will probably want to talk to us. Well, to you." Mum shifted her weight as she looked towards Luke. "But you're not to go in alone, my dear, I'll come in with you.

And you must tell them everything you know about Farley. That way you can be free of suspicion."

Luke was angry at Farley,. so why did his heart sink to hear those words from his mother's lips? He looked towards Teresa, who was watching him closely. He said, "Can I talk to you outside? For a minute?"

"Of course," she said, looking relieved at the prospect of getting out of the place. As they walked out, Luke could feel Mum's gaze burning into his back.

The cold bit at them even as they huddled by the sheltered side of the police station. Above, the sky was dark blue, a thumbnail moon standing out impossibly bright yellow against it. Luke blew at his bare fingers, and Teresa, seeing that he had indeed forgotten his gloves as she had feared, took his hands in her gloved ones. He looked down at her, as though startled, but did not pull away.

"What is it?" she said, gently, once a minute or two of silence had passed. "What did you want to say to me?"

Luke frowned, as though he himself wasn't sure of the answer. "I'm sorry," he said at last, which, unfortunately, the very last thing Teresa wanted to hear right then. *He* was sorry, for trying to do something for her? *He* was sorry, when she had nearly betrayed him that morning? She forced herself to focus as he kept speaking.

"If I'd kept a closer eye on Farley, this wouldn't have happened. I should have known he couldn't have a good reason for wanting to see the minister that badly."

"I was the one who brought him here in the first place," Teresa pointed out, and Luke bit his lip and shook his head as though that didn't satisfy him. She went on, chafing his hands with her own as she spoke, "So you think it was him?"

Luke looked down at her again and slowly nodded. "He said something earlier when I was seeing him to his train. I said I hoped he wouldn't try to see Mr. Albright again and he said something about it being 'all over.'"

Teresa swallowed as she took this in. She sensed Luke's careful gaze on her, but when she looked back, he had moved his eyes away again and she thought she might have imagined it. He was silent, however, as though waiting for her to say something. All at once she knew that this was her opportunity. This was the opening that she had been waiting for, to be honest with him. "There's something I have to tell you about, too."

He met her gaze warily. In a moment he would let go of her hands in disgust. He would look at her differently or, worse still, with that old blankness that he used to have, up until a few months ago. All this time Teresa had thought that she and Mr. Albright had made no progress with Luke, and yet now she could see it. It was all laid out before her, the long road they had travelled down since getting married, and now she was about to be shunted back to the start again. She lost courage at the last second and said instead, "I had an argument with your mother earlier."

Luke sighed. He didn't look particularly surprised. "Is that all?"

"I said some pretty hard things to her," Teresa said. "About you. I think I really upset her."

"She's said some hard things to you, too. I wouldn't worry. And just now, when we were driving here…" He cast his eyes up at the sky before continuing, "… she told me I should say I was in Birmingham all day today. Hang Sarge out to dry."

"It's not your fault that he did whatever he did. If he did it."

"I can't think who else besides him would have had the chance to do it, or who would have wanted to. But I just wish I knew what it was all about." Luke looked at Teresa out of the corners of his eyes. "Something happened in that prison camp in Rangoon. Something Farley can't get out of his head. And I can't say I don't understand the feeling. Of something possessing you, you know. Something taking hold of you. I…"

Luke stopped. Teresa had shuddered without meaning to, and slowly he took his hands out of hers, and put them in his pockets instead. "Farley's my friend. Whatever he's done, he's still my friend. I can't just leave him alone, so I'm not going to lie."

"You'd be caught out, anyway, if you did," Teresa said, struck by a sudden thought. "They rang me from Dr. White's office earlier, wondering why you hadn't shown up. All the police would have to do is ring that number and they'd know you didn't go to your appointment. And Mrs. Henshall saw you, too, outside the house."

"Then it's settled. I'll tell the truth." Luke touched a hand to her elbow and nodded at the door. "Let's get back in, it's cold."

Once Mrs. Henshall had emerged from her questioning, Detective Sergeant Gamble, a mild-mannered man who was sweating quietly into his brown suit, told everyone else that they could go home. He did not watch them go but returned his gaze to his notebook, flipping through the pages as he walked away in the other direction.

No one spoke as they rattled home. Luke was sitting up front, and Teresa saw his mother reach across to squeeze his hand every now and then, with a half-glance at their back passenger before dropping it again.

At home, once they were sitting in front of cups of weak tea, Mrs. Parrish started in on her own line of questioning. "What were you two talking about, at the station?" She seemed to be addressing the question to both of them but was looking only at Teresa.

Teresa looked at her husband, who gave a confirming nod. "We were talking about what Luke is going to say to the police."

"I thought we already decided on that, dear," said Mrs. Parrish, turning to Luke. He blinked and then, avoiding her gaze,

He blinked and then, avoiding her gaze, said, "I can't just lie. I was with Farley all day. I didn't know what he was planning to do, of course, but I knew something wasn't right when he left Albright's house. I could have said something, done something.

"I've told you before this is not your fault." Mrs. Parrish's voice was one of deadly quiet.

"Still, I can't lie. Teresa says Dr. White's office telephoned her earlier today anyway to ask why I missed my appointment, so even if I pretended I was in Birmingham, no one could back me up –"

"Well, the solution is simple there." Mrs. Parrish brandished her teacup at Teresa before taking a sip. "You don't tell the police about that telephone call."

"But they can just telephone the office to confirm," she spluttered, looking at Luke, whose expression was unreadable.

"And then it'll be your word against the word of Dr. White's secretary. You stick to your story, and no one can accuse you of anything." Mrs. Parrish put down her cup and leaned forward, watching the silent Teresa. "Or maybe you're not willing to do that? Maybe you're not willing to tell a little lie for your husband's sake?"

"of course I don't want Luke to get in any trouble but I'm not very good at lying anyway, and won't it make matters worse if they catch *me* lying, too? I just-"

"I think you're underestimating yourself, my dear." Mrs. Parrish leaned back in her chair again comfortably. "I think you're better at lying than you give yourself credit for."

Teresa stared at her. Luke set down his cup on the saucer with a crash and said, "*Stop.*" He had been staring at the table for the past few minutes, but now he lifted his gaze and looked at them each in turn. "I'm tired of this. Mum, Teresa's sorry for the things she said to you today. Now you say sorry, too."

"Luke, dear," said Mrs. Parrish, who had clutched at her heart at the loud sound, and now gave her son a bewildered smile. "If I thought I'd said or done anything to be sorry for, of course I would apologise, but as it is –"

"I'm not blind, Mum. I'm not stupid, either." Luke shook his head, running a hand up the back of his head, and said again without looking at his mother, "Just say you're sorry."

"Very well." Mrs. Parrish turned her gaze to Teresa, and said, slowly and deliberately, "I'm sorry, Teresa. You're a good wife to my son, and a good daughter-in-law. We're so very lucky to have you."

"Thank you, Joanna," said Teresa, feeling sick to her stomach. Luke cleared his throat and rose from the table.

"That's it, then. We should all get some sleep for tomorrow." He left the kitchen, the door swinging behind him.

Silenced, and a little baffled by his newfound authority, Teresa and Mrs. Parrish sat opposite each other for a minute or two after he had left. It was Mrs. Parrish who got up from the table first and began clearing the cups away. She said nothing, but gave Teresa a small, contemptuous smile before moving to the sideboard. Teresa picked up a tea towel and, as her mother-in-law washed, she began to dry. Still, they did not speak, and the clatter of crockery was impossibly loud to Teresa's ears. She felt her skin prickle every time Mrs. Parrish cast one of those quick glances in her direction, glances that seemed to say that she knew everything, that there was no hiding from her.

DESERVING THE HONOUR

*B*ill Farley didn't think he would ever get used to seeing his reflection in shop windows. First there would always come that moment of alarm, followed by genuine confusion as to *who that man was*, with the sunken cheekbones and pouchy skin and straggly grey moustache, and then, finally, would come the familiar dismay as he remembered that the man was him, that his young face had collapsed in the space of a few short years. For that reason, he tried not to look in shop windows where he could avoid it. The trouble was that when you were wandering around Birmingham at seven in the morning, when everything was closed, there wasn't much else to do besides look in shop windows. And so, as he walked along the cold street, skirting around window-washers and delivery men, his old man's reflection bobbed along beside him.

He had got back yesterday evening around half six, and, figuring that it was too late to visit Lizzy, had stayed in a hostel overnight. The place was an old air-raid shelter that had been repurposed after the war to cope with the large number of homeless people flooding into the cities. Bill supposed he qualified now as one of that number. He slept in a bunk bed in a room with a dozen others. One of the windows wouldn't properly close, and besides dragging in the cold, it kept up an awful rattle all night. Even if Bill hadn't had his share of bad dreams, this alone would have been enough to make for a disturbed night. As it was, he probably spent more time staring out at the blurry lights of the city, that were visible through a gap in the curtains, than he did sleeping.

The following morning, he left the hostel with the vague intention of walking to Lizzy's, but it soon struck him that it would be too early. Deciding that he would wait until eight at least, when the kids would have departed for school, Bill was left to wander the town with nothing to do. And when the clock above the train station struck nine and he was still wandering, he knew that it was neither too late nor too early to visit now, yet here he still was. It was plain and simple. He wasn't up to the task.

He might have been wandering forever if he hadn't passed that gaggle of schoolchildren. A mix of girls and boys, they had been split into pairs and were holding hands while their teacher led them somewhere. Their chatter, high and piercing, washed over him, and Bill felt like laughing and wincing at the same time. He looked after them as they went, thinking that little Billy and Dora might have been among them, and he wouldn't have even known. And, finding that thought more frightening than the thought of seeing his wife again, the thought that he was forgetting the faces of his own children, he didn't delay any longer.

Their row of houses had escaped the war relatively untouched. It had been built in the shadow of a factory a hundred years before, but that factory had long since closed down, and though its long chimneys and brown brick were still visible from Bill's street, it seemed the Germans hadn't considered it a worthy target. Either that, or it had benefited from that thing which had blessed all survivors of the war at one point or another, the sheer randomness of good fortune.

He stood on a step for some minutes before working up the courage to ring the doorbell. Almost as soon as he had done so, the door was wrenched open, and out stared his wife. Her fair hair hung down in dishevelled strands around her face. She had been crying, and her face was now locked in cold fury. Bill almost turned on his heel and fled there and then.

"You've really gone and done it now, Bill, haven't you?" she said, finally. As he stared at her, uncomprehending, she added, "You've just missed them. The police. They left not ten minutes ago."

"The *police?*" Bill repeated.

"Tell me you had nothing to do with it, Bill," she said, blinking away fresh tears. "With – with that man dying. Tell me!"

Teresa tried to get it all straight in her head. She would never speak to Tim again. She would never listen to his war stories again, or drink tea with him in his parlour. She would never be able to ask his advice about Luke, or even entertain the briefest fantasy about running away with him, because something like that wasn't even within the realm of possibility anymore. So, knowing that, why couldn't she feel anything? Why did she feel just as if some distant relative had passed away, and that all she could do was murmur, over and over again, that it was sad and shocking?

Mrs. Henshall didn't seem to be faring much better than her, although she, at the very least, was feeling *something*. She had shown up at their house in the middle of breakfast, but, incapable of eating, had just sat in the corner and started talking on and on about how impossible it was. She kept repeating herself. "He never hurt anyone," she would say, gazing at Teresa as though she expected to be contradicted. "He only ever helped people." And her hands would creep up over her eyes and she would start sobbing again, and Mrs. Parrish would hand her another cup of tea that she wouldn't drink, and Luke and Teresa would just sit there, lost in their respective thoughts. It was a relief when the doorbell rang.

The feeling didn't last long, however, as when Teresa opened the door, she saw D.S. Gamble standing outside and a squad car waiting in the street behind him. He was wearing the same brown suit as the day before, and there were beads of sweat on his forehead despite the cold. He cleared his throat. "Ah, Mrs. Parrish. We'd like to speak to your husband."

"We were about to drive to the police station ourselves, sergeant," said the older Mrs. Parrish, coming up in the hall behind Teresa. "Don't you want to interview all of us?"

"It's just Mr.Parrish we're interested in speaking to at the moment, ma'am," said Gamble. With a glance at the waiting car, he continued, "We thought we'd save you the drive."

"Is my son under arrest?" Mrs. Parrish said then, sharply.

"No, no. We're asking him to come with us of his own free will, just to answer some questions."

"I'll go fetch him," said Teresa. She climbed the stairs and knocked at Luke's door, letting herself in when she heard his faint reply.

He was lying on his bed, fully clothed, holding at arm's length a letter. There were envelopes scattered on the bedclothes around him, and in the corner of the room, the lid of the trunk was propped open against the wall. Teresa tried not to look too curious. "Luke, the police are here. They want you to come into the station and answer some questions."

"I know," he said, without moving. "I saw the car through the window."

Teresa shifted on her feet and spoke as gently as she could. "Well, they're waiting. You'd better go down."

"I'll go in a minute. I just…" Luke folded up the letter and sat up, so suddenly that Teresa was startled. His eyes were wide and bloodshot. None of them had gotten much sleep last night, of course, but he looked particularly ragged. He gestured around to the envelopes. "Look at all these. He wrote to me every week for the past four months." At Teresa's questioning look, "Farley. And all his letters say the same thing, pretty much, inviting me to the ceremony in May, saying how important it is for everyone to get together again."

"Did you take your embutal last night?" Teresa asked.

"No, I didn't. Must have forgotten." He shrugged off the question and went on, staring at her, "If Farley was so keen on getting to the ceremony, – if it was so important that he wrote me…" He did a quick count and then went on, "… *sixteen* letters about it, then , why would he do something like this, Teresa? Why would he make sure *he* couldn't go? Because he had to have planned this. Why else would he have tried to see Albright, before? And if he wanted to kill him, then, well..."

"It doesn't make sense," Teresa said as Luke trailed off. "But then, *he's* not making sense, Luke, is he? You'd better go down. Come on."

Luke sighed, put away the letter, and followed her out of the room.

The detective was friendly enough on the drive to the station, asking Luke about where he had served in the war and easy questions like that, but when they arrive, Luke was directed to the interrogation room and left there alone, waiting, for nearly an hour. The quality of the light in the room was strange, too. There were no windows, of course, but it wasn't just that. The light was grainy and hard on his eyes. It must have been that the lack of sleep was getting to him. His nerves were as raw as the winter air outside. The distant slam of a door somewhere in the station would make him snap up in his seat, only to slump back down when he realised no one was coming. He bit his fingernails down to the quick, one by one, and wished he had a cigarette.

The detective, when he eventually showed up, actually offered him one from his own box, but Luke shook his head and tried not to inhale too deeply as the man lit up his own cigarette. Gamble was as pleasant as he had been on the drive over, talking about the weather and complaining about paperwork. "Tired?" he said eventually, after Luke had given a one-word answer to yet another remark about the weather. Luke nodded.

"Couldn't sleep."

"I see." Gamble tapped out the ash from his own cigarette, holding it well away from his notebook. "Did you know Mr. Albright well?"

"No. He sometimes came over for tea. I went to his house once, too, I think, with my wife, but I mainly saw him at church."

"Are you a religious man, Mr. Parrish?"

"Yes," Luke said shortly.

Gamble, who seemed to have been waiting for more, nodded after a moment and leaned back in his chair. He cleared his throat. "You know that the Reverend Albright served as a military chaplain in Burma, of course? Did your paths ever cross there?"

"No. But I knew him from before the war." At the detective's questioning look, "From church. And he was there when my father died, in the hospital."

"I see. And may I say I'm sorry for your loss, Mr. Parrish."

Luke muttered his thanks, and that it had been a long time ago. D.S. Gamble put out his cigarette and brushed the ash from his fingers. Then he propped his chin on his hand and said, "We've conducted a search of Mr. Albright's house, and we have come to the conclusion that whoever killed him was probably known to him. There were no signs of a struggle or forced entry. We found a poker discarded in the back garden which we think likely to have been the weapon used in the attack. Can you think of any reason why someone might have wanted to harm Mr. Albright?"

"I don't know. He seemed like a good man."

"Seemed?"

"Well, like I said, I didn't know him well."

"I'm sorry to ask you all these questions, Mr. Parrish. I know this must be a very trying time. But since you and Mr. Farley were among the last people to see Mr. Albright alive…"

"I didn't see him," Luke said, looking the detective straight in the eye. "I didn't even go in the house. I waited outside."

"I see." Gamble wrote something down and looked back up at Luke.

"Listen," Luke said, before the detective could start in on another round of questions, "I know what it looks like. I know it looks like Farley must have done this. And I don't know that he didn't. But I never knew him to be violent before. I think there might be something else going on."

"Never knew him to be violent? But you fought alongside each other, isn't that right, yourself and Mr. Farley? He was the sergeant of your troop?"

"War's different." Luke held the detective's gaze, determined not to drop it. In the end it was Gamble who looked down first.

"You said that something else might have been going on, Mr. Parrish? What do you think that 'something else' is? Who do you think killed Mr. Albright?"

"I don't know. They'd have to have a grudge against him. And they'd have to... I don't know." Luke, gesturing with his hand, saw that one of his nails was bleeding, and lowered the hand to his side.

"In our search of Mr. Albright's house, we also found that some of his war medals are missing." The detective leafed through the pages of his notebook. "Can you think of who might have taken them?"

"His medals?" Luke stared at Gamble. "No, I can't think."

"Your friend Mr. Farley, perhaps?"

"But he has his own. Why would he..." Luke screwed up his face as he shook his head.

"Well, once we have located Mr. Farley, we can settle that question." The detective sergeant took out a handkerchief and mopped the sweat from his brow. Luke watched the movement.

"You haven't found Farley yet?"

"Not yet, no. A representative from Birmingham P.D. visited Mrs. Farley's house this morning, but she said she hasn't seen her husband for some time." With a quick glance up at Luke, "Of course, if you have any idea where he might have gone…"

Luke shook his head. "I'll let you know if I think of anything."

"Thank you, Mr. Parrish. You've been very helpful." D.S. Gamble stood, the legs of his chair scraping back along the floor. After a moment's hesitation, Luke followed suit.

As they were walking to the door, the detective dropped his notebook. Since Luke was closer, he bent down to get it.

"Butter fingers," Gamble said, with a rueful smile as he took the notebook off Luke. Then, pointing to his hand, "You're bleeding, Mr. Parrish. Would you like me to fetch you a plaster?"

"Oh, no, it's all right, thanks." Luke looked at his hands. "It's just from biting my nails."

"Nervous habit, I suppose," said the detective, still smiling. "Well, P.C. Carling will show you out."

It had been a long morning. The only thing that gave it any kind of shape was when Mrs. Henshall's sister arrived at the Parrishes' house around eleven to pick her up and bring her back home. After that, Mrs. Parrish said she would go next door to Mrs. Lyndon's for a while, and Teresa, having nothing to do, wondered aloud if she should go and meet Luke at the police station.

"Oh no, my dear," said Mrs. Parrish, who was in the middle of buttoning up her coat. "Why, you might be waiting for hours. You can never tell how long these things might take."

"But surely they won't have that many questions to ask him?" Seeing the guarded look on her mother-in-law's face, Teresa pressed on. "Unless... they can't honestly think that *Luke* did it?"

Mrs. Parrish sighed. "I know it's hard to imagine. But now that they can place him there, at Mr. Albright's house, around the time of the attack, well, *this* is why I wanted him to say he was in Birmingham for the day. If they know he was here instead, then it looks like he might have helped that man, Farley, been a lookout for him, at the very least. Can't you see that, my dear?"

Teresa shook her head. Mrs. Parrish took her arm, steering her to the kitchen. "Come and sit down for a minute, my dear. You're still in shock, I daresay. You're not thinking straight. Now." When they were sitting, the older woman resumed, "Tell me honestly. When you heard about the attack first, and when you heard that Luke had been seen there, at the house, didn't a part of you doubt him? Even for just a second?"

Teresa shook her head again, more vigorously this time. "No. I know he would never hurt anyone." She lifted her eyes to Mrs. Parrish's.

"But he *has* hurt people before. Think of Blackpool." As Teresa opened her mouth to protest, Mrs. Parrish held up a hand. "I'm *just* trying to look at it the way the detectives might. Of course *I* know Luke couldn't have done it. I never doubted him. But a mother's love, well, it's stronger than anything in the world, a mother's love."

Teresa fidgeted at this last part. "I've never doubted him," she said again, quietly but forcefully.

"And I'm sure that's to your credit." Mrs. Parrish leaned forward, and her hand came down on Teresa's, where it was laying inert on her lap. She patted it a few times, her eyes fixed on Teresa's face. "I'm so glad we've made it up, you know. Now we can talk frankly with each other. My dear, I know about you and Mr. Albright."

Teresa withdrew her hand in a flash. "There's nothing *to* know," she said, automatically.

"Now, Teresa, you don't have to pretend to me. You were seen together, yesterday morning. Mrs. Henshall saw it all." As Teresa covered her face with her hands, Mrs. Parrish went on, "But it's all right, my dear. I don't blame you, not at all. I'm sure it's a good thing you didn't let things get any further than they did. But you know you will have to tell Luke."

"I tried to tell him yesterday," Teresa said, her voice muffled behind her hands. "I really did."

"I believe you, my dear."

"I tried to tell him but I couldn't. I'm too much of a coward."

"You will have to tell him, sooner rather than later." For the first time, Mrs. Parrish's voice tilted into severity. "You know that, don't you? Mrs. Henshall will be obliged to tell the police what she witnessed between you and Mr. Albright. If she hasn't told them already, that is. And if you don't give Luke warning, if you don't prepare him for this, then how do you think he'll react, if that detective springs it on him? It could look very bad for Luke."

Teresa lowered her hands slowly as the full horror of it sank in. "They might see it as a motive," she said, staring at Mrs. Parrish. "They could say that Luke, out of jealousy... Oh, God, what have I done?"

"You will have to tell him," said her mother-in-law again, calmly. "The sooner you tell him, the sooner he can make his peace with it. And then it can't be used against him."

She rose to her feet, smoothing down her coat. She was moving for the door when Teresa said, in a small voice, "I can't imagine what you must think of me."

Mrs. Parrish halted but did not turn. Teresa went on, winding her hands in her lap, "But I love Luke. I really do. You have to believe me, Mrs. Parrish."

"I'm afraid, my dear, it doesn't really matter what I think." Over her shoulder, Mrs. Parrish gave her an apologetic smile. "It all comes down to whether Luke believes you or not."

When Luke got back, the house was quiet. Figuring that his mother and Teresa must have gone next door or to Mrs. Henshall's, he hung up his coat and climbed upstairs. It was just as well, he reflected, because he wasn't in the mood to talk to anyone. All the way home, he had been possessed by a gradual, sinking feeling, which was weighing him down so much by the time he came into their neighbourhood that every step was a struggle. He could feel that the questioning had not gone well. He had been too nervous, wired from lack of sleep and from not taking his meds. He kept seeing, again and again, the smile on the detective's face when he was leaving. What had it meant? Did he think Luke was guilty?

In his bedroom, the trunk was still open from where he had been rifling through Farley's letters this morning. He gathered up the letters now, some within their envelopes and some without, and tossed them back inside. He was about to close the lid again when the gleam of a medal caught his eye. Remembering what the detective had said about some of Albright's medals going missing, Luke reached inside the trunk and took out the one he had spotted. It was the Burma Star, awarded to every soldier who had served in the Burma campaign between 1939 and 1945. For that reason, it had never seemed particularly special. And yet, the thought of someone taking it made him close his hand over the bronze star, so tightly that the points dug into his palm. Perhaps, he thought, he should get a lock for this trunk.

"Luke? Are you there?"

He had not closed the door of his room fully, and Teresa knocked on the other side before letting herself in. "How did it go?"

"I don't know." Luke, with his back to her, put his medal back in the trunk and then closed the lid carefully. He rested his hands on the top and went on, "I was nervous. It made me nervous, that place."

"Of course it would. And you're tired, too." Teresa took a few steps towards him. He heard her approaching. "Did the detective say they'd be bringing you in again?"

"No. He just said I was helpful, whatever that means." Luke shook his head and finally turned. "Teresa."

"Yes?" Her eyes were wide and fearful, as though she was expecting him to say something harsh to her. And could he really blame her? Had he given her reason to expect any other treatment from him?

"I don't know what's going to happen," he said at last, quietly.

"Oh, Luke." Teresa's voice was barely louder than a whisper. "Luke, there's something…"

"What is it? Are you crying?" He took a step closer to her, holding up his hands. "You are. Teresa, don't cry. It's going to be all right. I'll make it all right soon, I promise. Just, don't cry."

"It's not that." She was shaking her head, her eyes squeezed shut. "I did something. Or I nearly did something, I don't know. And I've got to tell you. Luke, I'm all mixed up."

"Slow down," he told her, stopping a few inches away from her. "Just slow down, and tell me what's happened."

Luke was strangely calm as he listened to Teresa speak. It was particularly noteworthy that he didn't shout or cry out, because with every word she uttered, she was cutting him further adrift. There had been a time in Burma, floating down the Irrawaddy River at dawn in a flat-bottomed boat, when all the other soldiers were asleep. He remembered the cold, and the way the mist had looked, pouring down from the hills. He remembered thinking that it might swallow him up forever, and no one would ever know. He supposed that he was floating down that river still, but for a short while there had been someone else with him in the boat, and because she had been by his side the whole thing hadn't seemed so frightening.

She was gone now. Luke pushed away Teresa's gentle hands and turned away from her pleading. He lay on his bed, and turned over on his side, staring straight ahead until she had left him. He wanted to get lost in that mist, and never have thoughts again.

AN ACT OF GRACE

It was, in all probability, not going to be a white Christmas. Rain and sleet had been battering the Midlands for the past week. In Coventry, some of the streets had been partially flooded. Mrs. Henshall felt very sorry for young Mrs. Parrish when she came into the church soaked to the skin, her mackintosh dripping.

"Didn't you have someone to drive you, dear?" she called as the girl walked up the aisle towards her looking like a drowned rat.

"My mother-in-law has the car today," said Teresa. "She's with Luke at the station. The police called him in for questioning again."

Mrs. Henshall tutted. She was standing at the front pew, flicking through a missal. The church was empty, but at the foot of the altar, the flowers had been arranged for the funeral tomorrow. "Well, hopefully now that that man Farley has been caught, that detective will leave all of you alone." Pausing in her search, she looked up at Teresa. "I can't say it enough, dear. I *am* sorry I ever told the police I saw your husband that day. If I'd known they'd plague him like this –"

"You had to tell the truth." The girl looked very tired as she said this. "Luke was just in the wrong place at the wrong time."

"How is he bearing up, your husband?" It seemed an innocent enough question, but the silence that greeted it was so long that Mrs. Henshall eventually looked up again. Teresa had averted her gaze, and was biting her lip as though trying to think of what to say.

"Had a row, did you?" said Mrs. Henshall, kindly. "Well, never mind, dear, these things will happen. He'll get over it soon enough and come back to you. My own Bert always did, no matter how badly we rowed."

Teresa was looking at her strangely. Mrs. Henshall supposed she must have said the wrong thing without realising, and quickly moved on. "Anyway, my dear, here's the psalm I'd like you to read tomorrow." She took a sheet of paper out of the missal and handed it to Teresa. "'By the rivers of Babylon, there we sat down and there we wept, when we remembered Zion.' Beautiful, I always thought. And it was one of Mr. Albright's favourites."

"Are you sure," said Teresa in a low voice, staring at the paper, "that you want *me* to read it?"

Mrs. Henshall blinked. "Well, of course, my dear. You were a good friend to him. And I know for a fact that he was very fond of you."

"Thank you." Teresa looked as if she didn't quite believe her, but she folded up the sheet and put it in her bag, away from her wet coat. "I'll practice it a bit tonight and do my best."

"I'm sure you will, my dear." Mrs. Henshall turned back towards the altar and went up the steps. She halted at the top and turned back to look at Teresa, who was still standing by the front pew. "What is it, Mrs. Parrish? Was there something else?"

"There was something, yes," the girl said hesitantly, looking unsure. When she spoke next, her words came all in a rush. "Mrs. Henshall, I was wondering if you could lend me the key to Mr. Albright's house? You see, I promised to help him with his book and there was just the indexing left to do. I was thinking, maybe if I can finish that then we could still get it published."

Mrs. Henshall was silent for a long moment as she considered. "I hadn't even thought about his book." She suddenly felt close to tears as she looked back at Teresa. "Do you think we might really get it published?"

"I think it's worth a try," said Mrs. Parrish.

Grey flakes of snow were drifting down from the sky now, but they did not stick to the dirty ground. Teresa unlocked the door of Mr. Albright's house and stepped inside. She had thought for sure that there was no way Mrs. Henshall would agree to her request, knowing what she knew. But it seemed now that Mrs. Henshall *mightn't* know anything to begin with. Why, after all, would she want Teresa to read at Mr. Albright's funeral if she thought there had been something sordid between the two of them? Which left the question of why Mrs. Parrish had told Teresa that Mrs. Henshall knew more than she did. Maybe she had made it all up just to get Teresa to be honest with Luke about what had happened.

As these thoughts began to circle her mind with increasing speed, Teresa advanced forward, making her way to the study. She was very aware of every sound that she made, the drip of her mac onto the carpet, the squeak of her shoes. Then there were the sounds of the house, the ticking of the clock on the mantlepiece as Teresa stepped into the study, and the occasional groan of the pipes in the walls.

Mr. Albright's desk was neater than it had been the last time she had seen it. He had been reading through documents then, she remembered, and had said that he had something to tell her, but there was no sign of those documents now. The police must have taken them as evidence. She stepped around the patch on the carpet where Mr. Albright's body had been found and did not look at the stains that she knew were there. She came closer and closer to the desk until she was standing behind it. Without touching the surface of it, she reached her right hand down and opened the top drawer. She carried on like that with each drawer, slow and careful, until she had finally laid her hand on the manila folder that she knew to contain the manuscript. She took that out, and then took out the black, leather-bound book that contained his notes.

Mr. Albright's neat, curly handwriting was by now familiar to her, but there was something strange about seeing it when she opened up his notes, and knowing that the warm hand that had moved across the page, quite recently, was now cold. On one page he had written something about the formatting of footnotes. On another he had written something about the epigraph of the book. He wanted it to be an extract from Psalm 137. Teresa's heart began to beat faster, and she put down the book and rushed to the bookcase. She took out Mr. Albright's Bible and thumbed through the thin pages, careful not to rip them, until she had found the psalm. She read:

By the rivers of Babylon –

there we sat down and there we wept

when we remembered Zion.

On the willows there

We hung up our harps.

For there our captors asked us for songs

and our tormentors asked for mirth,

saying, 'Sing us one of the songs of Zion!'

How could we sing the Lord's song in a foreign land?

If I forget you, O Jerusalem –

Teresa shut the Bible, because it was becoming impossible to read when her eyes were blurry with tears. She had not cried yet for Tim Albright over the last week. She cried now, for the man imprisoned, freed, and then killed, for the man who had had so much more to give to the world, and who would now never get that chance.

In the end, it was the rain that had driven Bill Farley to give himself up to the police. He had given himself up rather than being caught. He thought that distinction was quite important. After Lizzy had told him about Mr. Albright's death, he had tried to protest his innocence, but it was no use. Figuring that if his own wife didn't believe him, he didn't have much chance of convincing the police, and so he went on the run, which, since he didn't have much money, meant, effectively, staying in a number of different hostels in Birmingham over the course of a few nights. On the fourth day, when the rains came and didn't cease, Bill listened to the *drip-drip* from a hole in the ceiling and, after a night of tossing and turning on a sodden mattress, finally made his decision.

The Birmingham police, after holding him for a time, handed him over to some constables in the Coventry police department, who bundled him into a warm car and drove him back to the town that he had just left days before. They stopped on the way for something to eat and uncuffed Bill's hands so that he could eat a sandwich. All in all, it could have been much worse.

He told all of this to D.S. Gamble and D.I. Fleming when he was in front of them in the interrogation room. They had wanted to know why he hadn't given himself up right away and so he answered to the best of his ability.

"And I'll answer any more questions you have, gentlemen," he said, spreading his hands, which was a bit difficult with the cuffs on, but he managed all the same. "I've got nothing to hide."

The detectives exchanged glances. One of them, the sergeant, was sweating profusely, and the other, the inspector, looked rather too young to be a detective. He must have been in his early thirties. According to Gamble, he had been called in from Scotland Yard to help with the investigation.

"The medals we found on your person, Mr. Farley," said D.S. Gamble at last. "Did you steal them from Mr. Albright?"

Bill shook his head. He had been expecting that question. "No, I didn't steal them. He gave them to me."

Gamble looked pained, and the detective inspector actually smiled for a split second. Bill turned his gaze on him, raising his eyebrows. "You don't believe me?"

"It does seem unlikely, Mr. Farley," said Gamble. "Why would Mr. Albright give you his medals?"

"He didn't give me *all* of them. Just the ones he said he didn't think he deserved. The Burma Star and the DCM. The Distinguished Conduct Medal, that is."

"And why didn't he think he deserved those medals?" Gamble asked.

Bill was silent for a long time as he tried to find the right words. He wound his fingers together and then said, "Because he was a good man, but he failed. He fell short. Those were the words he used, anyway. He 'fell short'. I would have put it a bit less politely." He looked up at the detectives again. "I thought he didn't deserve them, either. But when he offered those medals to me, I didn't want to accept, either. I didn't want to take what belonged to another man."

"So why did you accept them, then?" asked the Scotland Yard detective.

"Because he made me. He wouldn't take no for an answer."

"I see," pursued Fleming. "So you expect us to believe that, after you had been intimidating this man with visits to his house for several days up to his attack, he not only let you inside but actually gave you his medals."

"I barely believe it myself," said Bill, quietly. "When I think about it hard enough. I went in that house wanting one thing and left with my head all mixed up." Pointing at the wall as though Mr. Albright was standing just on the other side, "*He* mixed up my head, with all his talk of forgiveness and…" He trailed off.

There was a silence. "When you visited the Reverend Albright were you seeking his forgiveness?" D.S. Gamble asked, quietly.

"No! I wanted to tell him that *I'd* never forgive *him*. I wanted him to know just what I went through, because of what *he* did." Bill, in his vehemence, had started spitting, and he wiped his mouth, the movement awkward because of the handcuffs.

"We can take those off if you want," said Gamble, indicating the cuffs. "Just while we're here." His colleague turned to stare at him, but he just shrugged. Then, calling in a constable, he got Bill's cuffs unlocked and offered him a cigarette.

"We found some documents on Mr. Albright's desk, which he must have been looking over shortly before he was attacked," said D.I. Fleming, while Gamble was lighting his and Bill's cigarettes. "There was a report on the living conditions at a prisoner-of-war camp in Rangoon, Burma. There was also a firsthand account from the staff officer in the 28th Field Regiment of an incident that occurred around the time that you and the Reverend Albright would have been interned there, in 1943."

"Oh, good, you know it all already," said Bill, taking a puff of his cigarette. "Then I don't have to explain it to you."

"We're interested in hearing your version of events, Mr. Farley," said Gamble.

"It's a long story," said Bill.

"We have nothing but time, Mr. Farley."

Bill took one more puff of his cigarette and then put it out in the ashtray, feeling their eyes following the movement carefully. He sighed. "All right, then." Looking up at them, he began.

"I'd been in Rangoon close to a year when some men from our camp tried to escape. Three Australians and a Brit. They managed to get a boat, but they were caught again out at sea and brought back. The Japs tried to make us all sign a no-escape pledge after that, but we refused, every single man in that prison camp. There were thousands of us, and the Japs marched us to another barracks, built only for a few hundred men. We had barely any room to sleep, sit, breathe. We sat for hours under the sun and got no water. They executed the men who'd tried to escape,– made a bloody mess of it too, used so many bullets. We could hear the screaming all the way down on the beach. And the smell, you wouldn't believe the smell, with all us men packed into that one spot. You wouldn't have liked it at all." Bill glanced at Gamble, who was noticeably paler than he had been before. The Scotland Yard man looked impassive.

"Four days and four nights we sat in that barracks. We were starving, we got rained on, we roasted in the sun." A faint grin spread across Bill's face. "But we were winning. They knew they couldn't keep us there for ever. And then," His grin disappeared. "Albright went and signed the no-escape pledge. He couldn't stick it any longer. He said he had a duty to protect the lives of his men, but we all knew he only cared about saving his own skin. After that, it was all over. More and more men went to sign, and the ones who stayed, the troublemakers – me and some others, stubborn fools – we were shipped off, and if we'd thought Rangoon was bad, well, Singapore was ten times worse."

Bill was quivering now from head to toe, as he always did when he told this story. He wondered if he would be telling this story for the rest of his life. He wondered if he would ever have any other story to replace it, a cleaner story, a story that didn't reach into his chest and scoop out another piece of his soul with each telling.

"You hold Mr. Albright responsible for you and those other prisoners being sent away," said D.S. Gamble.

"I don't just hold him responsible. *he was* responsible. The men looked up to him, as their guide, and he knew it. The second he signed that pledge, it was all over, and everything we went through over those four days was for nothing."

"And did you tell Mr. Albright all of this? When you went to see him that day?" Gamble asked.

"I did. And he…" The breath caught in Bill's throat, and he shook his head. "He listened. He listened, that was the odd thing. When I was finished, he said, 'Bill, it's just like you said. I was trying to save my own skin.' He said that what happened was a 'failure of courage' and that he didn't expect me to forgive him, and then he offered me those medals."

"And then you picked up the poker and hit him over the head with it," said D.I. Fleming. Bill looked at him, and calmly shook his head.

"No, sir. I took the medals and walked out of that house, met Lucky, Luke Parrish, I mean, and went for a drink."

"And what was Mr. Parrish doing outside Mr. Albright's house at that time?" asked Gamble.

"He was waiting for me. I tried to get rid of him, but he wouldn't hear of it. He was worried about me, I think."

"Did Mr. Parrish know about the history between you and Mr. Albright?"

"No. I never told him." Bill saw the look exchanged between the detectives, and leaned forward, suddenly urgent. "Parrish isn't your man."

"Then who do you think our man is, Mr. Farley?"

"*I* don't know," Bill said, leaning back in his chair again, weary. "I haven't the faintest idea. I'm sure Tim Albright knew a lot of people in this town. And, you understand," Looking between them, " I can't say I'm altogether sorry he's dead, but I wouldn't have wished to do him harm."

There was a long silence. "Thank you for your honesty, Mr. Farley," said D.S. Gamble at last, with another glance at his colleague. "And thank you for your service."

Luke didn't know that it was nearly Christmas. He didn't even know what day it was, but then, that didn't matter much anymore. Mum knew all of those things; she had always been good at keeping track of them. She was sitting beside him now, in the waiting room at the police station. She was wearing that lavender perfume she liked so much. The smell was comforting and familiar. Every time it drifted into Luke's nostrils, he felt himself relax a bit more. He told himself that he would not be a bundle of nerves this time. He had taken his embutal last night and slipped into deep, dreamless sleep, a luxury he could not have imagined a year ago.

As they were waiting, Luke caught sight of Farley as the man was being escorted from the interrogation room to the holding cells. Hands cuffed in front of him, Farley slowed his pace a fraction as the P.C. led him past the open door to the waiting room. His pale eyes alighted on Luke and he called, "Chin up, Lucky."

"Don't you dare speak to him," said Mum, flaring up, but in another moment Farley had disappeared again. Not long after that, Luke was called.

"You'll be all right?" Mum clutched at him as he started to rise from his seat. "You're sure you don't want me to come in with you?"

"I'll be fine." He put her hands away from him, gently, and followed the policeman down the same corridor Farley had come up minutes before.

It was the same interrogation room as before, but instead of D.S. Gamble at the other end of the table, there was an unfamiliar detective, who looked not much older than Luke. He introduced himself as D.I. Fleming, and spoke with a London accent. His eyes rested on Luke as he embarked on some preliminary questions, and there was a querulous tone to his interrogatives, so that Luke began to feel like he was back at school and being needled by one of the other boys.

"Are you aware of the fact that the Reverend Albright and Mr. Farley were interned in the same prison camp from 1942 to 1943, before the latter man was transferred to a camp in Singapore?" the detective inspector asked at last, and Luke nodded. "Do you know anything about an incident that occurred during that time?"

It struck Luke that he would have felt burning curiosity on that very point a week before. Now, however, he shook his head and listened dully to the detective's explanation. When the other man had finally finished speaking, he said, "You don't look very surprised, Mr. Parrish. Is it possible that you *did* know about this before?"

"I didn't know," said Luke in a low voice. "Farley didn't tell me anything."

"But you already had your suspicions about Mr. Albright? About his not being all that he seemed, I mean?"

Caught off guard by the accuracy of this perception, Luke could only blink at him, and the other man pressed on, "Was Mr. Albright close to your wife Teresa?"

There was an expectant look on the detective's face. He almost looked like he was smiling as he waited for Luke's answer. The urge to reach across the table and grab him by the collar was almost overpowering. "They were friendly," said Luke. "I don't know what else you're suggesting."

"Oh, I didn't mean to suggest anything, Mr. Parrish. I'm just trying to get a picture of your family's relationship with Mr. Albright. We interviewed your mother yesterday and she seemed to think very highly of him." Fleming paused for the barest of seconds and then added, "I apologise if I've offended you."

"You haven't offended me," Luke said, stiffly, and the rest of the interview proceeded in a similar fashion. The detective inspector would ask some needling question, then Luke would struggle to overcome his initial reaction and give some non-committal answer. By the time it seemed to be winding down, Luke wasn't thinking anymore about the impression he must be giving. Curbing his temper in the face of the other man's insolence was taking all of his concentration.

"Just one final thing to ask you about, Mr. Parrish, before you go," said Fleming, at last, his voice casual. "You and your wife spent your honeymoon in Blackpool. We've been in touch with the police department there, who informed us of an incident during your stay in which you broke another man's nose. Can you tell me a bit more about that?"

Luke was frozen. Words would not come. The detective, watching him, continued,

"According to a statement your wife gave one of the officers on the scene, you were in, I quote, 'a kind of a fog' at the time. The fire alarm had gone off in the hotel where you were staying and this apparently caused some confusion. Would I be right in thinking that you mistook Mr. Fletcher for someone else?"

"I thought he was the enemy," said Luke, his tongue loosened at last.

"The enemy?"

"Yes, like you said, I was confused."

"We spoke to Mr. Fletcher on the telephone and he told us that he never received any apology or acknowledgement from you after the incident, only from your wife. He said that he decided not to press charges out of sympathy for her situation."

"I should have apologised," Luke murmured.

"Can you speak up, please, Mr. Parrish?"

"I should have apologised," Luke said, much more loudly. He made himself look the detective in the eye. "I just didn't think of it at the time. Teresa handled everything."

"Do you think she was alarmed? At your behaviour?"

"Alarmed? No, I don't think she was."

"And have any other incidents like this taken place?"

"No," said Luke. "No, I'm not – I'm not like that."

"Very well." Fleming stood up from his chair and picked up his notebook without looking at it. "You're free to go, Mr. Parrish."

Teresa had put away Mr. Albright's notes in her room as soon as she had gotten home, being unable to face reading them yet. She went downstairs to the kitchen, where it was warm, and looked again at the psalm on the page Mrs. Henshall had given her. She had just put her stockinged feet up to the stove to warm them when she heard a surprising sound, a knock at the back door.

Straightening her skirt and drawing down her feet again, Teresa hurried to the door and opened it. More surprising still was the sight of their elderly neighbour on the doorstep. "Mrs. Lyndon! Is something wrong?"

"Nothing, nothing, my dear. I just made too many scones and thought you might like some." Mrs. Lyndon held up a plate, covered with a tea towel.

"That's very kind, Mrs. Lyndon. Here." Teresa took the plate from her and glanced at the grey sky. It had stopped raining, except for the occasional solitary drop. "Won't you come in for some tea? Mrs. Parrish and Luke are still at the police station, and I wouldn't mind some company."

She expected her neighbour to refuse, since Mrs. Lyndon never spent time in other people's houses if she could help it, but to her surprise, the old lady accepted and stepped into the warmth of the kitchen. Teresa bustled about, fetching the tea things, and didn't notice that she had put down the psalm until Mrs. Lyndon had picked it up.

"What's this, dear?"

Teresa explained about being asked to read the psalm, watching Mrs. Lyndon's face carefully, but the old lady's expression did not change, and she merely nodded solemnly and put it down again. "It's only right that you should be asked. Mr. Albright was very fond of you, I hear."

"Mrs. Henshall said that too," Teresa said, and then, as the kettle began to whistle, she went to attend to it. When the tea was drawing in the pot, she pulled her chair near Mrs. Lyndon's and resumed, "Can I ask, did she say anything to you?"

"Who, dear?" Mrs. Lyndon was staring contentedly at the flickering light of the stove.

"Mrs. Henshall. Did she say anything to you about..." Teresa's face had gone hot, but she made herself continue. She had to know. "About Mr. Albright and me?"

Mrs. Lyndon looked confused for a moment, and then her wrinkled face broke into a smile. "Oh, goodness, you don't mean that rumour? I'm sorry that ever got around to you, my dear. Mrs. Henshall was so embarrassed when the minister found out she had started all that nonsense about you and him."

"Then you do think it's all nonsense?" Teresa said carefully. "Because if people thought there was something between us, then it wouldn't be right for me to read tomorrow."

"Dear girl." Mrs. Lyndon put a hand on Teresa's. "Don't worry your head about it. It was only ever gossip. And if Mrs. Henshall thought there was anything to it, she wouldn't have asked you to read in the first place."

Teresa was never quite sure why she couldn't have just left things there, but ever since she had told Luke the truth, it was as though the floodgates had opened within her, and there was no way to stop it escaping. She took her time, though. She rose to pour the tea, and only when they were both sitting again with their full cups did she say, "There *was* something to it."

Mrs. Lyndon was stirring sugar into her tea, and the movement of her spoon gradually stilled as she looked up at Teresa.

"It was nothing so very bad," Teresa rushed on. "Though I know it was wrong. That day, the day he died, I'd gone to visit him in the morning. I was upset. I put my arms around him, and he held me, and Mrs. Parrish told me Mrs. Henshall had seen us."

Mrs. Lyndon's eyes were wide as she took in Teresa's words, and then slowly she shook her head. "She can't have done. Maggie, I mean. She would have said something to me."

"So then it must have been Mrs. Parrish who saw us," Teresa murmured. "But why would she pretend it was Mrs. Henshall? What difference does it make, who saw us?"

She had been talking more to herself than to Mrs. Lyndon, and was surprised, therefore, when the old woman made a noise as though she wanted to say something. Teresa looked up, eagerly. Mrs. Lyndon was avoiding her gaze, staring into her tea.

"My dear," the old woman said quietly. "There's something I think I ought to tell you."

She got no further. The sound of the front door slamming made them both start, and Teresa winced as she spilt a bit of tea on her skirt. She was still trying to dab it out when her mother-in-law and Luke came in, the former full of chatter as she threw down her wet things, the latter avoiding Teresa's gaze, just as he had been doing for the past week.

"You're very cosy here!" Mrs. Parrish declared. "Well, don't let me interrupt. Oh, Agnes, are you leaving already? I'll walk you to your door."

"How did it go?" Teresa asked Luke quietly, once the two women had departed. He looked down at her and shrugged, before heading out the kitchen door. She supposed she hadn't really expected anything else.

On the drive home from the police station, Luke had been quiet, which, of course, was not unusual for him. Naturally, Mrs. Parrish knew her own son's moods better than anyone. She was anxious, however, to get a picture of how the interview had gone, and finally broached the topic, with what she considered to be a pretty harmless question, when they were stuck in a line of traffic. "Did you have the younger detective or the older one? Or both together?"

"The younger one," said Luke, and he slid down his seat a bit, as though trying to get as low as humanly possible.

"Oh, I didn't like him at all. I had both men questioning me yesterday, and the D.S. was all right. Good manners, you know. But the younger one, the fellow from Scotland Yard? So rude! The way he looked at me, as if he expected everything I told him to be a lie! And the questions he asked me!... Some of them were, " Mrs. Parrish glanced at her son, who was staring straight ahead at the unmoving car in front of them, "well, they were not very nice. There was one about Teresa."

She waited. When Luke said nothing, she sighed. "Now, darling, don't pretend. Anyone can see that something's happened between you two. You've barely spoken to one another this last week."

The car in front of them began to move again. Mrs. Parrish put her foot to the accelerator, at the same moment that Luke burst out with, "Teresa's done nothing wrong."

Mrs. Parrish glanced at her son, who slumped back in his seat and resumed his former blank expression. Dully, he said, "She's just in love with someone else, that's all. Or she *was* in love. I don't know how to say it now that he's dead."

"Is it Mr. Albright you're talking of?" Mrs. Parrish asked, gently. When her son gave a small, almost imperceptible nod, she sighed again. "I did suspect something. I didn't want to say it to you, of course, until I was sure. But all that time they used to spend together…"

"Teresa's done nothing wrong," Luke said again, and, for the first time, he turned to fix his eyes on his mother. "And you're not to get after her about it."

"I wouldn't dream of doing that, darling," said Mrs. Parrish, keeping her eyes on the road.

"Because I never told her she wasn't allowed to love anyone else," Luke went on, as though his mother hadn't spoken. "I just thought, when we got married, I thought that was the one thing she wouldn't do. She mightn't understand, or know how to help, but she'd love me. Just me, no one else."

"So did I. We were all fooled by her." Sensing that her son was about to protest, Mrs. Parrish went on, quickly, "I know you don't want to hear anything against Teresa. That's because you have a loyal heart, my dear. but you can't expect me to look at things the same way you do. I have a mother's feelings, Luke, and all I see is that this girl came into our lives making promises that she couldn't keep, making herself so important to you that you'd have no choice but to marry her. Now she's let you down, just when you needed her the most."

"I shouldn't have married her," Luke said quietly, leaning against the headrest as though the conversation were making him tired. "That's true."

"Then why don't we do something about it?" said Mrs. Parrish, encouraged.

They had pulled up to the house on Wragby Row now, but neither of them made any move to get out of the car. "Do you mean," started Luke, looking at his mother again, "a divorce? Because I couldn't do that. It would look bad for her, for both of us."

"Not a divorce, dear. Not one of those horrible, messy things. I'm talking about an annulment."

Luke frowned, but said nothing, which showed that he was at least considering her words. Mrs. Parrish turned towards him more fully, propping one hand on the steering wheel. "You could qualify, you know. There are certain things about your marriage,– well, things I suspect rather than things I know for sure, so perhaps you can tell me..."

Luke's ears went red, and soon the rest of his face followed. "Mum," he said, in a pained voice, shaking his head. "Mum, please..."

"I know you're embarrassed, Luke, but this is important. *If* you wanted to get an annulment then it's possible you could qualify on grounds of non-consummation, but they *would* have to investigate whether you and Teresa ever..."

"Mum." Luke was covering his face with his hands now. Mrs. Parrish sighed and went on,

"Of course, in cases of non-consummation it's usually wilful refusal by the wife, and with you and Teresa it's obviously quite a different,– well, a different situation..."

"You know a lot about this." Luke had removed one of his hands and was looking at his mother out of the corner of his eye.

"Of course I do, Luke," she said calmly. "I've been looking into what we can do. And if you just forget about being embarrassed for a minute and think about it, an annulment might be the best thing for all of us." She leaned forward. "We could get out of this place, Luke." This drew his attention. His eyes flashed towards her, the hope in them unmistakable. "We could finally move somewhere else. I've been thinking about it for years, you know. We have only bad memories here. We could live in a nicer place, maybe by the sea. You always liked the sea, Luke, didn't you? We could live by the sea, you and I, and your sister could visit us there too, when she's back in England, and we could be all together, the three of us, just like before."

Luke was silent. Mrs. Parrish watched him, hungrily, waiting for his response. When it came, it was not in the form of words. He gave a slow nod. Mrs. Parrish let herself smile, then, just a little. Gladness was flooding through her, gladness such as she had not felt in a long time.

"Come on, my dear," she said finally. "We'd better go inside, or Teresa will start wondering what we're doing out here."

It was the second time she had cried that day. She had better get it together, Teresa chided herself, drying her eyes and putting away Luke's handkerchief. There was plenty to do, and she wouldn't be able for any of it if she fell apart now. She checked on the potatoes in the oven. Mrs. Parrish had allowed her to cook dinner, a rare concession which she had only made since she and Luke would be at the station most of the day. She judged that they still needed another half hour and went upstairs to her room.

There was no desk in her room, so she put her back to the headboard of the bed and read Mr. Albright's notes where she sat, checking the manuscript every now and then. She tried not to do the latter too often, because every time she read his writing she would get sucked in and forget to be critical. His first chapter discussed his early ministry in Coventry, and Teresa was at the end of it before she realised that more than half an hour had passed. She sprang to her feet so quickly that she nearly upended the black leather-bound book, and in the process a piece of loose paper slipped out. Teresa snatched it up.

Dear Mrs. Parrish, the note began. Was it for her? Why did it look scrawled like that, as though he had been in a dreadful hurry? It and went on:

I am writing to apologise for my rudeness earlier. It was indiscreet and unworthy of me to dredge up things long past. Whatever happened back then, I'm sure it's none of my concern. Those were dark times for us all. I hope you will forgive me for mentioning the matter, and believe me when I say that I will never do so again –

The note ended there, and the pen had made a long line down the rest of the page as though he had been interrupted while writing.

Suddenly it was very clear to Teresa what she had to do. She folded up the note and kept it in her hand as she went downstairs. She passed the door of the parlour, which stood ajar. Luke and Mrs. Parrish were in there, talking. Their voices stopped when they heard her footsteps, and she heard them start up again as she went into the kitchen.

There was a tinge of smoke in the air, and Teresa held her nose as she opened the oven and took out the tray of potatoes with her other hand. They were a little burnt, but not unsalvageable. She left them on top of the oven, covered them with a tea towel, and then slipped out the back door.

Next door, Mrs. Lyndon was listening to *It's That Man Again* on the BBC, a faint smile on her lips as the comedians' voices bantered back and forth. She put down her knitting when Teresa came in. "Dear, I'm sorry, I didn't hear you knock."

"That's because I didn't knock," said Teresa, and going over to the wireless, she switched it off. Mrs. Lyndon's jaw dropped. "There's no time to lose. Here, read it." She thrust the note into the older woman's hands.

"Where did you get this?" said Mrs. Lyndon quietly, after she had finished reading. She looked up at Teresa.

"I found it in Mr. Albright's house. He was going to send it to Mrs. Parrish, before he died. He was apologising for something,– I don't know what, but it means that she must have visited his house that morning. *She* must have been the one who saw us together." Teresa stopped to catch her breath. Her heart was racing. Mrs. Lyndon was looking down. "Mrs. Lyndon, I think you know something. You were going to tell me earlier, weren't you?"

Her neighbour was silent. Teresa sighed. "You're frightened of her, aren't you? And she's worried you might say something. That's why she bundled you off as soon as they came back. Has she threatened you?"

"Joanna Parrish doesn't frighten me," said Mrs. Lyndon sharply, meeting Teresa's gaze. "You're the one who'd better be careful what you say."

"I'm not worried about being careful anymore," said Teresa. The words flooded out of her before she could even think them. "And I don't care if I've insulted you. None of that matters now. My husband is well on the way to being locked up for something he didn't do. Are you going to let that happen?"

"No," said Mrs. Lyndon, tightly, "And neither will Joanna. You'll see. She loves Luke more than anything in the world, and she loved her husband just as much, when he was alive. She loves him still." Her eyes were boring into Teresa's now. "What do you think you're doing, coming over here and bothering an old woman with your suspicions?"

"I never said anything about Mrs. Parrish's husband," Teresa said quietly. Mrs. Lyndon swallowed. "And the note said nothing about it either. You *know something*, Mrs. Lyndon. You were with her that day. She went to your house after we had an argument, or at least she said she was going to your house. You've got to tell me –"

"And then what?" Mrs. Lyndon crashed to her feet, the knitting falling to the floor and her joints clicking. "What would happen if I told you what I know, child? If I told the police?" Pointing at Teresa, she said "I'll tell you what. Your family would be destroyed, just the same. Your husband would be destroyed, just the same as if they locked him up. Only he'll never get over this. Do you want that for him, Teresa?"

"He loses either way," Teresa whispered. "*We* lose either way."

"You don't know that," said Mrs. Lyndon. "They're still looking at that other man, aren't they? Farley. Chances are he'll get the heavier sentence. Luke might just get a few years, and people know he's not a monster. He bled for our country." She hesitated for a moment before going on, her eyes still on Teresa, "His wife betrayed him."

"I didn't –"

"She's all he has left, Teresa," Mrs. Lyndon said. "His mother. You won't take that from him too, will you?"

Teresa had a bitter taste in her mouth. "There's nothing I can do if you won't tell the truth. That note, by itself, I don't think it will be enough."

"No," agreed Mrs. Lyndon. "But, just in case…" Under Teresa's horrified eyes, she tore up the note and let the pieces flutter to the floor.

"Go home to your husband, Teresa," she said, with a sad look in her eyes. "Go home to Luke. He needs you now more than ever. Go home and be with him."

Teresa had made the dinner that evening and seemed to be waiting for someone to praise the food, her eyes darting between her neighbours at the table as she lifted a fork to her mouth. Neither Luke nor Mrs. Parrish obliged. Luke wouldn't even look Teresa in the eye, but, Mrs. Parrish noted with some concern, when Teresa got up from the table and turned her back on them to get more potatoes, her son's eyes followed her all the way out of the room.

She knew it was not going to be the work of a few days, or weeks, or even months, to get Teresa out of Luke's head completely. The girl had gotten her hooks in him a long time ago, and would not be letting go any time soon, no matter how much distance might be put between them. Mrs. Parrish's vague hope was that perhaps, in a year's time, when they were settled down somewhere else, Luke would meet some other, much more suitable girl, and that, bit by bit, Teresa would fade away until she was just a distant memory. Mrs. Parrish could not really tell, of course, what this more suitable girl would look like or how she would act. She just knew that Teresa had never, and would never, fit the bill. That was about as deeply as she had thought on the matter.

She reached out and squeezed Luke's shoulder. He raised his head, startled, and for an instant she was reminded of how he had been as a little boy. His position slightly hunched, he looked up at her now just as he had looked up at her then, with eyes wide and trusting. The army had shorn off his lovely curls, of course, but those curls had grown back now. Missing, and probably gone forever, were the freckles that she used to love, and in their place were lines, lines along his forehead and cheeks, and two thin lines between his eyebrows. She wished she could iron them away just like she ironed the creases from his shirts.

"What are you thinking about, dear?" she asked, without really expecting a response.

Luke's frown deepened and he said, "They asked me about Blackpool today."

Something pierced the cloud of content that had been surrounding Mrs. Parrish for the past minute or so. "About Blackpool? What do you mean, darling?"

"Something happened there," Luke said, looking at her out of the corner of his eyes. "Teresa and I didn't tell you. But I hurt someone. I broke a man's nose. I wasn't thinking. I was still half-asleep, in a muddle, and I thought I was back in the war."

Mrs. Parrish tried to pretend that this was new information to her. "But darling, that's different. No one in their right mind would hear that and think that you'd be capable of killing someone. And how did the police here even know about it?" The first thing to do, she thought to herself, would be to ring up the landlady in Blackpool and tell her she would never be taking her business there again.

"They've been thorough, Mum. They looked into Mr. Albright and Farley's pasts too. There was something that happened in the prison camp in Burma…"

Mrs. Parrish wasn't interested in anything that had happened in a prison camp in Burma. This was the here and now. She focused her eyes on her son's face, and tried to keep the urgency from her voice as she said, "Why didn't you tell me this before? That they knew about Blackpool?" She didn't want to scare him.

Luke ignored the question and went on, "There was a no-escape pledge that the Japanese wanted the prisoners to sign. They refused to a man and went without food and water for days. They might have won better conditions if Mr. Albright hadn't signed…"

"Luke, this is important. What else did they ask you in the interview today? Do you think they actually, seriously suspect you? Because if they do, then we have to act fast. We have to decide –" Mrs. Parrish stopped as they heard Teresa's footsteps coming back from the kitchen, and she widened her eyes at her son as though to tell him that the conversation would be continued later.

Then the doorbell rang, and they heard Teresa's footsteps divert to the hall. They heard her pull the door open, and a man's voice greeting her. They heard her cry out, and Mrs. Parrish shot up from her chair.

"Luke, come on," she hissed, and her son stared up at her, uncomprehending. "Luke, they've come for you! You've got to run, come on! You can hop the wall and –" she gestured to the back garden visible through the window, " – I'll tell them something, I'll make something up. Come on, Luke." He was still staring at her, without moving. Leaning down, she tugged at his arms, tried to pull him up, but he was too heavy. Mrs. Parrish started crying at the futility of it all, short, bitter sobs that sounded as though they had been scraped from her throat. "Luke, *please. Please.*"

The door to the hall opened, and Teresa, treacherous little witch that she was, stood there, framed in the sunlight. It seemed unnaturally bright for the time of evening and for the weather that they had been having. Beyond Teresa, Detective Inspector Fleming stood in the front door, his long shadow slanted across the hall floor. Teresa was crying.

"Don't let them take him," Mrs. Parrish spat at Teresa, and then she began to howl as the detective stepped over the threshold and into their house. She sounded like a wounded animal. She could not recognise her own voice, or understand why her chest hurt so much, as though she was being torn up inside. Luke was on his feet now, and white as death as he stared at his mother. She cried, "Don't take my son! Don't take him!"

D.I. Fleming halted in the kitchen. "I'm very sorry for this," he said to Teresa and Luke, and then he looked at Mrs. Parrish. "Joanna Parrish, I'm arresting you on suspicion of the murder of the Reverend Timothy Albright."

Mrs. Parrish's sobs had stopped. Her mouth hanging slightly open, she put her hands behind her back and let Fleming put the handcuffs on her without so much as a struggle. She let herself be led out through the hall, and only when she was about to step into the sunlight did she look back. She did not see Teresa, or the detective inspector, or her own hallway. She only saw her son, with tears streaming down his face. She knew what to do. She gave him a small, brave smile.

"Don't cry, Luke," she said. "Don't cry. It's going to be all right."

THE TRUTH WILL SET YOU FREE

rs. Lyndon knew the difference between right and wrong, and she thought of herself as having lived a pretty good life, all things considered. It was downright unfair, though, how people seemed to expect her to be good and virtuous all the time. When you were older, you were supposed to be closer to God, and an older woman had even more of those expectations piled upon her. But Agnes Lyndon, at seventy, didn't feel any closer to God than she had done at twenty. She felt Him there, most of the time, but He always seemed to be busy with something else. On His watch, her Bert had been killed in the war that had been meant to end all wars. Twenty years later, her only son and her only grandchild had been lost to another war. All the family she had left in the world these days was her daughter-in-law Rosie, who, rather than staying in Coventry as Mrs. Lyndon had wanted her to, had chosen to move to a grotty flat in London and work in a homeless shelter.

Rosie was nearly forty and pretty plain-looking, so it wasn't as though Mrs. Lyndon suspected the girl of gadding about in London or of getting over the loss of her husband too quickly. No, Rosie's time was undoubtedly being well spent helping the poor, but Mrs. Lyndon resented, all the same, that it was being spent away from her. The poor in London's East End were needy, yes, but then wasn't she needy, too? She was all alone in this house. Family was supposed to stick together in times like these.

It was for this reason that Mrs. Lyndon had been happy to go along with things at first. She had not felt any guilt over indulging Joanna Parrish by telling a little white lie. The whole point of a white lie, after all, was that it did not harm anyone, and Mrs. Lyndon knew what it was to have a daughter-in-law who resisted your management at every turn.

And so, when Joanna Parrish had come next door to Mrs. Lyndon's one day, very distressed about her daughter-in-law and feeling that the girl had gotten herself into some kind of trouble, Mrs. Lyndon had offered her old friend tea and sympathy. She had agreed not to say anything when Mrs. Parrish told her that she was going to go over to Mr. Albright's house to "see what was going on." A bare hour afterwards, by which time Joanna had returned to Agnes defeated, reporting that she had seen nothing,

Maggie Henshall rang up in a panic, telling them that she and Teresa had found Mr. Albright's body. Joanna stayed very calm throughout it all, and Agnes did not need to be told that the promise of secrecy extracted from her was now sealed in cold fear. She did not want to touch it; she did not want to look at it.

Lying to the police was not such a frightening thing to do when it did not feel like lying at all. Mrs. Lyndon, like many other women of her generation who had seen the world come apart twice, and lived to tell the tale, was capable of holding two contradictory truths in her mind at once. She had hated God and loved Him, hated her country and loved it, and now she hated Joanna Parrish but also loved her, and lied for her, and told herself that it was not lying.

Someone else could easily have killed Mr. Albright, a shell-shocked soldier whose wife's infidelity had driven him over the brink, or a former prisoner-of-war who was now a drunk, or both men together. Mrs. Lyndon told herself these things over and over in the days that followed Mr. Albright's death, and at times really believed them.

When the girl, Teresa, not Rosie, who was still in London and remained unaware of the whole story's connection to her mother-in-law, began to figure things out, she also illuminated some new aspects of the business that Mrs. Lyndon had not known before. Mrs. Lyndon had not known that Joanna had in fact visited Mr. Albright's house that morning, too, meaning that she did not merely suspect Teresa and the minister but had actually seen them together. And this meant, in turn, that she had lied to Mrs. Lyndon while asking her to lie for *her*, and that she had gone over to Mr. Albright's house that afternoon with some intention other than catching him with Teresa.

The note Teresa brought Mrs. Lyndon made things clearer. It became clear that Mr. Albright had known about Joanna's little mistake years before, and that he had threatened her with his knowledge of it. Following on from this, it also became clear to Mrs. Lyndon that the lies were not over. The lie she had told would now have to be followed by more lies, lies upon lies, and, bitter in this conclusion and hating Joanna more than ever as she did so, Mrs. Lyndon tore up the all-important note and let the pieces of paper flutter to the floor.

What young Mrs. Parrish did next, however, surprised Mrs. Lyndon. Rather than going into hysterics or shouting at Mrs. Lyndon, Teresa got down on her hands and knees and gathered up the pieces of paper, one by one. When she had them all in her hands, Teresa looked up at Mrs. Lyndon and asked her, nonchalantly, where she kept her tape, as if she expected the old woman to tell her, as if she was unafraid of Mrs. Lyndon attempting to stop her.

So Mrs. Lyndon told her, numbly, and when Teresa went out to the kitchen, she followed her. She watched the girl spread out the pieces of paper on the chequered tablecloth and tape the note back together.

The whole thing took about twenty minutes. Mrs. Lyndon's legs had gotten tired by then, and she had collapsed into her rocking chair. Teresa flattened out the taped-up note. Then she looked up at Mrs. Lyndon.

"The potatoes are going cold," she said, indicating next door with a jerk of her head. "I need to go back." Holding up the note, "You can keep this. It's up to you what you want to do with it."

Teresa got to her feet.

"When you've lived in this world as long as I have, dear," Mrs. Lyndon said, wearily, "You'll understand that sometimes, it doesn't just come down to telling the truth or lying. Sometimes, you've got to think about what will hurt people the least. And then you've got to do your best to stick to that."

Teresa looked at Mrs. Lyndon. There was something about those steady blue eyes of hers; the memory of those eyes stayed with Mrs. Lyndon for a long time afterwards. They were not shocked or offended by her morality. They did not narrow in contempt or judgement. They took you in, took you at your word, and then seemed to say, "And?"

After Teresa had departed, Mrs. Lyndon went back to the wireless. *It's That Man Again* was still on; she was glad she could catch the end of it. She took up her knitting and tried to laugh along with each punchline, tried to smile indulgently at the silly voices of the comedians, but she found that she could not do any of those things. At last, as the strains of the programme's ending music began to play, Mrs. Lyndon rose to her feet with a painful creak. She made her way to the telephone in the hall, and dialled for the police station. She waited as the operator put her through, her hand trembling on the receiver, and then finally, the London-accented voice of D.I. Fleming greeted her politely.

She told him everything.

When Teresa later learned how close the police had come to arresting Luke that night instead of Mrs. Parrish, she felt sick with relief.

"When the call from Mrs. Lyndon came in, we were almost out the door," D.I. Fleming told Teresa on the day of Mr. Albright's funeral. The detectives had come to the service, sitting quietly in the back of the church, and in the cemetery after the burial, the Scotland Yard detective had sought Teresa out. She was puffy-eyed and exhausted and not in the mood to talk to anyone. Even as Fleming spoke to her, her eyes kept straying over to Luke, who was standing some distance away with the Carmichaels and Mrs. Lyndon. His shoulders were hunched, his hair dishevelled. He had probably not slept a wink last night.

"D.I. Gamble was the one who suspected your husband," Fleming told Teresa, following her gaze. "Of course, we thought Farley was our man at first. He seemed the most straightforward suspect, and as you find in this line of work, Mrs. Parrish, the most straightforward answer to a question tends to be the right one. But Farley was honest with us about his past with Mr. Albright. Everything he told us matched up with the accounts we had of conditions at the camp in Rangoon. Once we'd talked to him a while, it just seemed there must be more to it. We started to think, then, that Farley might have been a reluctant accomplice, or that, perhaps, after he'd left Mr. Albright's house, your husband might have come back and confronted Albright himself, alone."

The crowd of mourners was now moving towards the gates of the cemetery, towards the waiting cars. Luke's auburn head soon disappeared among a sea of hats. Teresa and D.I. Fleming followed at a slower pace.

"It was D.S. Gamble who advanced the theory about your husband being the sole culprit. He was under the impression that your husband's nervousness, particularly in his first interview, which Gamble conducted alone, marked him as the more probable suspect, while Farley's confidence showed that he had nothing to hide."

Teresa had drawn breath, as if about to protest, and Fleming glanced at her in acknowledgement.

"*I* thought, on the other hand, that your husband's nervousness might have had another, simpler explanation. When I interviewed Mr. Parrish myself, I found him to be quite different to how D.S. Gamble had described him. He was evidently angry at me for the suspicions I was casting upon him, which I found to be a good sign. It showed he hadn't accepted those suspicions as a given, as a guilty man might do. A guilty *individual*, I should say. I also spoke..." Fleming hesitated before going on, as though embarrassed, and Teresa glanced at him in confusion. "I also spoke to your husband's doctor, and he informed me that the sleeping medication Mr. Parrish is taking can have a side-effect of anxiety, particularly when the patient is under acute stress, as I imagine Mr. Parrish must have been in his first interview. Unfortunately..." The detective coughed. "Unfortunately, Dr. Jackson's reputation has been somewhat compromised by what has recently come to light regarding his relationship with Mrs. Parrish, so I don't think he can now be called on as a witness."

"No," said Teresa quietly. "I suppose not." She said nothing more, because, detective or no detective, Fleming was effectively a stranger, and she did not want to be drawn into a conversation with any stranger about her mother-in-law's apparent infidelities.

They were nearly at the gates of the cemetery now. Teresa could see Mrs. Lyndon hesitating by Mrs. Carmichael's car, the two women looking back at her while Luke, standing beside them, averted his gaze.

"I've been telling you all this, Mrs. Parrish," said D.I. Fleming, with an air of finality to his tone, "because there is a long road ahead of us. Joanna Parrish has hired a solicitor, and they are bound to fight us every step of the way. We need to have a solid case in order to convince a jury of Mrs. Parrish's guilt, and as a witness, Mrs. Parrish, you're invaluable to us."

"Call me Teresa," Teresa said, with a half-smile. "It's less confusing."

"Together with your account and Mrs. Lyndon's, we can get a picture of Mrs. Parrish's movements that day. The coroner's report put Mr. Albright's time of death at early afternoon. Your husband and Mr. Farley left the vicinity of Mr. Albright's house no later than 12 p.m., according to eyewitnesses who noticed Mr. Farley's distressed state after his visit to Mr. Albright. Then there's your argument with Mrs. Parrish, around 2 p.m., as you told us, Mrs. Parrish telling Mrs. Lyndon that she would be paying a covert visit to Mr. Albright's house, around half past 2, and your telephone call to Mr. Albright's house, which went unanswered, made at approximately 3:15 p.m."

D.I. Fleming had his notebook out now, and appeared to be absorbed in the details.

"I'm not the only witness you have," Teresa pointed out. "You said so yourself, detective. There are eyewitnesses and Mr. Farley, too, and Mrs. Henshall and Mrs. Lyndon. Surely I'm too close to it all?" A note of desperation had come into her voice. "Surely, when it comes time to give evidence, the jury will be more convinced by someone who's more –"

"Impartial?" Fleming suggested, with a humourless smile. "In a case like this, Mrs. Parrish, there's no such thing. The Reverend Albright was a public figure, well-loved, widely known through his military service. Emotions will be running high throughout this whole case. And I might as well warn you now that as soon as the details of this get into the papers, you and your family will have to think about how best to secure your privacy. You'll have to stay put until the inquest, of course. That will probably be in March, – but after that, I would advise you and your husband to get away for a time."

Teresa stared at Luke's back. Mrs. Carmichael and Mrs. Lyndon were getting into the car now and beckoning to her. *If I condemn his mother, he's not going to want anything to do with me, much less get away with me*, she thought. Aloud, she said, weakly, "Isn't there any way I can get out of this? Giving evidence?"

D.I. Fleming was silent for a minute or two. "No one's going to force you," he said at last. "Least of all myself. I'll be going back to London soon, in any case, and leaving this in the hands of Detective Sergeant Gamble." He sighed. "I know this is a difficult case, and I do have sympathy for your predicament, Teresa. But this is the best, and perhaps the *only*, way of proving your husband's innocence."

Teresa lowered her head and nodded. Out of the corner of her eye, she saw D.I. Fleming tip his hat. "Merry Christmas, Mrs. Parrish."

"Merry Christmas," she said, a little incredulously. How could it be Christmas with all this going on?

They parted ways, and Teresa went to join the others, But as she was coming up to the car, Luke glanced over his shoulder at her, and then told Mrs. Carmichael, who was leaning out of the car window, "I'll get a lift with Bill." Without another glance at Teresa, he walked across the gravel to where Farley was standing with his wife. Farley met Teresa's eyes briefly and gave a grimace which could have been read as either sympathetic or condemnatory.

As she sat into the backseat of the car with the two Carmichael children, Teresa began to think about her own capacity for pain. These last few days, these last few *years,* she kept thinking that she had hit the bottom of it. And then she would end up plumbing new depths within herself, as she was doing now, reaching further down into that dark well.

It wasn't much of a Christmas. No sane person could have expected it to be, under the circumstances. Of course, Luke wasn't entirely sure that he counted as a sane person.

But still, he was prepared for Christmas to be the miserable affair that it was and didn't even mind too much. Most of his Christmases from 1939 on had been spent at the front. He didn't remember much about the Christmas of '43, the year he had been shipped home with a hollow head, except that his sister Lily had been just about the only thing to make it bearable, and last Christmas was more distant still.

Teresa packed up her things in a small bag on Christmas Eve night and told Luke that she would be going to her sister's early the next morning, and that, of course, he would be welcome there too. He said nothing, only reflected to himself that after all these years, Teresa Evans finally seemed to have learned how to tell when she wasn't wanted.

Farley's wife Lizzy, who had apparently forgiven him, had come to Coventry for Mr. Albright's funeral and, upon learning that Luke would be spending the day alone, invited him to Christmas dinner at their house instead. Finding it suited him, Luke agreed, and he drove to Birmingham with her and Farley the next morning. They had to pick up the children from Lizzy's mother's house first, as well as Lizzy's mother herself, and soon there was quite a squash in the backseat.

Luke didn't mind the bright chatter so much, finding that it distracted him. He did mind the curious gazes, though, and those continued all through dinner. There was tinned chicken, water cress and apple jelly, followed by tinned jelly for dessert, And then there were Christmas crackers. Thinking that his friend would have been disconcerted by the loud noises, Luke saw with surprise (and a little envy) that Bill was entering enthusiastically into the festivities. His face, alive with laughter, even looked younger. Luke absented himself not long after that.

Winson Green Prison was not very far from Bill's house, and Luke was able to walk the distance. His mother had been remanded to the women's holding unit there, and when the guards brought her out to the visiting room, she had no makeup on and her hair, uncurled, looked limp and stringy.

Apart from the initial alarm of her appearance, though, Mum seemed to be her old self, and settled down to complaining about rationing for a while. Everything they had been served for Christmas dinner had been tinned, apparently. When Luke told her he'd enjoyed the same fare at the Farleys', she smiled with grim satisfaction and said it was a shame how some women couldn't make do. She, for her part, had never used rationing as an excuse to deprive *her* children of the nutrients they needed, and on she talked, while Luke listened with growing relief, realising that some things didn't change.

When their time was up, Mum put a hand to Luke's cheek and said, "Don't look like that, dear."

"Like what?"

"So worried." Mum dropped her hand again at a warning glance from one of the guards, but kept her eyes fixed on Luke, smiling. "You don't need to worry about anything, dear. I've got a very good solicitor, Mr. Harvey. You'll see him when you come to visit again next week. Merry Christmas, dear."

She was being brave, Luke thought, just as she had been the night they arrested her. In reality she must have been terrified then. She must be terrified now, but she was hiding it for his sake.

There was a photograph that had been taken outside Coventry General Hospital in 1939. It had hung on the wall in the parlour for a while, displayed in prominence equalling that of the portrait of the king. Luke remembered noticing it when he was home on leave. To find it again, now, required some digging, but since he had nothing but time these days, and since there was no chance of Mum coming back and disturbing him, he set to it one morning. Rifling through the chest of drawers in the master bedroom, he found plenty of other things that he had not been looking for: railway ticket stubs, old lipsticks and bottles of clumpy rouge, food coupons that had gone out of date, and even a few of the letters he had sent Mum during his first year overseas. He did not look at those letters. A stranger had written them, after all, and he continued with his search. He finally found the photograph buried under one of Dad's old winter coats.

In the photograph was his father, looking just how Luke would always remember him, not thin and sad as he would become a little over a year later, but hale and hearty; Dad the businessman, shaking the hand of the hospital director as he presented him with a cheque for donation. Behind Luke's father and the director, among the hospital staff, stood Dr. Jackson, his hair untouched by grey. He was grinning, and slightly angled towards Luke's mother, as though he had been saying something to her when the bulb went off. Mum looked pretty. Her face was fuller, her nose and chin less sharp and pronounced. She was not looking at Dr. Jackson, but there were the beginnings of a smile on her face.

The harsh cry of the telephone bell sent Luke shooting to his feet, and his heart had not slowed its pounding by the time he got downstairs to answer.

"H-hello?"

There was some background noise on the other end, the click of a typewriter and the sound of voices conversing, and then a third voice said, "Mr. Parrish?"

"Yes?"

"It's Theobald Harvey." When Luke said nothing, the man continued, "Your mother's solicitor? I thought we might travel to Birmingham together today. You're getting the eleven o'clock train, I take it?"

"I..." Luke shook his head as though to clear it. He had been trying to get better at remembering appointments, since lately there was no one around to help him keep them. But the only thing that stood out for today was that Mrs. Henshall had invited him and Mrs. Lyndon to her house to see out the Old Year, as she'd put it. "I thought the visit was supposed to be tomorrow."

"I changed it to today. I thought you would have been informed. Some things have come up, you see, which I thought better to discuss sooner rather than later." Mr. Harvey spoke so rapidly that Luke felt like anyone trying to listen to him must necessarily be left far behind, in the clouds of dust thrown up by the speeding wheels of his thoughts. "So I'll meet you at the station at eleven o'clock, Mr. Parrish?"

"Yes," Luke managed to get out, and then there was a burst of noise on the other end. Somewhere in the midst of that noise, Mr. Harvey must have officially closed the conversation, but Luke didn't hear any farewell.

In person, Mr. Harvey was even more overwhelming. He was a small man. Luke towered over him as they walked down the platform together. He was probably around as old as Luke's father would have been if he were still alive, but rather than having that quiet, authoritative air that Luke was used to seeing in older men, Mr. Harvey was brimming with eager energy. He talked rings around Luke, complaining about the quality of the coffee served in the station tearoom before proceeding to order more of it, progressing, in the blink of an eye, from poor coffee to rationing to the incompetence of the new Labour government. Then he turned his attention to Luke, and by the time they'd found a carriage, they'd covered school, university, the army, Luke's father's death, Burma, and his marriage to Teresa.

"We'd better get on to matters of business, Mr. Parrish," said Mr. Harvey at last, signalling an end to the small talk, though, in Luke's view, there had been nothing particularly small about it. "Now, as I told you, I've worked with other murder suspects in the past, and up until yesterday, I would have said that your mother had a better chance than any of them of gaining a jury's sympathy." The carriage door opened, and a man with a suitcase made as if to come in. Mr. Harvey said sharply, "Excuse me," and the man backed out again. The solicitor continued, as the train began to move, "That's all we need, as you know, Mr. Parrish. We don't need to prove your mother's innocence; we just need the jury to be in reasonable doubt as to her guilt. And as to proving that anyone else is guilty, again, that is beyond our purview. Of course, it might happen as a result of our winning the case, but that is not our aim."

"I don't care what happens," Luke felt the need to interject at this point. "I mean, to me or anyone else, as long as they find her not guilty. I just can't see her locked up."

"And I'm sure any son would feel the same way." Mr. Harvey waved this off and glanced at his watch. "We'll cross that bridge when we come to it, Mr. Parrish. For the moment, let's focus on winning this case. Now, as I said, up until yesterday, I was quite optimistic about your mother's chances."

"What happened yesterday?"

"Two things. Firstly, Dr. Raymond Jackson left his post in the hospital without notifying anyone. Packed up his things and left Coventry, along with his wife and children. I'm attempting to have him tracked down, and when I succeed I shall try to persuade him to return. It would be inadvisable to call on him as a witness, of course. That would only serve to remind the jury of the affair, which, of course, would make them less inclined to be sympathetic to your mother."

Luke, thinking of the photograph, did not contradict the man. Perhaps he should have. But Mr. Harvey had said "affair" so matter-of-factly, as though it brooked no argument.

"The only person who might have knowledge of said affair, apart from Dr. Jackson and your mother, of course, is dead," said Mr. Harvey, "and the note written by Mr. Albright to Mrs. Parrish, in which he apologises for an apparent threat, is so vague that it might refer to anything. There isn't even a date on it; it might have been written weeks, months ago."

"What's the other thing?" said Luke, warily. While his head was beginning to hurt, he was, at least, able to grasp most of what the other man was saying now.

For the first time, Mr. Harvey hesitated. It was just for a second, but it was enough to make Luke dread what was coming next.

"The coroner's report was made available to the defence for the first time yesterday. It outlines that Mr. Albright was struck in the head with the poker several times before he died, as evidenced by the amount of blood at the scene, indicating that his attacker did not have sufficient strength to land a single killing blow."

Luke rose from his seat and moved to crank open the window. His need for fresh air was so sudden and overwhelming that he might have stuck his whole head out if another train hadn't come blaring by, shooting off in the direction of Coventry.

"This piece of evidence is quite troublesome for us, Mr. Parrish," Mr. Harvey went on, unperturbed by Luke's sudden movement. "The prosecution will likely use it to rule you out as a suspect, since they're bound to bring up the episode in Blackpool. And, considering that you were able to break a man's nose with one blow, as they will no doubt point out, why should you have had trouble dispatching Mr. Albright? Why should you have needed to hit him so many times, or, indeed, to use any implement besides your own bare hands?"

Luke grimaced as he sat back down.

"Anyone can see that you're a strong man, Mr. Parrish. Now, Mr. Farley, on the other hand, one might be able to believe that *he* would have needed to strike Mr. Albright multiple times before killing him. His period as a prisoner-of-war appears to have diminished his strength. He –"

"Farley didn't do it," Luke broke in.

Mr. Harvey looked more confused than annoyed by the interruption. "I thought it was clear enough already, Mr. Parrish, that I'm not interested in who 'did it' or 'didn't do it'. What I'm interested in is how the evidence put forward by the prosecution relates to your mother. And unfortunately, at present, a portion of it seems to point to her. So what *we* need to do is develop a strategy that deals with this evidence, piece by piece, and shows up its flaws so that the barrister arguing Mrs. Parrish's case in court will be able to induce reasonable doubt in the jury's minds as to whether or not she, as you would say, 'did it'."

"And how do we do that?" asked Luke.

"Well, fortunately, I have some ideas, Mr. Parrish. I'll outline them later when your mother is present." With that, Mr. Harvey lapsed into silence, turning towards the window as though he was actually interested in the passing scenery. Luke, watching him, couldn't help wondering why this entire conversation couldn't have waited until later, and after a few minutes of silence had passed, he voiced the question.

Mr. Harvey looked at him, surprised. "Why did I just tell you what I told you, Mr. Parrish? To prepare you, of course. I'm told you don't react well to surprises. And, while of course there's no easy way of broaching bad news, your mother will probably take it better if you and I both remain calm."

Luke took this in, frowning. As Mr. Harvey looked out the window again, Luke said, "Why am I here at all, then?"

"Because your mother wanted you to be present, I presume."

"No, but I mean, why didn't you arrange to visit her by yourself? If you were worried about my reaction?"

"I'm not worried, Mr. Parrish." Mr. Harvey gave a short, sharp laugh. "When I'm worried, I can promise you it will be difficult to ignore."

"But why –"

"I have already spoken to your mother on the telephone a number of times," said Mr. Harvey, with a relenting air. "We thought it would be best to have you present today when we are going through our strategy. And that is all I will say for the moment, Mr. Parrish."

Luke had been longing for silence for the past hour, but now that he had it, he felt itchy and restless. They couldn't get to Birmingham fast enough; they couldn't get off the train fast enough. Even when they had passed through the prison security and reached the visiting room, they seemed to be waiting forever for Mrs. Parrish to arrive. Mr. Harvey had his notes to look at, at least, but Luke had only his hands, his large, sinewy hands which had broken a man's nose, which were apparently going to save him and condemn his mother at the same time, which he spread out on the table now as he waited.

Mum gave Luke a funny look as soon as she was seated across from them, and at first, he thought she must have seen the torment in his expression. But then she said, "Where did you get that?"

Luke hadn't taken off his coat when they arrived. The heaters in the visiting room didn't seem to be working properly, and there was a damp chill in the air. He looked down at the coat now. "I found it in your room, in the bottom drawer of the chest."

"You were looking in my room?" she asked.

"It's warmer than any of my coats," Luke said, with a shrug, and then, as she continued to stare at him, "I didn't think you'd mind."

"I don't mind," Mum said quickly. "Of course I don't mind you going in there."

Mr. Harvey coughed pointedly. "If we could get started –"

"I can give you money to buy a new coat," Mum pursued, still looking at Luke. "You know where I put the money, for safekeeping? Under the Bible on the shelf in the parlour. Take what you need and go into Woolworths first thing tomorrow, no, better make it the day after if all the shops are closed tomorrow."

"Mum, I'm fine," said Luke, sensing Mr. Harvey's impatience.

"I just don't like you wearing your father's…"

"Mrs. Parrish," said Mr. Harvey, firmly. "We have a lot to discuss and not very much time on our hands. If you wouldn't mind. Please."

Mum relented, but as Mr. Harvey went through the developments in the case that he had been talking about on the train, Luke sensed her gaze flickering back to him several times. Whenever he met it, though, she would look away, quickly. She had gone a bit red, and since it was hardly from the non-existent heat of the room, he could only conclude that something had flustered her. It couldn't be what Mr. Harvey was saying, either, since she barely seemed to be listening to him. Was it just because he'd worn Dad's coat? Luke felt sorry and confused and annoyed all at once.

Were other people's mothers so hard to figure out? Did other people's mothers have secrets that lurked in their eyes whenever you caught them unawares?

At last, Mr. Harvey came to the 'strategy' that he had been so reticent about on the train. He talked, again, about the unknown origins of Mr. Albright's unfinished note of apology, how its contents did not prove anything, and how it would be fairly easy to undermine in court, how they might even suggest that it had been addressed to the younger Mrs. Parrish rather than the older. He talked about how any suggestion of an affair between Mrs. Parrish and Dr. Jackson would be only hearsay, since the prosecution, as of yet, had been unable to find a single person who had witnessed anything untoward between them. Then, with a glance at Mrs. Parrish, who gave a slight nod as if in permission, which Luke didn't miss, Mr. Harvey said, "With regard to the witnesses themselves, there's only one who gives me some concern, and that is your wife, Luke. She has been working closely with detectives this past week."

"I know," said Luke, shortly. He had seen Teresa on the day of Mr. Albright's funeral, talking with the Scotland Yard detective.

"It was Teresa who noticed the unusual amount of blood at the scene of the crime. The constable on duty that day failed to take a sample, and Mrs. Henshall told detectives that she was too distraught to have noticed anything herself. Of course, there are still the results of the coroner's report, stating that there were multiple lacerations to Mr. Albright's head. But then again, even experts can be mistaken, and if we can get another professional to analyse those lacerations, perhaps *his* findings might be different. It would mean applying for permission to have Mr. Albright's corpse exhumed, and that might take some time, but..."

"What else about Teresa?" said Mum. She was looking slightly sick. "What else has she been telling the detectives? You mentioned on the telephone..."

"Yes," said Mr. Harvey, with a wary glance at Luke. "Well, there is also the matter of the time of death. Between Teresa and Mrs. Lyndon's evidence, the detectives were able to pinpoint a time which fits with the coroner's report *and* with your apparent departure from Mrs. Lyndon's house, Mrs. Parrish. Now, my concern is that while Mrs. Lyndon's evidence, by itself, is questionable, as she is elderly, her memory may not be serving her well anymore, she may be confused, but Teresa's corresponding evidence strengthens it. Of course, it is all circumstantial, but any strategy to show it up as such would need to centre around Teresa."

"I'm sorry, dear," broke in Mrs. Parrish, before Luke could say anything. "I know you won't like this, but Teresa's not a reliable witness, and we need to be able to show the jury that. She lied to you, and to me, too. She lied to everyone."

"And in order to show the jury this," Mr. Harvey added, his eyes on Luke, "We need to show that while the rumours about your mother's infidelity are unfounded, the rumours about your wife's relationship with Mr. Albright are, unfortunately, very much true."

"You know I would never have done something like that to your father, Luke," Mum said fervently. "You know that, don't you? The very idea of me, with his doctor, no less, it's disgusting. I was always loyal to your father. I loved him so much. The only people on this earth who I loved more were you and your sister."

While she paused to let this sink in, her eyes still searching Luke's face, Mr. Harvey said, "Maybe we should give your son a chance to speak now. Mr. Parrish, why don't you tell us what you know about your wife's affair?"

"It wasn't…" Luke started. They were both looking at him, and now it was his turn to feel flustered. "It didn't get that far. She told me she was tempted. She told me everything."

"Are you sure?" Mum's voice was gentle. "Are you sure she told you everything?"

Luke looked down at his hands, still spread out on the table. He tucked them in his lap, and looked up resolutely.

"I'm tired," he said. "My head hurts. Can we stop talking in circles now?" He looked between them, Mrs. Parrish and Mr. Harvey, but their expressions gave nothing away. "Can you just tell me what it is you want me to do? Do you want me to get up on the stand and accuse her of adultery? Because I'm not going to do that."

"And we wouldn't ask you to," said Mum. "Of course we wouldn't, Luke. We just think – *I* just think it's time that you closed this chapter."

Luke stared at her, and went on staring at her. She continued, "If you sue for divorce by reason of infidelity..."

"Mum –"

"... and *tell the world* what she did to you, to us..."

"Mum, no!" Luke had raised his voice, and he saw, out of the corner of his eye, the guard at the door stirring. He ignored it, breathing hard. "You said divorce was horrible, messy. What happened to that?"

"Things changed, Luke." She spread her hands. The guards had uncuffed her for the duration of the visit, but as soon as it was over, they would put those metal clasps back on her wrists. There were marks there, from the chafing of the metal. Her skin looked raw and sore.

"We can discuss other options," Mr. Harvey said, glancing between them. "Since Mr. Parrish has made his position clear, we can take another ."

"Nothing's changed, Mum," said Luke, forcing himself to look away from her wrists and back into her eyes. The realisation came upon him as such realisations always do, with the sense that it had been there all that time, in the back of his head, waiting to be brought forward and recognised. He'd thought she was being brave, when she had told him not to worry on his last visit, but it was just that she'd had a plan, a plan that involved blackening Teresa's name in order to clear her own. "*You* haven't changed. A man died, a good man died and you've been locked up because of it and you're *still* the same. You're still after her. You're still after Teresa."

"And you're still defending her!" Mum burst out. "Why, Luke?" Her eyes were wide with despair. "Why? She never loved you. She lied to you and used you –"

"Used me?" Luke repeated. He couldn't help smiling at that. "And what exactly did she use me for, Mum? What exactly did she get out of marrying *me*?"

The prison guard had come up to their table now. Mr. Harvey had his chin propped on his hands and was shaking his head slowly from side to side. Luke got to his feet.

"I want to leave," he told the guard. "Please."

"Don't go." Now Mum looked frightened. Her eyes were damp and her lips and chin were trembling. "Don't go, Luke. Don't go!"

Her cries followed him as the guard led him out of the visiting room, just as they would always follow him, for the rest of his life. He would never be free of her. He would always owe her his life. If she was lucky, there was freedom awaiting her, somewhere in the distant future, but nothing of the sort for him. He would always carry her on his shoulders.

The strains of "Auld Lang Syne" spilled out of Maggie Henshall's house, through the door that stood open to welcome the New Year, and onto the dark street, where, in a few minutes, neighbours would gather to shake hands and gaze at each other for a minute or two. Luke knew the routine, even if he had not lived it in years, because it had been the same on his street. There was something he had always found unsettling about the New Year. It was all that gazing. He could see it now, as people held hands and sang. Their eyes were bright and searching; they dared to look at one another in a way they never would have at any other time of the year.

Maybe it had something with all the claret people were drinking, too. Mrs. Henshall had had a bit, her sister had had a bit, and her sister's husband even more. Luke had even had a glass. It had been a long time since he'd had a drink, and he could feel it swirling around his insides, tingling his skin. He reckoned that today, of all days, he'd earned it. His throat had felt dry all the way back from the prison. He'd vacillated between anger and regret a hundred times. He kept wondering what his father would have thought of what Luke had done, walking away and leaving Mum like that.

He couldn't stop that now, the wondering. Had his mother and father loved each other? Could someone who loved someone else hurt them so deeply and still call what they had "love?" Or was this all some horrible mistake? Was Mum, in fact, who she said she was, a good person, a good mother and wife?

He had lived with the two of them for a few months now, Mum and Teresa. Both had claimed to love him. Both had hidden things and interfered and later said it was all for his own good. Teresa had written to Bill Farley when Luke had let his unanswered letters pile up. Mum had gone behind his back to plan a strategy of defence with Mr. Harvey, and would happily have ruined Teresa's life to secure her own freedom.

Luke wanted to believe that his mother was innocent of both charges that had been levelled against her. One, if true, robbed his father of his last moments of dignity on this earth, and the other, if true, was too horrible to contemplate.

Yet *was* death such a horrible, alien thing to him? It shouldn't have been. He had been surrounded by it for years. It seemed horrible and alien to him now, maybe, because it had encroached upon his hometown, but Coventry was no stranger to death either. Just a few short years ago, bombs had rained down from the sky and made a blazing path through the city's streets. The skeleton of the cathedral attested to that fact today, and all the frenzied construction going on now couldn't replace what had been lost.

As Luke walked home from that New Year's Eve gathering, having said his goodbyes, he heard the cranes creak in the wind and the slats of scaffolding knock together. He had lamented all that building to Teresa before, as they had stood in Hearsall Common looking down at the city. He had wondered why people couldn't just leave things be.

But right now, he was getting the strangest feeling. Maybe it had something to do with knowing how quickly things had tumbled apart. Buildings could turn to ruins in a matter of minutes, the plaster cracking and the windows shattering and the brick crumbling until only the beams and rafters remained in place. Mum and Teresa had both said they loved him and cared for him, and neither was around anymore. Mr. Albright had had plans and duties and, presumably, hopes of his own. He had told Luke, the last time they'd met, that their work together was far from done. He'd been writing a book, according to Teresa. He'd stood at the altar and preached the word of God and people had gathered to listen to him. Luke had liked listening to him. And now all of these things, because they had been contained within one mortal man whose life had been extinguished before it was his time, were vanished, gone.

Maybe it had to do, too, with how he had watched the world come apart, and his own country with it. He had stood on the frontlines of that collapse, in fact, and had probably helped it along by firing shells at it. Because of this, because of all the destruction he had seen in Burma and the way that destruction had rebounded to his own corner of the world, Luke couldn't help but feel that it might be a noble thing to do, the *only* thing to do, to help rebuild. He was strong, he could lift things, and he could learn. He could climb scaffolding and breathe fresh air and look out over the city and know that he was leaving something of himself behind.

Luke hadn't the faintest idea how he would go about getting work like that, but in that moment, walking through his deserted city, the details didn't matter. It must have been nearly ten years since Luke had thought of what he wanted to do with his life, and actually felt excited at the prospect of work. University and the army had flattened him out, chipping off pieces of his soul until it fit with routines and regimes that had been made hundreds of years before. But maybe now, if he tried, he could start getting those pieces back.

He was still thinking of this when he rounded the corner and came onto Wragby Row, and at first, he thought that his eyes must be deceiving him. That warm, yellow light surely was issuing from one of Mrs. Lyndon's windows and not from one of his own. For the past week, he had been coming back to a dark, empty house. It had been up to him to turn on lights and make the place a home again.

Luke quickened his pace, and as he came nearer, saw that it was unmistakable. The light was coming from *his* parlour window, not from Mrs. Lyndon's. Suddenly he thought he might know what was going on, and he was surprised at the smile that spread over his face as he approached the front door. He had expected other emotions to take precedence. So much had happened between them, and things would never be the same again; things would never be all right again. But here he was, smiling. What did it mean?

Luke stepped into the dark hall. "Hello?" he called out. Footsteps came from the parlour, quick and eager; there was a delighted laugh as the door was wrenched open, and out from the lighted room stepped a young woman. She had short auburn hair, tanned skin and the weary smile of the traveller returned home.

"Happy New Year, Luke," said Lily Parrish, and she soon had her arms around him. She explained, in fragments of sentences, how she had wanted to surprise him, how she hadn't counted on his being out of the house, and asked if he had walked all the way from Maggie Henshall's, all alone? How silly that had been of him.

Luke, as he slowly returned his sister's hug, just listened. He did not trust himself to speak yet. The disappointment had been brief, and now happiness, happiness so pure it was frightening, replaced it. Now that Lily was here before his eyes, Luke realised that at some point, he had stopped believing that she would ever come home.

It was funny how quickly Teresa had found herself slipping back into the old rhythms of life. She had her old room back, the one that faced out over the shopfront and the housing estate across the road. Beyond that estate she could see the trees that marked the edge of Hearsall Common. It was not so far away, and yet it was also miles out of her reach, another life now, one that she had not lived for very long, one that might even have been a bad dream.

She woke up at six every morning, dressed quickly in the cold, and opened her curtains to see the morning light creeping across the rooftops. After knocking back a cup of watery coffee in the kitchen, she would go downstairs to find Brian already hard at work, unpacking a delivery or counting the money in the register. She would walk down the aisles stacking shelves, and at half past seven the blinds would go up. At quarter to eight, Brian would unlock the door, and then they would all come flooding in.

The post-Christmas rush was something to behold. Teresa knew from experience that it would eventually drop off as they got into January and people's pockets emptied, but for the moment, it was as though they wanted to delay the inevitable by throwing around as much money as they could. The day after Boxing Day went by in a flash. There was no time to sit down, barely any time to eat. Teresa staggered up to bed that night and fell asleep with a head blessedly empty of thoughts.

That was the thing she hadn't realised she missed about this kind of work. It kept you busy during the day and knocked you out at night so that you didn't have time for brooding. As well as that, even though Luke wasn't around to keep an eye on anymore, she still had plenty to worry about. She had missed the signs of exhaustion in her sister once before, and she wouldn't allow herself to be so careless again. She tried as much as she could to persuade Kathleen to take time off, showing her that she and Brian could handle things on their own. On days when her sister was working, Teresa studied her like a book, analysing every sigh and frown. She thought it was the least she could do. She thought that her sister would appreciate the gesture.

But she was, to put it generously, mistaken.

On New Year's Eve they closed up early and sat up for a while with a glass of beer each. No one made it till midnight. Teresa went to bed around eleven and fell asleep listening to the pop of fireworks in the sky. Kathleen and Brian had invited some friends for dinner the next day, and so in the morning they got up early to get everything organised. Kathleen started clattering pots and pans in the kitchen and Brian started moving chairs around. Teresa, who had risen a bit later than them, poked around the place, trying to make herself useful.

It was rather alarming when her sister set down the spoon she had been using to stir the gravy in the pot, and actually put her head in her hands.

"I'm fine, Teresa," she said, her voice muffled through her hands. "But if you ask me how I am *one more time*, I don't think I'll be fine anymore."

Teresa, struck dumb, could only stare at her sister. After a moment, Kathleen lowered her hands from her face and cleared her throat. "Did you invite Luke today?"

"I sent a note yesterday," Teresa told her. "Got no answer. And when I telephoned this morning, no one picked up."

"Maybe someone took him out," Kathleen said, picking up the spoon again. "Well, that's good news, I suppose." Teresa was still staring at her sister.

Kathleen sighed, meeting her gaze again. "Look, Tess, I know you mean well with all this." She gestured vaguely around the room, and Teresa's confusion only deepened. "But I don't need you watching my every move. Brian can do that well enough."

"I'm just worried about you, Kath. That's not a crime, is it?"

"You should worry about *yourself*. Worry about Luke."

"There's nothing I can do for Luke anymore." Teresa looked down. "He doesn't want to talk to me. He doesn't want to be near me. He's made that clear."

"So that's it, then?" Her sister had raised her voice slightly, and Brian appeared in the doorway with a wary look on his face.

"Kath..." he started to say.

"So what are we going to tell people today, about what's happened? Has Luke left you? Have *you* left *him*?"

Teresa gazed at her sister incredulously. "That's what you're worried about? What you're going to tell people?"

"Kath, leave it," Brian said, and Kathleen flicked her eyes towards her husband and jerked her head as if to tell him to leave them alone. With a sigh, he went back out to the sitting room.

"Of course I'm worried about what we're going to tell people. Especially since I barely know myself what happened."

"I thought that was pretty clear," said Teresa, coolly. "His mother was arrested for murder. I gave evidence to the police that's going to help the prosecution build a case against her, and now Luke won't talk to me."

"You did the right thing," her sister retorted. "And you're just going to let him and his mother go on punishing you now? After everything you did for him? After everything they put you through these past few months?"

"It wasn't just them," said Teresa, quietly. "It was me, too."

"You made a mistake. You thought you might be in love with someone who was kind to you. You didn't *do* anything. That's the important thing. Do you think you're the only married woman who's been tempted?"

Brian, who was evidently still listening from beyond the doorway, gave a pointed cough. Kathleen's cheeks went a bit pink, and then, refocusing her attention on Teresa, she said, more calmly, "Look. You can't just go back to the way things were. You're still married. Luke has to tell you what's going on, at least. He has to give you that courtesy."

The gravy in the pot was beginning to bubble. Kathleen turned back to it, adjusting the heat.

"He doesn't owe me anything," said Teresa.

Kathleen took this in, and then shrugged. Without looking at Teresa, she said, "All right, Tess. You can go on thinking that. And you can go on hiding here forever, if that's what you want. I'm not going to stop you. I'm not going to make you do anything."

"I'm happy…" Teresa began. But she didn't get any further. One look from Kathleen and her mouth snapped closed again. Her sister saw through her; she saw everything. And, in that moment, how Teresa hated her for that.

Tears were blinding her as she got to the coatrack by the door, and she just put on the first thing she could lay her hands on. The shape felt unfamiliar, the sleeves too long; it was one of her sister's. Teresa didn't care. She slipped her feet into the pair of house shoes that was lying nearby and put her hand to the doorhandle.

"Where are you going?" Brian asked, uneasily. Then, over his shoulder, "Kath, I told you–"

"Let her go," came her sister's voice, calm and authoritative. Teresa, grimacing at the new bout of tears that came, pushed through the front door, down the stairs and out through the dark shop.

The cold air dried her eyes. Teresa, putting her hands in her coat pockets, found that there were no gloves there. Kathleen never bothered with them because she said they always just got lost. Teresa kept her hands in her pockets as she cut through the housing estate where so many of the shop's regulars lived. She even recognised some of the houses, having brought deliveries to them in the past. And, in the more distant past, she had played on that low wall that separated the estate from the park. She had climbed that tree and swung on that length of rope that still hung from one of the branches. She had been so eager to prove that she was just as good as the boys; she'd thought that would get Luke Parrish to notice her.

Wet was beginning to seep through the thin shoes that she was wearing. She kept stepping in puddles because she wasn't really looking where she was going. A cold, soaking rain had started to drift down from the sky in the last few minutes. Wet from above and wet from below. Teresa smiled grimly.

When she reached Wragby Row, she saw straight away that the windows of their house were ablaze with light. As she drew nearer, she could hear laughter, and not just any laughter. It was the laughter of young people. It seemed Luke was, in fact, at home, and that he was not alone.

She had been planning on waiting inside until he came back from wherever he'd been. Her keys were in her coat pocket back at Kathleen and Brian's, but she knew where the spare key was kept, under the doormat, where anyone might have stolen it but which they had always trusted would remain untouched. There was no need of a spare key now, of course. She only had to stand on the doormat and ring the bell. Within seconds, the door had been opened and light flooded out. They had fixed the light in the hall, Teresa noted. The laughter was louder now, and she could see someone's legs through the open door in the parlour. They were sitting down, a hand gesturing as they talked.

"Teresa!" exclaimed the unfamiliar woman who had opened the door. "We were just talking about you." She moved forward as though to embrace her, and Teresa flinched back a fraction. The woman looked startled too, for a moment, but then she smiled and reached out to shake Teresa's hand instead.

"I'm sorry, it's been so long, hasn't it? And Luke says I look different since I went overseas. It's Lily, Lily Parrish."

"Lily," Teresa echoed. "Of course." She shook her sister-in-law's hand. Lily looked nothing like her mother, and only faintly like Luke. Teresa examined her face more closely. There were shadows under her eyes, as though she hadn't slept. So she'd heard about her mother, then. What a home to come back to. Teresa wondered if she should just turn and go.

"Well, come in!" said Lily at last, after they had been staring at each other for a moment. She smiled at Teresa as though she was all right with everything, as though it didn't matter to her that Teresa had condemned her mother. "You didn't walk all the way here, did you? I think it's starting to snow. Here, I'll take your coat."

Teresa, looking back out through the narrowing gap in the front door as Lily swung it closed, saw that her sister-in-law was right. What she'd thought was cold rain had actually been snow, drifting down and melting as soon as it touched the ground.

"I surprised Luke last night," Lily said, reaching for Teresa's coat. "Of course, I had a few surprises waiting for me, too. Oh, you don't want me to...?"

"I'll hold onto it," said Teresa, shrugging off her coat and folding it over her arm so that the wet seeped into the sleeve of her blouse. "Thank you."

Lily had that startled look again. How rude she must think Teresa was being, but she recovered quickly, as before, and went on, "I thought I'd get a few people together today. It's been so long, you know. This is –" For they were in the parlour now, before Teresa could have so much as a moment to collect herself, " – this is my fiancé, James Durham. I don't think you've met before."

"Wonderful to meet you," said the man, getting to his feet. He was handsome and fair-haired, and spoke with a posh London accent, like D.I. Fleming's. He had a very charming smile. Teresa smiled back automatically as he clasped her hand.

"And this is James's stepsister, Irene Carstairs." Another handshake, this time with a striking young woman with black hair, red lips and skin like porcelain. Teresa was suddenly very aware of the mud flecks on the backs of her stockings and the bedraggled state of her own hair.

There were more introductions, to Mrs. Lyndon's daughter-in-law, a tough-looking woman, to friends of James and Lily, who all seemed somehow pleased to meet Teresa, as if she could have meant anything to them, or they anything to her! She couldn't take in the names; there were too many. People kept laughing and smiling too. Even Luke had been smiling when she'd come in with Lily, because, of course, he had been the first person in the room she noticed.

Now he had broken off his conversation with whoever he'd been talking to, a glamorous-looking older woman, probably some other London connection, and was looking towards Teresa, uncertainly. As soon as their eyes met, she made herself hold his gaze. She indicated the kitchen door with a nod of her head and hoped that he would understand her.

Lily was mid-introduction, and Teresa had to extricate herself quite rudely. She escaped out to the kitchen while they all stared after her.

There were children playing out here, a boy and a girl. They were crawling around under the table, and squealed in delight at Teresa's entrance, giggling amongst themselves. Then, from the other end of the table, a man, evidently their father, straightened up and brushed the dust from the knees of the trousers. He smiled at the new arrival, his moustache bristling and his drawn face suddenly looking younger. "Teresa! I mean, Mrs. Parrish. We were hoping you'd come."

"Were you?" said Teresa, sharply, before she could help it. The children looked at her curiously from between the table legs, and a faint frown appeared on Bill Farley's forehead.

Then, from behind her, she heard a quiet voice say, "Teresa?" Luke had followed her after all. Farley, with a glance between the two of them, bent down again and reached out his hands to his children.

"Come on, Billy, Dora. Let's go out to your mum."

When they had left, Teresa turned around to face Luke. He looked well, she noted to herself. She was noting a lot of things today. He looked better than he had looked for a long time, as though a great weight had lifted from his shoulders.

She spoke first. "I sent you a note yesterday, inviting you to Brian and Kathleen's today. They're having a party too." She glanced towards the door, just as another round of laughs echoed through to them.

"Oh, yes." Luke looked contrite. "I was at the prison yesterday, visiting Mum. I didn't get your note till evening. And then I was at Maggie Henshall's for the New Year, and when I got back, with Lily and everything, I was distracted."

The corner of his mouth lifted until he was almost smiling. He was happy that his sister was back. Of *course* he was happy. How could she begrudge him that? Yet she did, all the same.

"It's wonderful," Teresa said, so flatly that a small part of her felt ashamed. "Wonderful that she's back. I telephoned this morning, but no one answered."

"Oh, well," Luke looked like he was concentrating very hard on remembering. "That's right, we were at the train station this morning, me and Lily. That must have been when you telephoned. We were meeting James off his train. You've met James? Lily's fiancé?"

"I've met James," said Teresa, her voice still flat. Luke nodded slowly. His head was inclined down, but he raised his eyes to look at her, and she saw that he was confused. Suddenly she knew that she could not stay there any longer. If she did, bitter, spiteful words were going to escape from her, about how this did not feel like her house anymore, how she had been gone a mere week and already it seemed like she had been forgotten, how the parlour was full of happy strangers and yet *she* felt like the interloper. Or she might even echo Kathleen's words. She might ask Luke why he didn't think she deserved to know what was going on, why, if it was all over and she was truly forgotten, he wouldn't just tell her and end her suspense.

But, in the end, she was glad she hadn't said anything, because Luke said, "We were going to come see you later today." He was still watching her, warily. "We were going to go to Brian and Kathleen's, honestly, Teresa. It's all just been... You know."

So that settled it, then. He had been about to come and see her, to end things officially. Her horrible suspense would not have lasted much longer. He had just been distracted by the return of his sister, and Teresa could understand that.

"There's no need now," she was even able to tell him, gently, before reaching out and putting something into his hand. She closed the fingers of his left hand over it. And then she held onto his fist for a moment. She allowed herself that, because she had to say goodbye. She looked into his eyes for one last time as his wife.

As soon as she was outside, she started running. The snow that was coming down was not really proper snow at all. It melted within seconds of landing on her coat sleeves. It was as though England was making some half-hearted, last-ditch attempt at a white Christmas, but it was too little, too late.

She went through the park this time, slowing to a walk as soon as she got under the shelter of its trees. She wanted to take the long way home. Here, where there was no one else around, she could cry as much as she wanted to. In a while, when she was able, she would go back to Brian and Kathleen's, join in the games, and put on a smile. She could feel it now, that she would be putting on a smile for the rest of her life.

But before she'd had much of a chance to think through what she had just done, she heard a distant shout. Someone was calling her name. Even though she didn't really think it could be him, Teresa sped up her pace, almost tripping in her haste to get away. She was glad that she had taken this path. It was muddier, and there were no views over the city, but it was flatter, too. As the shouts grew closer, the low wall at the edge of the park came into view, and Teresa decided to cut across the green to it.

As soon as she was out from under the trees, the snow started coming at her harder, and she knew she had made a mistake leaving the path. And then there was the sound of running footsteps right behind her.

"Teresa!" Luke exclaimed, catching her around the arms. His hands closed over her chest. She struggled, but of course he was stronger than her.

"Let me go. Let me go!"

"Talk to me first. Teresa!" Luke sounded so upset that, as he loosened his grip and came around to face her, she knew she could not try to run again, but she wished that he would not make things so difficult.

"What's this? Teresa?" Luke held out his hand so that she could see the glint of the wedding ring she'd placed into it a few minutes before. He was staring at her as he panted hard.

"I'm setting you free," said Teresa, in the same gentle voice she had used back in the house.

"Don't talk to me like that. Don't *look* at me like that! Don't I get a say in this too?"

"Of course you get a say. I just thought –"

"Stop thinking for a minute and just look at me." With his free hand, Luke took hold of one of hers and held it firmly, but he took so long to speak that all she felt was dread when he finally opened his mouth. He said, "Do you love me?"

Bitter tears sprang to Teresa's eyes, and she did her best to free her hand from his grip. But it was only when she said that he was hurting her that Luke actually let go, looking down at his own hands with a startled expression.

The tears were running down Teresa's face now. She put her hands back in her coat pockets and wished for this all to be over. She wished that she was back in her warm bed, that whatever words of farewell that Luke was gathering within himself now were said and done with.

"All right," said Luke, and now it was his turn to speak gently. When she risked a glance up, she saw that he was watching her, as he held out his free hand in a placating gesture. "All right, so you love me."

Teresa just cried harder.

"This is silly then, isn't it? Because if I love you and you love me, then we should stay together. Shouldn't we?"

Teresa went still. Her wide eyes sought out Luke again, and he looked back at her steadily. There was no hint of wariness or doubt in his expression.

"You don't love me," she managed to say.

"What, you want me to prove it? I'll prove it, then, I don't mind." With one arm, Luke tugged her towards him and drew her in. Teresa felt like a block of ice as he held her, her limbs stiff and locked together.

"I've been no kind of husband," he said into her hair, his hand at the small of her back, keeping her steady. "I know that. But that doesn't mean you can just leave me." He released her, but it was only to bring their faces level so that he could kiss the tears from her cheeks. Teresa's eyes drifted closed. Luke went on, "You can try." She could hear that he was smiling now. How could he be smiling when she was so miserable? "But I'm not going down without a fight."

"You didn't want to see me," Teresa reminded him, without opening her eyes, because she hoped, rather distantly, that he would go on with the kissing. "You didn't want anything to do with me."

"I was angry. I've been angry." Luke planted one last kiss on her forehead and then drew back a bit. Teresa opened her eyes again, reluctantly. He put a hand on the shoulder of her coat, brushing off the snow. "But Mum, well, she's not going to come between us anymore, Teresa."

Now the explanations came pouring out of her. "I only went to the police after she was arrested to help you. I didn't want you going to prison for a crime you didn't commit. I know you wanted to sacrifice yourself, but I couldn't let you."

"I know. I know." Luke pulled her in again, winding his arms around her properly this time. "Let's stop that now.

Let's stop talking about the past. Will you just stay like this for a minute? I nearly lost you today."

"You wouldn't have lost me," said Teresa, her voice muffled by his shoulder. "Not really. Not ever."

"You say that now, but you looked pretty sure when you gave me that ring. You gave me a good scare." Luke pulled back again and turned her chin so that she was looking at him. "I can't promise that things will be perfect. Or even,– well, good. But if you want to be with me and I want to be with you…"

"*Do* you want to be with me?" Teresa couldn't help asking.

Luke sighed. "Yes. *Yes*, I do, Teresa. I…" Shaking his head, he trailed off. "You know I'm not good with words." He held her gaze for another minute and then leaned in to kiss her lips. The movement was slow and uncertain at first. He kept breaking off, as though he thought he must be doing something wrong.

Thankfully, Teresa knew what she was doing, even if he did not, and the next time he broke away, she looped her arms around his neck and leaned in herself. She kissed Luke gently but deeply, her hands shifting to enclose his face instead of his neck. It might have been a few minutes before she took a break. Luke was breathless, at any rate, when she pulled away at last, and as she brought their foreheads to touch, he said, "I've wanted to do that for a while."

"I've wanted to do that for a while."

Teresa was silent for a moment, and then she blurted out, "Have you?" There was so much she wanted to know and understand, and for the first time, she thought he might answer her. "I thought that time when we had to share because you brought Farley home, I thought there was something, but I wasn't sure."

"I did. I wanted to hold you, to be with you." She felt Luke's exhalation on her neck, and could tell he wanted to say something else. He brought a hand up, curved against her warm cheek, and added, "But, Teresa, I'm not sure how much I can promise you. I love you. But the other things…"

"Whatever you can give," said Teresa, "it's enough for me, Luke." She brought him into her arms and hugged him to her. She was so happy that she wouldn't have minded staying like that until nightfall. She had thought that what she'd felt on their wedding day was happiness, but it was only a pale shadow compared to this. This was happiness untampered by fear. This time, she had reason to think that they might actually survive whatever the world threw at them next.

It was Luke who eventually stirred. "Will you put it back on?" he asked quietly, and Teresa realised that she had forgotten about the ring.

She watched as he placed it on her finger. The metal felt warm, probably because he had been holding it all this time. His hand was warm in hers, too, as he led her back to the house. They walked together like two children, dawdling, swinging their hands between them. They went unafraid, happy to be together, and feeling that everyone in the world must envy them. Innocence was not so easily won in those days, after all. But they had fought for it, and now they had it, and they were going to hold onto it for as long as they could.

EPILOGUE

O xford, 2005

Of course, Grandad didn't tell me the whole story on Christmas Eve. The others came back from church around about the time that *he* came into the story, which actually wasn't for a while. I was confused at first. I thought, when he'd started with a wedding, that the story was going to be about him and Granny, and instead he started telling me all about Luke and Teresa Parrish.

Then, on Christmas night, after everyone was lying around exhausted from all the eating, Grandad went on with the story. No one was really listening except me. David and Dad were playing chess, and Mum was reading a new Lee Child book that she'd gotten for Christmas. Molly was texting, and Susie tried to listen to Grandad at first but got confused and couldn't keep up with all the different people he was talking about.

I wasn't confused anymore. I knew that what he was telling me was the truth about what had happened to him after the war. But it wasn't just about him. Really it was about Luke and Teresa, and Luke's mother, and the minister who'd also been a prisoner-of-war, like Grandad, and Teresa's sister and brother-in-law who worked so hard in their shop.

"Luke saved me," Grandad told me that night. His eyes, very pale, I'd noticed, were shining with something. I felt a little scared that he might start crying. I didn't know what I'd do if that happened. Grandad said, "He was the best friend a man could have asked for." He paused, looking at me, and then said, "He died the year you were born. And you were named after him."

I was surprised that he remembered my name after all. All this time he'd never said it. And then Mum looked up from her book and said yes, that was right, Luke Parrish had died in 1995 and I'd been named after him because Luke had never had any children of his own.

"Luke and Teresa never had any kids?" I asked. Grandad had got out his handkerchief and was blowing his nose, but I don't think it's because he was crying. I hoped not, anyway.

"They couldn't," said Mum, quietly.

I wanted to ask why they couldn't, but Grandad interrupted, looking towards Dad. "We were going to name you after Luke but then Lizzy's father died, so we named you Daniel instead, after him."

Dad was absorbed in his chess game, and just gave a little jerk of his head when he heard his name called. "What's that?" he said, without looking away from the board.

"Never mind," said Mum, rolling her eyes, and then she looked back at Grandad and said that it was getting past my bedtime.

"Let me stay up a bit longer, Mum," I pleaded. *"Please*? I want to hear about what happened when Grandad went to see the minister. Was there a fight?"

Grandad said nothing, folding his handkerchief and putting it back in his pocket. He didn't seem to have even heard me. Then Mum got the others to gang up on me–David and Susie and Molly, the traitors, and I was bundled off to bed. I could hear them laughing downstairs, watching some film together. I kept my bedside lamp on and took out the book by the minister, the one with the really long title and all the stuff in it about God. I saw something that I hadn't noticed before. Teresa Parrish's name was in small print on the page with the details of publication. She'd helped to edit it, and she had written a bit at the end, too, talking about how it was important to publish Mr. Albright's book after what happened to him. That was when I found out that he had been murdered.

I barely slept that night. When I got up in the morning, the first thing I did was corner Grandad about it at the breakfast table. I couldn't believe he hadn't said anything about it before.

"Luke," said Dad. "Give your grandad a chance to eat his breakfast."

"But I've got to know what happened," I spluttered, still staring at Grandad. "Who killed Mr. Albright? It wasn't Luke, was it? Because of his wife and the minister?"

"I don't think this story is really suitable..." Mum started to say.

"It was the butler," my brother said, leaning across the table to wave his fork at me. "The butler did it."

"That's not funny, David," I said, and looked back at Grandad. He was either trying to smile or starting to say something, I wasn't sure which. But I didn't have time to find out. I went on, "Please finish the story."

"I'd say you've got enough for your school project now, haven't you?" said Dad. "More than enough. Miss Fullerton is going to be very impressed."

"The project's on World War Two," I said impatiently. "And Grandad's story is about what happened after. She'll say I did it wrong."

Something lit in my grandfather's eyes at this last part, and he glanced at me and then rubbed his mouth. "What happened after," he repeated, and then nodded. "Yes, of course. I need to finish the story."

Mum and Dad said he should get packing for his train back to Birmingham, but Grandad said there was plenty of time and that he'd like to go for a walk. We got all wrapped up, the two of us, in scarves and gloves and hats, and went out through the neighbourhood. The roads were quiet and the houses all lit up.

Grandad moved very slowly. I felt a bit bad for dragging him out and said that we'd better not go too far. He didn't really seem to know where he was going, but he peered down at me and asked if there was a war memorial near here.

I said yes there was one. We'd passed it on my school tour a few months ago. He said he'd like to go there. As we kept moving, at a snail's pace, he carried on with the story, picking up where he'd left off last night. By the time we'd gotten to Marston Road, I knew all about what had happened in Burma with the Japanese and Grandad and the prisoners-of-war. I knew about Mrs. Parrish lying to her son and Teresa and everyone. I knew about Luke and Teresa deciding to stay together and be happy.

The war memorial was huge, around nine feet tall, with steps and red tiles around it. It had so many names on the front, and on the right side there was an inscription: GREATER LOVE HATH NO MAN THAN THIS, THAT A MAN LAY DOWN HIS LIFE FOR HIS FRIENDS.

I couldn't believe that the story was really over. "What happened to Luke?" I asked Grandad. "Did the nightmares stop? Did he get better?"

Grandad was quiet for a long moment. The wind rustled dead leaves around us. They skittered over the tiles and my hands felt cold even through my gloves.

"I don't know," Grandad said at last, which wasn't exactly what I'd been hoping to hear. "I don't know if he got better. We didn't talk much about those things, after Mr. Albright died, but we wrote each other letters. The last time I saw him was at the commemoration, the 50-year commemoration. That would have been..."

"1995," I supplied. Grandad's eyes widened.

"Yes, 1995. He died not long after. D'you know..." He made a sound that might have been a laugh or a cough, looking down at me. "D'you know how old I am? I'm eighty-nine years old. I never thought I'd live this long. I never thought Lizzy'd die before me. And Luke's gone too, and Teresa..."

I scuffed my shoe along the stone. I wasn't really thinking about what he was saying, but worrying instead about what I was going to tell Miss Fullerton when we presented our projects. I hadn't really learned much about World War Two at all. I started, "Maybe we'd better head back home. Mum and Dad said –"

"I think it was a good life, though, for Luke," Grandad continued, as if I hadn't spoken. "No children, but he helped rebuild his town. He did more than I ever did, and that's a fact. I never stuck to anything in my life. I worked in factories, shops, whatever put bread on the table. All I ever had was Lizzy, and the kids."

"And now us," I added. Grandad reached down and ruffled my hair through the hat.

"I'm going to die very soon. That's a fact, too." He stared at the stone memorial, and I stared at the ground, embarrassed and sad because of what he was saying. "I'm eighty-nine. I've seen a lot of things. The war, and everything that came after. More war. More death. London bombed again, just like it was all those years ago."

I shivered. I still didn't fully understand what had happened last July. People had died on the London Underground, and Dad told me that "terrorists" had done it, and that the problem might be getting worse. It scared me to think of the same thing happening in Oxford, where everything was so old and beautiful.

"Will you promise me something, Luke?" Grandad asked then. I craned my neck to look up at him. In a slow, creaky movement, he turned his back on the memorial and put a hand to my shoulder. "When I die, and when people ask you about me…"

"You're not going to die, Grandad," I said automatically, because I thought it was the polite thing to say. But he just continued, as we walked back down the road,

"... don't tell them what I told you about Burma. Don't talk about the war. Talk about your father, your uncles and aunts, your brothers and sisters. My family. That's what I've got to show for all these years. Not some dusty old medals, but *you*, all of you." He stopped, took out his handkerchief to blow his nose again, and he took so long doing it that I thought he'd said all he was going to say, but then he went on, "The war was a long time ago. And I've lived a life since then. You'll see when you grow up. A man's life has more than one story to it."

My grandfather, Bill Farley, died a little over a year later. We got to have him for one more Christmas before he went to the hospital. Mum and Dad said I was lucky I'd got to spend so much time with him. It was my first big funeral. I cried and cried as they carried out the coffin. I didn't feel lucky, not lucky at all. I think it would have been easier if I hadn't gotten to know him so well.

But I was glad I'd written his story down. And, as I got older, I learned to be glad for the time that we'd had. Nowadays, I try to live a life that Grandad could be proud of, and to write stories he could be proud of, too.

Thank of reading. We hope you enjoyed this beautiful story of resilient love against the odds.

If you would like to continue reading Gracie Shaw's wartime stories, why not grab her fabulous 3 book boxset, Victory of the Heart?

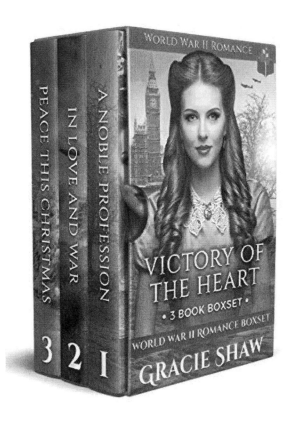

A historical romance boxset filled with love against the odds, and beautiful romantic tales of overcoming adversity. Three beautiful stories in one bundle, free to read on Kindle Unlimited.

Read Now on Amazon
Free to read on Kindle Unlimited

OUR GIFT TO YOU

AS A WAY TO SAY THANK YOU WE WOULD LOVE TO SEND YOU THIS BEAUTIFUL STORY FREE OF CHARGE.

Click here for your free copy of Whitechapel Waif

PureRead.com/victorian

At PureRead we publish books you can trust. Great tales without smut or swearing, but with all of the mystery and romance you expect from a great story.

Be the first to know when we release new books, take part in our fun competitions, and get surprise free books in your inbox by signing up to our free VIP Reader list.

As a thank you you'll receive a copy of Whitechapel Waif
straight away in you inbox.

Click here for your free copy of Whitechapel Waif

PureRead.com/victorian

Printed in Great Britain
by Amazon

17531996R00176